HOMELAND
INSECURITY

HOMELAND
INSECURITY

RICHARD & EVANGELINE ABANES

HARVEST HOUSE PUBLISHERS

EUGENE, OREGON

Evangeline Abanes is published in association with the literary agency of The Literary Agency East, Ltd., 51 E. 25th Street, Ste. 401, New York NY 10010.

Richard Abanes is published in association with the literary agency of The Literary Agency East, Ltd., 51 E. 25th Street, Ste. 401, New York NY 10010.

This is a work of fiction. Names, characters, places, and incidents are products of the author's imagination or are used fictitiously. Any resemblance to actual persons, living or dead, or to events or locales, is entirely coincidental.

Cover by Left Coast Design, Portland, Oregon

Cover photo © Third Eye Images / Solus Photography / Veer

HOMELAND INSECURITY
Copyright © 2007 by Richard Abanes and Evangeline Abanes
Published by Harvest House Publishers
Eugene, Oregon 97402
www.harvesthousepublishers.com

Library of Congress Cataloging-in-Publication Data
    Abanes, Richard.
    Homeland insecurity / Richard Abanes and Evangeline Abanes.
       p. cm.
    ISBN-13: 978-0-7369-1469-7 (pbk.)
    ISBN-10: 0-7369-1469-2 (pbk.)
    1. White supremacy movements—United States—Fiction. 2. Militia movements—United States—Fiction. 3. Domestic terrorism—United States—Fiction.
4. Journalists—Fiction. 5. Investigative reporting—Fiction. 6. Mississippi—Fiction.
I. Abanes, Evangeline. II. Title.
    PS3601.B353H66 2007
    813'.6—dc22

2007002495

Printed in the United States of America

07 08 09 10 11 12 13 14 15 / LB-SK / 11 10 9 8 7 6 5 4 3 2 1

A WORD FROM THE AUTHORS

We, the authors, denounce all forms of bigotry and prejudice, believing that racist ideologies are based primarily on hate and ignorance. Furthermore, *Homeland Insecurity* does not support, advocate, or condone racism, anti-Semitism, or white supremacy.

Readers should be aware, however, that this particular work of fiction contains accurate descriptions of the beliefs held by white supremacists, and uses direct quotes and paraphrases of statements that have been made by racists. The individuals quoted or paraphrased include Klansmen, neo-Nazis, and members of the hate-based Christian Identity Movement. Consequently, readers may find certain portions of this volume to be offensive.

Some white-supremacist leaders mentioned within the narrative are, in reality, notable figures in the racist community. These personalities include Robert Matthews, Richard Butler, William Pierce, and Louis Beam. It must also be noted that various hate Web sites linked to racism, anti-Semitism, and the neo-Nazi movement in America are referenced. Our intention is not to offend the reader, but rather to truly depict a very real danger that currently exists in the United States.

—*Richard Abanes*
—*Evangeline Abanes*

1

Nothing drives people harder than a fear of sudden death.
ADOLF HITLER (1889–1945)

★★★

No one moved after the light turned green, not even the leather-clad motorcyclist poised to zoom away on his Ninja. Finally, somewhere around the two-minute mark, a black-and-white L.A.P.D. unit with "to protect and to serve" emblazoned on its doors rolled forward, cutting off one car after another. The bored cop behind the wheel knew he'd go unchallenged. No one wanted to hear "Can I see your license, please?" in the middle of gridlock, a common sight around Los Angeles—especially so near Christmas. *Only seventeen shopping days left.*

The choicest spot to be under such circumstances, as every L.A. driver knows, is right behind the creeping police cruiser. And on this day, fate had smiled upon an old van, a silver BMW Z3 coupe, and a "Buginators.com" pickup. They all managed to slip past the cross traffic along with the cop just before the signal flipped back to red. But none of them got very far, maybe a few yards, at most, thanks to the dense row of brake lights flashing for at least five blocks in every direction.

ReichMan resumed his course, shooting a quick glance back over his shoulder at the crowded scene. It was so amusing. From the frustration on each face to the anger in every horn blast. He hated this holiday. To him it was nothing more than a profane season of hypocrisy and lies.

Goodwill toward men? Peace on earth? Never. Not as long as a single Jew still sucks breath. Vampires, one and all. Parasites. Leeches living off the lifeblood of hard-working Americans, stuffing their pockets with cash that rightfully belongs to others. Crooks. Liars. But you can't fight 'em. They control the government. They make the laws. Filthy scum. Zionist Occupational Government. ZOG.

Like the others who'd been waiting for the signal to change, ReichMan was forced to detour around the cars clogging the crosswalk on Beverwil Drive. But this was a minor inconvenience. *The oppressed righteous ones won't have to suffer much longer,* he assured himself as he weaved between the hoods and bumpers in his path.

As he reached the other side of the street, everything suddenly appeared more in focus than usual. Closer to his senses. Saturated by colors he'd never before noticed. The world had gained a disturbing measure of clarity…three dimensions had expanded to four, then five, then six. Reality, it seemed, was making a final appeal for mercy—a last plea for him to alter his course.

He continued his march along the cracked sidewalk, its inner edge slowly being overtaken by a narrow strip of shade—a lightless boundary inching outward from the buildings, ignored by everyone but him. It would take only a few hours, he estimated, for that band of darkness bordering the storefronts to transform the whole sunny neighborhood into a gloomy den of sin and misery.

ReichMan walked on, noticing the cracks and crevices in the cement beneath his feet. Old friends. He stared at them, head down, as he went along Pico Boulevard, amazed by the erratic patterns and distorted cuts. The streets were bringing back a lot of memories—all bad. His days and nights as a homeless teen. The heat. The boredom. The danger. Wandering back and forth from Santa Monica to Hollywood, hoping to scrounge up enough change to stay alive. And when begging was unsuccessful, there was always his reliable backup donor: the nearest restaurant dumpster.

An oily stain in the concrete unexpectedly grabbed his attention, stopping him in his tracks. It was shaped like an eagle. He liked eagles and recalled how, when he was eleven, he used to watch them soar and dive all afternoon from a rugged hillside around Bakersfield where he grew up. He wasn't ReichMan back then. He was James Patrick Miller, a lonely little boy who had no idea why his mom and dad had abandoned him.

As ReichMan continued his trek, he couldn't help but think back on his so-called childhood. He'd thought the ordeal would never end. The torture began when he was three years old, not long after his parents left. He was shuttled from one abusive foster home to the next, beginning with the Nelsons, who beat and demeaned him, ignored and confused him.

Stand up! Stop crying! Don't you scream! Don't you dare scream, you worthless piece of trash!

He spent most of his early youth miserable and alone. No brothers or sisters. So at fourteen years old, James Miller decided to make a break for what he hoped would be a better life. But he ended up on the streets—just another scared and hungry runaway. Vulnerable to everyone. That's when he turned to hate for companionship. It was always there for him. Empowering him. Consoling him. Protecting him.

By seventeen he was living in a cardboard box propped up under a freeway overpass. That's where a neo-Nazi recruiter found him. He took James in and accepted him. No questions asked. He made sure the boy had three meals a day, a warm place to sleep, and friends to hang out with. He also laid out a smorgasbord of scapegoats on which James's hate could feast: Jews, blacks, foreigners—anyone who wasn't like him. It was *their* fault that he was so miserable.

Finally, a couple of Klansmen who met James at a cross burning provided him with spirituality and self-esteem. They helped him understand that no matter what his enemies had done to him, no matter what they'd robbed him of, there were two things they could never do: steal his white pride and deny his white power.

"You are the product of a superior race," his mentors taught him. "A race of rulers created by Almighty God. In your body flows the blood of royal ancestors." The proof, they said, was clear enough. "Look at the greatest civilizations that have ever been! You have the Vikings. Then England. Then America. ALL WHITE!"

But James still felt like a loser. His gut kept telling him that his total worth was less than nothing. So he upped the ante by getting involved with Yahweh's Army and dedicating himself wholly to its Revolutionary Battle Plan. He followed through with his vows so zealously that by twenty-six he'd served two jail terms and had an impressive record: carrying a firearm during an unlawful assembly, malicious destruction of property, obstructing an officer, resisting arrest, assault.

Eventually, the Nordic Brotherhood—an elite underground racist group—noticed ReichMan and asked him to join their ranks. He agreed, and once more followed up his vows with action, this time obtaining various badges of honor for more serious crimes: attempted robbery, robbery, battery, possession of illegal weapons.

ReichMan had finally become the kind of ruined human being that unfailingly elicits either a shake of the head or a shrug of the shoulders from members of "civilized" society. Neatly classified and stamped DEFECTIVE by the system's quality control department, and written off as a lost cause. *Oh, well. What are you going to do? Next case.*

But after today, ReichMan would never again feel the pangs of insignificance and hopelessness. The world would forever view him differently. People would never again say his name as if they were talking about roadkill at the side of the highway. No one would ever again think of him as anything less than ReichMan, the brave soldier. ReichMan, the hero. ReichMan, the martyr.

2

Cowards die many times before their deaths;
the valiant never taste of death but once.

WILLIAM SHAKESPEARE (1564–1616)

★ ★ ★

Special Agent Christine Carlyle and her partner, Eddie Stark, had just finished discussing the reliability of revolvers versus the firing capacity of semi-autos when SamuraiHack left his apartment. The computer nerd—also known as SamHack, Sammy, or simply SH—had been under the Secret Service's watchful eyes for months via telephone taps and computer monitoring, but this was the first time anyone had ever seen him outside. He was a gangling guy, frail and exceptionally pale, a true geek if there ever was one, sloppily dressed in a bagging pair of blue jeans and a bright orange T-shirt that said "Extreme Indoor Enthusiast." It looked like he hadn't washed his hair in a month.

The twentysomething-year-old rarely left his cheap, one-bedroom hole-in-the-wall, preferring the quiet calm of isolation to the strain of social interaction. He usually ordered out for Chinese food or pizza when hungry; and for income, played Internet video games. He'd create numerous characters and play them nonstop for a few weeks, sometimes slightly longer, until they were a high-level wizard, or Jedi pilot, or whatever, complete with loads of combat skills, powerful weapons, and in-game treasures. Then, he'd sell the characters on eBay for real-world money to lesser-skilled players who would've had to play for countless months to obtain such a level of advancement.

SH was grossing more than two thousand a week. And it was tax-free since he only dealt in cash and money orders. He kept himself totally independent with a portable generator for home power, a stash of disposable cell phones, and a DSL he'd tapped into using the guts of an old radio. His mail was delivered to a different post-office box every few months, each one acquired through the use of fake IDs he'd purchased from a dozen different places around L.A. He was completely off-grid, detectable only by those who *really* wanted to find him—like the Secret Service.

It had cost the government a lot of money and man-hours, but now six federal agents were watching SamHack's every move. Two of them were nearby in an unmarked sedan, while four more were several blocks away in a van loaded with more electronic gear than a NASA space capsule. The operation, known as "5P," was given the go-ahead after the Department of Homeland Security red-flagged "President Peter Piper's Pickled Peppers" Internet blog, designed and maintained by SamuraiHack.

The Web site, dedicated to exposing the truth about President Peter Beckett's "totalitarian regime," as SH called it, initially appeared to be no different than a million other Web sites created by self-styled political commentators with an axe to grind. But in recent months the 5P blog had become more threatening toward not only the president, but also members of Congress and other political figures.

The first post that grabbed the Secret Service's attention declared, "YoU, dear mR. PrEsiDenT. HeY, ARE YOU LIS-TENING? YoU, aloNg WiTH yOUr eNtire rOyaL CoUrT of coNGresSioNal KillErs, desErvE to DIE."

But for all of his tough talk, SamHack had so far failed to show a desire to personally commit acts of violence. He hadn't even crossed that thin line between freedom of speech and committing a felony by making an actual threat against the president of the United States. He'd merely stated that the president *deserved* to die, not that he'd kill him. Perhaps he was hoping that someone else might do the job, or maybe he was simply letting off steam in a terrifically unwise manner.

Either way, the Department of Homeland Security wanted to make sure that the computer know-it-all was not going to make some kind of aggressive response to what he perceived to be the criminal misdeeds of President Peter T. Beckett.

"There he is," Stark said, passing the binoculars to his partner. "Take a look."

"Yep, that's probably him," said Carlyle. "Looks like a real winner, doesn't he? He's probably heading for that corner market."

Carlyle was still a rookie, at least by Secret Service standards. She'd started her career by joining up with the Bureau of Alcohol, Tobacco, and Firearms fresh out of the university. A few years later she upgraded to the U.S. Secret Service, thanks to some openings in the agency's newly created Division of Domestic Surveillance. It also helped that she'd graduated third in her class and spoke several languages.

For two years, Stark had been teaching Carlyle everything he knew about the Secret Service's job to investigate and protect. He was a seasoned agent whose career stretched back nearly thirty years, six presidential administrations, and eight Secret Service directors. But times had changed. *He'd* changed. And he was ready to get out. Early retirement was calling loud and clear. Before crossing the finish line, however, he wanted to pass on what he'd learned.

Stark had no family. His one and only marriage had ended years earlier. No kids. So Special Agent Carlyle would be his legacy—the daughter he'd always wanted but never had. She was sitting with him in a black, unmarked car about fifty yards from Sammy.

"That's not going to help our boy get a date," Carlyle commented, as she spied SH coming out of the store. "Looks like he's taken up smoking—nasty habit."

"Can you see the brand?"

"No. Too far away." Carlyle kept up her vigil as SamHack lit up, then began walking back to his apartment. "I think he's just heading back home."

Stark took back the binoculars and peered through them. "Hmm. No, I don't think so."

"Why not?"

"Because he's crossing the street now."

Stark threw the binoculars into the backseat and was out of the car before Carlyle could even open the door. By the time she finally emerged from the alley where they'd parked, her partner was already halfway down the block, waiting for her next to a Chevron station.

"Hey, a little warning next time, please," Carlyle said after catching up.

"You just need to work on your reflexes, Chris. You'll never get promoted if you keep reacting like that."

SH stood at the corner of the busy intersection, taking long drags off his cigarette and looking around.

"What's he doing?" Carlyle muttered.

"I don't know. Looking for something…or somebody. Maybe he's just getting some fresh air. You know he stays cooped up in that stuffy room of his staring at a computer screen all day long— and his nights aren't much different."

Carlyle squinted and shielded her eyes to get a better look at him. "There are worse things he could be doing."

"Well, maybe he's already doing it, but we just don't know about it yet."

Stark had seen just about every kind of antigovernment plot in his three decades of impeccable service. But the whole Internet angle was new and challenging. Technology was moving faster than law enforcement. Worse yet, there were countless hackers like SH who did nothing more than spend their time trying to figure out ways of staying three steps ahead of everyone else.

The twenty-first-century's computer whiz kids seemed to have an entire network of brilliant but mischievous (and often criminal) minds dedicated to circumventing computer security systems. They were constantly endeavoring to tap into the Defense Department database, attempting to steal someone's identity, or seeking to launch a new virus to erase every credit card number in Chase Bank. The world was far more dangerous and untamable than it had ever been.

"Hey, Chris, do me a favor. Go get our sound box. If he's meeting someone I want to know what they're saying."

"Got it," she replied, then turned quickly and headed back toward the car.

3

★ ★ ★

The day had been selected carefully—Martyrs Day—so designated in honor of Bob Matthews, who in 1984 became one of the most revered "martyrs" in the white-supremacist community. His drift toward legendary status began after he decided that hurling verbal threats at blacks and Jews was no longer good enough. Action needed to be taken; a definitive move against the enemies of the white race had to be made.

So Matthews recruited nearly two-dozen members of the Aryan Nations into a clandestine society called The Order. They condemned "race mixing," saw blacks as little more than subhuman beasts, and embraced various conspiracy theories about how the Jews were the behind-the-scenes rulers of the world, the prime instigators of evil.

Matthews hoped to start a revolution, a race war, that would ultimately topple the U.S. government, which he believed to be a Jewish-controlled political entity called ZOG (Zionist Occupational Government)—a shadow government of sorts dedicated to the destruction of the white race. He further held that ZOG's defeat would pave the way for a new Aryan Republic led by key racist leaders—a kingdom of intolerance wherein every Jew would be executed and every black shipped back to Africa.

The Order tried to launch Armageddon by first machine-gunning to death Jewish talk-show host Alan Berg. They subsequently moved on to robbery, stealing $500,000 from an armored car in Seattle and $3.6 million from a Brinks truck in Ukiah, California. But instead of kick-starting the end of the world as we know it, every member of The Order was captured and sent to prison, except for Matthews, who suffered a fiery death at the hands of federal agents after they'd tracked him to a ramshackle house on Whidbey Island in Washington state. He instantly became an icon of the radical racist right—a veritable fountainhead of white-supremacist lore and legend.

ReichMan idolized Matthews and concentrated hard on the Aryan rebel's great achievements and revolutionary teachings, hoping to direct his every thought back to the destination that lay ahead: the Museum of Tolerance in The Simon Wiesenthal Center.

Almost there. Not too far away. Just past the next stoplight. Keep focused.

A few more steps took him to the base of a street lamp just outside a neighborhood deli. ReichMan saw some pastries in the window, and he knew they'd taste good. But he had no money so it didn't matter.

Just then a blue El Camino turned the corner. Gaudy red and yellow flames were painted along both side doors, and double exhaust pipes tricked out the back end. The driver had his 32-speaker system cranked to the max. Razor-sharp gangster rap lyrics boomed out from the car's sleek chassis.

No one can reach you. No one can teach you.
No one can feel the pain that eats you, the pain that defeats you.
Every day you live for the demons that eat you.
You're a Killer.
Don't you know they've beat you?

You're a Killer.
No one left to beseech you.
You're a Killer (You're a K-i-l-l-e-r).
You're a Killer (You're a K-i-l-l-e-r).
Killer (Killer). Killer (Killer).

A blob of bubble gum, already compressed by a million other shoes, bore the full force of ReichMan's weight. He watched it disappear under his foot, and suddenly became very conscious of the harsh thud reverberating from the pavement each time it was struck by the soles of his heavy, steel-toed jackboots. The rhythmic pounding of the hard leather heels jolted him again and again, like electric shocks to his spine. The loud smack of each step hit his eardrums with a message that seemed to rise from the earth itself: *No. No. No. No.*

Stop, James. Stop, it went on. *It doesn't have to end this way. You don't have to do it. You don't have to die.*

But ReichMan didn't stop. He couldn't stop. It was too late. His thoughts turned back to the mission. *Where am I? How long has it been? Ten minutes? Twenty?*

He paused in front of an antique store to catch his breath. Through the window, a cuckoo clock. *1:55 p.m.*

He was right on time. No rush. No obstacles. No excuses.

After a few more moments, ReichMan stepped away from the window, and continued moving toward his target on West Pico Boulevard. He noticed how many eyes were meeting his. They made him feel uneasy. He was seeing something in them he had never allowed himself to see—souls. Some were afraid. Most were confused. And they had hopes and plans as important and special as the ones he used to carry around.

"White Power," ReichMan mumbled. "White Power...Hail Victory..."

He said it over and over in his head, reminding himself of why the war had to begin. Why there was no more time to delay.

Whites founded this country. Whites built this country. Now we're second-class citizens, practically servants of the stinkin' Jews and their black lackeys.

"White Power," he intoned more firmly. "White Power!"

ReichMan hoped that the words, like a sacred incantation, might dispel the inner voice continuing to attack his resolve. But the holy chant wasn't as inspiring or hypnotic as it was when recited in unison with others at rallies, marches, and cross burnings.

The faces of passersby kept lingering in his mind. *Who are these people? Where are they going? What do they see?*

He thought perhaps the sun was getting to him. Temperatures had hit ninety-five degrees and there was no breeze. The black trench coat he wore only made things worse. The garment was one of the few things ReichMan owned that brought him any pleasure. He'd gotten it after seeing *The Matrix*. It was uncomfortable, but he couldn't take it off since it was the only thing concealing the fifty pounds of explosives strapped to his body.

Now he was struggling with the weight. Sweat ran freely from all his pores. Every muscle ached under the burden. But the responsibility was his. Aryan brothers and sisters worldwide were relying on him. *Just do it.*

4

★ ★ ★

Frank Delafield—reporter for the *Bizarre Times International*—couldn't help but notice the brawny skinhead across the street. The menacing figure, who had a swastika, a pair of double-8's, and *W.A.R.* tattooed on the back of his head, was peering through the window of Forever Collectibles, shifting his weight back and forth as if searching for something.

Now THAT'S unusual, Delafield mused. *A neo-Nazi with a fondness for antiques.*

Frank continued watching the peculiar scene, realizing that a feature story on the white supremacist might be ideal for part three of his *BTI* series on Christian Identity, the religion of choice for Klansmen, neo-Nazis, white supremacists, and hard-core anti-Semites. Like so many other alternative religious groups, Identity had co-opted the term "Christian" in hopes of securing some degree of respectability, even though there was nothing very respectable or Christian about it.

The disparity between CI and genuine Christianity had hit Frank after only a few interviews with some of Identity's most notable and influential preachers: Bill Billingsly, leader of the

Colorado-based Christian Action Foundation; Dwight Long, pastor of the Church of God's Righteousness outside of Phoenix; and Pastor Brian Phillips, a real piece of work whose eclectic and zany brand of odious dogma included Hitlerian worship, numerology, hatred of homosexuals, end-time extremism, and surprisingly, UFOism.

They all spouted Jesus-lingo as confidently as any Christian fundamentalist he'd met and quoted Bible verses as accurately as most born-againers. But that was where the similarities ended. And Frank wasn't afraid to say so. In part one of his *BTI* series he wrote, "Christian Identity, also known as CI, is a truly foul faith—a hate-based religious system of self-righteous drivel built on little more than acute racism, misinterpretations of the Bible, and wildly distorted versions of history."

After its publication, Frank had received two anonymous death threats on his answering machine, several warnings from other reporters about the need for caution, and nearly two hundred letters of complaint—all written by members of Yahweh's Overcomers, a racist church in Muskogee, Oklahoma. Frank kept the letters in a file he labeled *Hate Mail: Racists (good for quoting)*.

"Whites are being wiped out," one missive declared. "Slowly, but surely, we are being systematically eliminated from the face of the earth. The civil-rights movement started it. Then came race-mixing, which is an abomination, thus saith the Lord. Intermarriage is NOT the way God intended people to live."

Another letter ranted, "You, sir, are a race traitor, and your lies are the lies of the Zionist Occupational Government (ZOG) now ruling America. You'll be sorry, either in this life, or in the next, or maybe both!"

A third note, which for some reason questioned Frank's heterosexuality, went on to theorize, "You must be a Jew, Delafield. You certainly lie like one. But your propaganda won't change the fact that God has chosen whites as His covenant people, and we will free America from its enslavement. When that day comes, you will be one of the first ones tried and hung for treason. Repent! Stop slandering God's people!"

Frank disliked threats. So in part two of the series he wrote his opinions even more forcefully. "Adherents to Identity may love to mouth pious platitudes," he began. "But all of their 'God this' and 'God that' ramblings are an elaborate deception, a mask skillfully wrought to disguise the hideousness of their hate and prejudice. Their creeds—far from echoing the sentiments of love and forgiveness found in the Bible—reverberate instead with the poisonous rhetoric and deadly delusions popularized by Hitler, then parroted throughout the South during the 1960s by ignorant thugs and KKK sympathizers."

Looking at the skinhead across the street, Frank felt certain that he'd truly found the fresh angle needed for his next article. He followed the hulking man at a safe distance, eager to get the scoop on why this racist had been window-shopping at Forever Collectibles. Delafield could already see the headline in his highly creative, if not overactive, mind: "Aryans and Antiques." Or maybe he would lead off his piece with something more historical sounding. A real attention-grabber like "A Hobby for Hitler."

Regardless of the title, he knew it would sell magazine copies. But first he had to figure out how to bag his quarry.

Excuse me, sir, could I have a word with you? I'm a reporter.

Or should he roughen up his intro a bit?

Hey, man, I work for a magazine and I was hoping I could interview you.

The last thing Frank wanted was a punch in the nose, or worse. The skinhead outweighed him by at least forty pounds—and all muscle.

The journalist finished the last bites of his lunch: a cold Big Mac and an even colder cup of Starbuck's holiday blend—black, with a double espresso caffeine-booster. This disgusting combo was part of what Frank called his madman's diet, a fabulously unhealthy regimen that was, in truth, slow suicide. "If you think your workouts are gonna save you, Delafield, you've got another thing coming," his boss, Angus Reid, would say. "The big one's just around the corner." But Angus would always get the same response from Frank: "Hey, someone's gotta eat it."

After dropping his half-empty cup and greasy wrapper into a corner trash bin, he saw the skinhead was outdistancing him. The guy seemed to be walking really fast. Instead of crossing over to Mr. Racist's side of the street, Frank began jogging down his side of the block to at least get within shouting distance. Finally, he pulled up level with him, but only because the guy had stopped to stare at another building.

Frank watched. *Now what's he doing?*

As usual, the first thing that popped into his mind ended up coming out of his mouth—"Hey, you! You in the coat! I want to talk to you!"

A few bypassers turned, but the guy across the street didn't seem to hear him, and he immediately disappeared inside the door. That's when Frank realized where he was standing. "Oh no," he whispered.

5

A thing is not necessarily true because a man dies for it.

OSCAR WILDE (1854-1900)

★ ★ ★

The Simon Wiesenthal Center came into view.

Jew lies. That's all that's there. Fake history and blasphemies against Der Führer, the bravest and wisest leader of all time.

ReichMan quickened his pace, cursing under his breath—at a Hispanic garbage collector, at a jewelry store called Rosenberg's, at the whole world. He walked faster as a vision opened up to him of the four other soldiers completing their missions at that same moment. Each of them had been handpicked based on their dedication, zeal, and prior demonstrations of bravery.

They, too, had adopted new names upon joining the elite army of Aryans; names that expressed their faith, hopes, and hate. VampireKiller was heading for the offices of the Anti-Defamation League in downtown Seattle. AryanUndertaker, in Montgomery, was nearing the main entrance of the Southern Poverty Law Center. In Baltimore, WhiteFury was already inside the NAACP's national headquarters. And PsychoSS, a native New Yorker on his home turf, was approaching the Congress of Racial Equality.

They knew they'd receive a glorious immortality as reward for their sacrifice. The Jew World Order, after all, would feel the wrath of the Aryan people through them. And the war was going to start. America would never be the same.

As ReichMan neared his target, he imagined Bob Matthews looking down from heaven. Like Matthews, he too was willing to give up everything for the cause. He had never felt so important. Then he heard, or thought he heard, someone calling to him from far in the distance: "I want to talk to you!" The voice was different from the one inside his head that had been hounding him all day. Was it the spirit of Matthews? *Maybe.*

ReichMan tried to stay calm, but as he approached the entrance, his heart began to pound. He opened the door and started whispering a line from the *White Warrior's Training Manual:* "Courage to do the thing that's right, is what separates the Jew and the n——r from the white." Now it was his turn to do what was right.

White Power! Hail Victory!

The Center was packed. The crowd filled the lobby— Christians, Jews, Muslims. Young and old. Men, women, children.

Children. ReichMan noticed them as soon as he walked though the front doors.

A class of seventh-graders were there on a field trip. The eleven- and twelve-year-olds should have already been at the La Brea tar pits several blocks away, looking at dinosaur bones and talking about fossils. But heavy traffic had gotten them to the museum late and they were only now beginning their tour.

ReichMan felt a twinge of doubt. But it lasted only a moment, and only for the white children. They would be casualties of war— unavoidable collateral damage. As for the young Jews, they were evil to the core anyway. Better to get rid of them now before they grew up to inflict yet more harm on God's chosen race. And the blacks, well, they weren't even children; just little n——rs: little apes, little dogs. They didn't matter. He looked at his watch: *2:00 p.m.*

Afternoon, sir," he heard the guard say. "Would you please step through the security gate."

"What?"

The officer, frowning, came out from behind the front desk. "You need to step through the gate and show your ID before entering the museum."

ReichMan took two steps back and began opening his jacket.

"Sir, please step..."

Time slowed to a continuum of drawn-out seconds. ReichMan ducked and sprinted through the metal detector, which shattered the calm with its ear-splitting alarm. The security guard ordered ReichMan to stop, then drew his gun and threatened to shoot.

James Patrick Miller headed straight for an orthodox Jewish rabbi standing near a photograph of Holocaust victims.

"RaHoWa!" he shouted as loudly as he could. "RA-HO-WA."

It was the war cry of countless white supremacists—a reference to their Racial Holy War against all nonwhite races. Then he pulled the red cord hanging from the vest under his coat.

The last thing ReichMan saw was a brightly colored Star of David on the lobby's east wall. Final thoughts rushed through his mind like a bolt of electricity: *Eagles...Jews...Brotherhood, life, honor...Glory.*

★★★

After watching ReichMan disappear into the building, Frank pulled out his cell phone and ran inside a florist shop down the block. He sprinted toward the back, almost knocking over an elderly woman holding some daisies. He punched 9-1-1.

"911. What is your emergency?"

"This is Frank Delafield, I'm a journalist...in front of 9786 West Pico Boulevard. Nearest cross street, Roxbury."

"What is the nature of your emergency?"

"I think there might be some trouble about to happen at the

Simon Wiesenthal Center, the Museum of Tolerance, I saw a guy that I—"

A deafening explosion blew Frank's Nokia out of his hand. Everything went dark as he flew through the air. Glass shattered. Concrete and drywall crumbled. The world around him disappeared in an instant. It sounded like a freight train was speeding by him at a hundred miles an hour. A sharp pain sliced through his arm as he began to choke on dust and dirt. It was like drowning in a sand dune.

His first contact with anything solid was the corner where the wall met the ceiling. He was then blown into some kind of storage area near the shop's loading dock, knocked unconscious by the concussion waves that ripped through the air around him.

The area that had once been filled with beautiful fragrances and displays was now an open-air graveyard. A few body parts lay about, grim indicators of the horror at ground zero. No one except Delafield knew what had happened in those first few moments of chaos. As he began to come to, he already knew The Simon Wiesenthal Center no longer existed.

SamHack dove for the ground when he heard the blast and felt the sidewalk rumble beneath him. *An earthquake? A gas leak?* The pack of cigarettes in his pocket was crushed as he struggled toward a patch of shrubbery like a terrified soldier under fire. "What the…" he mumbled amid the car alarms and neighborhood dogs barking uncontrollably.

Down the block, Carlyle looked back at Agent Stark. But her partner was already running up the street toward an enormous plume of smoke rising into the distant sky.

"Stark!" she called out. No response.

She ran back to the car and jumped in behind the wheel. "This is Carlyle," she yelled into her headset. "You guys hear that?"

Three blocks north, Agent McBride responded from inside the van that held the group's surveillance equipment. "Already on our way, heading northwest on San Vincente. Not sure what it is, but I guarantee you it's not good."

"Keep me posted."

"Watch yourself, Chris. That sounded like some of the battle-field explosions I heard in Kuwait."

Carlyle peeled out of the alley and headed up the street. "Let me know if you find anything. I'm picking up Stark now," she explained, pulling over as Stark darted out from a driveway.

He snapped open the door and jumped in. "Go west on Pico, fast."

Carlyle turned the corner, blowing past other vehicles that sat in the middle of the street.

"What about Sammy?"

"We'll pick him up again later. Right now we got bigger problems." Stark took out his spare revolver and checked it, then called the central office. "This is Stark. We have a major explosion west of La Cienga, probably on or around Pico. I'm three to four miles from there now and heading in with Carlyle."

Two miles from the blast zone, they could see dozens of buildings with windows blown out and hundreds, maybe thousands, of people fleeing in terror. Ahead of them a huge cloud of dust, ash, and smoke was rising ever higher.

"Hurry," Stark said. But the debris, cars, and people jamming the road were slowing them.

They finally had to stop about a mile out. Guns drawn, the two agents ran the rest of the way to ground zero, dodging the outward rush of people. Sirens could be heard approaching from all directions. The billowing cloud over Pico Boulevard was at least twenty stories high. Elsewhere small fires were starting to break out, which only added more smoke and heat to the already thickened air. The sound of screams and crying was everywhere.

On what used to be a sidewalk, Stark yelled to Carlyle through the throngs of panic-stricken people, "Try to keep everyone moving! Keep them *moving...*" Stark pointed east, "...that way!" He disappeared into the smoke.

Carlyle began making sure that those who were fleeing didn't trample each other. "Keep going. Everyone keep moving," she yelled. "Go go go. Don't look back. I'm a federal agent," she yelled. Then she looked down and froze. Lying at her feet was the leg of a small child.

6

War Crimes: Attack, or bombardment, by whatever means, of undefended towns, villages, dwellings, or buildings; seizure of, destruction or willful damage done to institutions dedicated to religion, charity and education, the arts and sciences, historic monuments and works of art.

STATUTE OF THE INTERNATIONAL TRIBUNAL FOR THE PROSECUTION OF PERSONS
RESPONSIBLE FOR SERIOUS VIOLATIONS OF INTERNATIONAL HUMANITARIAN LAW COMMITTED
IN THE TERRITORY OF THE FORMER YUGOSLAVIA (MAY 25, 1993)

The soldiers in the War Room argued back and forth about the future, making speculations about why they had been gathered together. Perhaps a final battle plan had been drawn up and would be presented to them. Maybe a new member was being inducted into the elite order.

All of them had received a personal invitation from the Reichsmarschall:

THE WAR ROOM. 0100 HOURS. OPERATION SPRENGBOMBE.
HAIL VICTORY.

But something was amiss. Their commandant was now almost an hour late. The chatter spiraled upward into a cacophony of indiscernible words, until a voice from the crowd shouted above the noise. "Die Welt gehört uns!" *The world belongs to us!*

Loud cries of "White Power!" and "Hail Victory!" reverberated against the damp walls of the bunkerlike structure, lasting for several minutes, dying down only to be re-energized by another shout from someone else of "Heil Hitler!" or "Sieg Heil!"

Suddenly, one of the soldiers started singing: *"Deutschland, Deutschland, über alles. Über alles in der Welt..."* Pride filled every heart. And the others, one by one, joined in:

> *Wenn es stets zu Schutz und Trutze*
> *Brüderlich zusammenhält!*
> *Von der Maas bis an die Memel,*
> *Von der Etsch bis an den Belt:*
> *Deutschland, Deutschland über alles,*
> *Über alles in der Welt!*

Raucous praise for the Fatherland and Der Führer erupted even before the hymn's last lines filled the War Room—*Germany, Germany above all. Above all in the world!*

Then the chanting began once more.

"Heil Hitler!" "Heil Hitler!" "Heil Hitler!"

"Sieg Heil!" "Sieg Heil!" Sieg Heil!"

Suddenly, everyone realized their commanding officer had entered. He'd been standing there for some time inspecting his troops, but went unnoticed until that moment. Uncontrolled fervor was turned into awe and reverence.

"Fellow soldiers of the Fourth Reich," he slowly began. "Today is a glorious day. The flame of the Fatherland burns brightly again. The destiny of our superior race, first envisioned by the Great One, looms ever nearer on the horizon. The war effort, after these many years, has been renewed. And this time we—will have victory!"

The Nazi salute that the Reichsmarschall gave to punctuate the end of his opening declaration brought thunderous replies of "Sieg Heil," until he raised his hands and quieted the uproar.

"Today, five warriors of unmatched bravery gave their lives for our cause," the leader continued. "And in doing so, they moved the Fourth Reich much closer to triumph. Like the many men and women who have gone before them, these martyrs now enjoy their reward in the realms of eternity, and will forever have their names recorded in the pages of history. Very soon you will all understand their degree of commitment. Let us never forget their sacrifice."

The room became still. No one moved. No one spoke. No one knew who had been chosen to lead the way.

"VampireKiller," shouted the Reichsmarschall. "He gave his life without hesitation." Several soldiers directed their gaze downward, while a few others looked at each other. "As did AryanUndertaker, WhiteFury, PsychoSS…and ReichMan. They all died valiantly." He paused. "WE HONOR YOU."

Everyone came to attention, and gave a silent Nazi salute. The names were well-known. It had been a great loss, but a necessary one. These martyrs would not be the last freedom fighters to pay the ultimate price. Each member of the Nordic Brotherhood knew that as they paid their final respects.

After a few seconds, the Reichsmarschall slowly lowered his right arm. "And now, my fellow warriors, the time has come for us to do our part. Each of you will be given orders in due time. You will be expected to carry them out without question, without doubting, without fear. You have already shown yourselves worthy of these tasks." He gazed intently at his followers. "You, my brothers and sisters in arms, will bring about the long-awaited empire."

"Heil Hitler!" shouted a lone voice from somewhere in the back of the room.

"Yes. Heil Hitler, indeed. Our glorious forefather had the vision, but he was betrayed by incompetence and cowardice in his ranks. Today there is no such hindrance to establishing God Almighty's superior race to its rightful place. And I promise you, my young warriors, my brave fellow soldiers, that the Fourth Reich *will* be established by us—never to be destroyed."

A lengthy pause hung in the air, finally broken by the Reichsmarschall's percussive voice. "It is our destiny!"

Cheers crested in unison as the Reichsmarschall once more gave the Nazi salute. *"Ein Volk,"* he bellowed to his devoted warriors.

The men and women lifted their voices together: "One People."

"Ein Reich!"

"One Empire!"

"Ein Führer!"

"One Leader!"

Roars of adulation for the Reichsmarschall and the movement's new martyrs continued as each soldier headed for the room's narrow exit. The meeting was over. The war, however, had just begun.

7

The world is too dangerous to live in—not because of the people who do evil but because of those who look on and do nothing.

ALBERT EINSTEIN (1879–1955)

★ ★ ★

L.A.'s renowned Museum of Tolerance was a work of art and inspiration. The high-tech experiential learning center emphasized two themes: the dynamics of racism and prejudice in America; and the history of the Holocaust: "the ultimate example of man's inhumanity to man."

In the Holocaust area, a tour recapped the events of World War II by moving visitors from exhibit to exhibit so they could relive the prewar years, the rise and fall of the Third Reich, and finally, Europe's liberation. This encounter with Germany's past was further dramatized by passport cards handed out to guests. Each one bore the photo and story of a child whose life had been changed by the Holocaust. Throughout the tour, these passports would be updated. And at the exhibit's conclusion, the fate of each child was revealed. Some of the stories did not end happily.

There also was a re-creation of a 1930s prewar street in Berlin as well as a room where visitors could hear about the courage and sacrifice of Holocaust survivors. In the "Articles and Documents of the Holocaust" display, the writings of Anne Frank were featured, along with artwork from the Theresienstadt ghetto, a bunk bed from the Majdanek death camp, artifacts from Auschwitz, and a flag sewn by Mauthausen inmates for their American liberators.

It was all obliterated by madness.

The high-tech bomb exploded outward at around 27,000 feet per second, destroying everything in the immediate vicinity, leaving only a deep, sizzling crater where ReichMan had self-detonated. The blast had reached a temperature of nearly 4000 degrees C.—enough to incinerate everyone in the building in less than a second—and had leveled most of the block, hurling rubble in every direction for more than a mile. Windows were shattered three miles from the blast.

No amount of training could have prepared L.A.'s emergency personnel for the destruction awaiting them.

There was nothing left of the two-hundred-seventy-six victims inside the museum, ninety-seven of whom were children. The same thing could not be said for those in the street or in nearby buildings. Tons of glass, concrete, and steel buried hundreds of them. Most were crushed instantly. Others, not so quickly. Those who died outside would eventually account for another eight-hundred-twenty-three lives lost.

Frank realized that he must have been out for at least a few minutes. He wasn't quite sure where he was, although he knew he was no longer in the florist shop. He could hear sirens, screaming, crying, and a man yelling for someone named Katie.

The stunned reporter got up and checked himself. His head throbbed and his right arm had a jagged cut, but otherwise he seemed okay. He had somehow ended up on a pile of garbage bags and old mattresses behind what used to be the store, which he figured was the only reason he'd survived. He worked his way out of the rubble and stumbled across the pavement, trying to find a place from which to get his bearings. Finally, after rounding a corner where a café used to be, Frank stopped.

His mind wanted to disengage, shut down. Most of the wounded were sprawled out on the ground—some unconscious, others groaning in pain, oblivious to the carnage. Of those who could still walk, many were in shock, wandering aimlessly around overturned vehicles or among smoldering remnants. Hot ash filled the air, now heavy with vapors released by the explosives.

"You okay, mister?" a voice called. A fireman, standing about twenty yards away, took a couple of steps closer. "Hey! Are you okay?"

"Yeah," Frank answered. "Yeah…I'll be alright!"

"You sure?"

Frank looked at his arm. *Others are hurt a lot worse than me.* "I'm okay! Go on."

The fireman gave a final directive as he moved away. "There are paramedics down the street. Just walk that way on Pico until you reach 'em."

The journalist headed away from the danger, trying when possible to help others along the way, frustrated that he couldn't do more for them. He reached emergency personnel about a hundred yards down the block and saw they were already managing a steady stream of men, women, and children. Several people were loading their SUVs and pickups with the less seriously injured and transporting them to the hospitals.

Frank sat on the curb for two hours as the surreal tragedy continued unfolding around him. More bodies. More waiting. More suffering. *I can't believe this is happening.*

Live coverage of the bombing had already started playing nonstop on every major network. He saw a FOX News van rounding the corner and a CNN team being ordered behind a barricade by an exhausted cop. ABC arrived, followed by CBS. Next, the newspaper reporters showed up. Then the photographers. Soon they almost outnumbered the police and rescue personnel. Cameras and microphones were shoved in people's faces.

The world sat watching the results of yet another terrorist attack against America. Another nightmare. The president was already meeting with his closest advisors. Law-enforcement agencies and the armed forces were on high alert. Leaders worldwide were expressing sympathy and outrage. Pastors were calling their congregations to prayer. Teams of counselors were being dispatched, and candlelight vigils were beginning to be held.

Not until five hours after the explosion did Frank finally leave Cedars-Sinai Hospital. He had a minor concussion, ten stitches in his arm, and a bottle of Darvon tucked into his pocket. His clothes were a wreck, and his cell phone, along with his microcassette recorder, was missing. He also had no idea where his car was. But he was fortunate. He was alive.

Frank called for a taxi, and by seven o'clock he was back in his tiny apartment, thankful to see its cluttered floors, leaky bathroom faucet, and worn-out green carpeting. *The life of a bachelor.*

He tried for the next half hour to contact the police about the skinhead who'd entered the museum, but no luck. He'd been trying ever since his arrival at the emergency room around four o'clock. A waiting-room payphone. A borrowed cell phone. Nothing had worked. The taxi driver had even tried to use his dispatch radio to ring somebody for Frank. Anybody. L.A.P.D. Sheriff's department. Highway patrol. No use.

Guess I'll just have to go down to the station in person tomorrow, he thought to himself.

After taking a shower and microwaving a frozen dinner, he sat down in front of the TV with a beer in his left hand and a pen in his right. He flipped on CNN, ABC, MSNBC. Everyone was saying the same thing. It was the worst terrorist attack on Americans in U.S. history.

And the information he'd heard at the hospital was true: Los Angeles wasn't the only place hit. The terrorists had pulled off a coordinated bombing, much like the ones that in years past had rocked Spain, Italy, Greece, and London. This time it was America's turn.

> **CNN:** It has now been confirmed that the U.S. was attacked earlier today by terrorists who coordinated simultaneous

bombings in L.A., New York, Montgomery, Baltimore, and Seattle. According to Secretary of Homeland Security Duncan Phelps, this was an unprecedented act of "aggression and barbarism." National Security Advisor William Cooper has also spoken out forcefully against the terrorist act, calling it "senseless slaughter" and vowing that those responsible will "pay dearly for their actions." The nation is currently on its highest alert status and will remain so until the possibility...

MSNBC:...here, live on the scene in lower Manhattan, trying to make my way through what is absolute bedlam, as New Yorkers are once again having to deal with a nightmarish tragedy that is horrible beyond description. The entire city has been shut down from 57th Street all the way south to Battery Park. The reason, of course, is the obliteration of an entire section of Broadway near 14th Street. No one is exactly sure where ground zero is, but some have been speculating that the target was near the Congress of Racial Equality building. The blast, an apparent terrorist attack, occurred at approximately 5 p.m. New York time, just as thousands of people were on the streets heading for subway stations and getting on buses. The death toll at this time is incalculable. We now go to...

FOX: ...recap our top story this hour, hundreds, perhaps thousands, are dead, dying, and missing in five major U.S. cities. Estimates of as many as 5000 to 7000 dead and perhaps 5000 injured are coming in...

CBS: ...for those just joining us, that the latest statement from the FBI has identified what they believe were the five terrorist targets. First, in Baltimore, the NAACP headquarters...

ABC: ...FBI Director Craig Malone has not ruled out al-Qaeda or any other Middle Eastern terrorist organization. At the same time, however, experts are saying that the choice of targets is uncharacteristic of such groups...

Every network continued airing news breaks and updates,

gradually moving from straightforward coverage to speculations even before anyone knew much about what had happened. It was the kind of journalism that pulled in viewers, but it turned off Frank big-time. He always stressed hard evidence in his stories, no matter how outrageous the subject matter. He might throw out an opinion here or there, but never in the absence of facts.

"Middle Eastern, blah, blah, blah...sure, right," he mumbled to himself.

Didn't anyone else know? It wasn't another 9/11. Not even close. He slowly got up from the couch, sore and barely able to stand. The kitchen seemed far away from the living room. Every joint and muscle ached. After a few agonizing steps, he made it to the refrigerator and grabbed a second beer. He knew a third and a fourth would follow. It was going to be a long night.

8

★ ★ ★

President Beckett had been looking forward to spending the evening with his grandchildren. Instead, he found himself wrapped up in a series of emergency meetings. Cabinet members needed debriefing, and more than a few high-powered senators were demanding some answers, particularly those from California, Maryland, New York, Alabama, and Washington.

For the current meeting, the president had called in law-enforcement-agency leaders to account for the situation—the head of the FBI, the Attorney General, and the CIA director, as well as Lance Vaughn, director of the Secret Service, and Duncan Phelps, Secretary of Homeland Security.

"Gentlemen," he began, "you said these people were under surveillance and that there was *no way* they could make a move like this. I want someone to tell me—tell me *exactly*—what happened."

"Mr. President," Vaughn began, "we were doing everything possible to monitor their actions. The information we received from our informant was absolutely accurate."

"But apparently incomplete!"

The Secret Service director shifted uncomfortably in his chair.

This evening he was not going to be able to give any responses that would satisfy the president. "Unfortunately, yes."

"Well, that's not going to cut it, Lance. In less than twenty-four hours I'll be standing in front of the American people, and I'd better have something better to tell them than just 'Sorry, everyone, we knew this was going to happen, but we decided not to take down the terrorists because we wanted to trace their financial ties.'"

"There were complications that prevented us from pinning down the *exact* day," Vaughn added.

"You think the public is going to care about that? We had the terrorist group identified and we knew about their targets. And let's be honest, we had a pretty good idea of the day too."

"In my briefing to the national-security team last month I made it very clear to everyone present that we had to find their War Room or else they'd be able to organize an attack," countered Vaughn. "We should've dedicated more men to finding it."

"You'll forgive me if I'm still a bit skeptical about this so-called War Room," Phelps snapped.

"What's your take on this whole thing, Duncan?" The president turned to him.

"My feeling is that the place doesn't exist. When did they put it up? How, and from where, did they get their supplies to construct this secret hideout? We can't trace any building materials. That would be basic to any structure large enough to house the kind of numbers we've been talking about. Satellite imagery is turning up nothing. We have no leads of any kind except a single conversation between two redneck Nazis that one of our agents overheard. An agent, by the way, who searched every inch of Karl Gruber's compound. And even he can't find any War Room. It's just not there."

"That doesn't mean the building doesn't exist," said Vaughn. "Maybe it's located off-site. The terrorists could be using any one of a dozen different ranches within a twenty-five-mile radius of the camp."

Secretary Phelps was losing his patience. "So what do you want us to do, Lance? Break down the door of every home near Rosamond, or Mohave, or California City?"

"Don't be ridiculous. Of course not."

"That's enough," the president said, stepping in. "Phelps, what does Homeland Security propose?"

"I think we need to focus on where they got their explosives and give up this whole search for the mythical War Room. If we can trace the explosives route into the U.S., we'll probably be able to find their domestic contacts."

"Do we have any intelligence on the origin?"

Phelps reached across the table and pulled out two files. He gave one to the president and one to Vaughn.

"This is our latest information. The materials probably came from the Middle East. About three weeks ago a load of high-grade military explosives was shipped from Egypt by al-Jihad. And it still hasn't shown up at any of the locations we usually track such shipments to. I have a feeling it was somehow diverted to the U.S."

"So now we might have al-Jihad working with a domestic group?"

"Maybe. Or maybe al-Jihad is just acting as a middleman."

"Then get on it. If that shipment came here I want to know where it landed and how it ended up getting distributed to a bunch of white supremacists in five major American cities."

"Yes, sir," replied Phelps.

Vaughn sat up. "And what about our operations, Mr. President?"

Beckett looked at his friend of twenty years. He trusted him completely, but his performance of late, particularly on this particular case, had not been as reliable as usual.

"You tell me, Lance. Do you think it's worth it for us to keep looking for this War Room?"

"Yes, Mr. President, I do."

"You still believe that the War Room is where this Nordic Brotherhood is holding its meetings?"

"Yes, sir."

Beckett paused. He walked to the window overlooking the White House lawn and surveyed the distant lights of the D.C. area. Almost eight years had passed since he'd become the most powerful leader in the free world. And despite all attempts at engraving his name in the annals of history as one of America's best presidents, his popularity rating was at an all-time low.

"Alright," he finally decided. "You locate the War Room, if it exists, and do it as soon as possible. Put every available agent on it. But keep me informed. I want to be updated on a daily basis."

"Absolutely, Mr. President."

"Anything else, gentlemen?"

Phelps stood up from his chair and started gathering up the files he'd passed out during the meeting. "Sir," he said as he tucked his papers into a black briefcase. "What are you going to say to the American people?"

The president hesitated. "I'm open to suggestions."

"I think..." Director Vaughn slowly began as he, too, stood. "I think we need to be careful."

"Agreed," Phelps said as he clicked his briefcase closed. "We should give them the Middle Eastern connection and nothing more. It'll do no good to start a panic. This isn't Israel. Our people aren't used to living on red alert."

"I want these terrorists caught, gentlemen," replied Beckett. "And I want them caught soon."

Both Vaughn and Phelps nodded.

The Secretary of Homeland Security then shook hands with his commander-in-chief and exited the office. It was late, and his family was waiting for him at home. Vaughn, however, lagged behind to have a final word with Beckett.

"Mr. President? Sir, I want you to know how truly sorry I

am about this whole mess. Let me assure you that we *will* get them."

"I know, Lance. I have confidence in your judgment. You've never let me down."

The two men patted each other's shoulders, remaining locked in an extended handshake, until Vaughn broke his grip. He turned and began walking away, adding with a final glance, "Give my best to Jean."

"I will," the president said, giving his friend a half-smile. He stood there for a moment and watched the director of the Secret Service disappear around a corner before re-entering his office to prepare for the next day.

Although it was already 10 p.m., the president would not be seeing his wife, Jean, for several more hours. There was too much work left to do. The F-16s patrolling D.C. airspace told him as much, as did the Homeland Security Advisory System, which was set to red. And the military was on high alert—DEFCON 2—only one click shy of all-out war. It hadn't been that elevated since the Cuban missile crisis.

For the first time in his political life, Peter Beckett wished he had chosen another career path.

9

★ ★ ★

Angus Reid hated it when events as newsworthy as the L.A. bombing disrupted his routine. Such incidents meant that his job as senior editor of *Bizarre Times International* would be reduced to just trying to stay sane in the midst of insanity. Unscheduled stories would have to be approved and written. Witnesses would have to be tracked down. And pictures, the biggest hassle of all, didn't just appear out of thin air. Photographers had to be called, shots chosen, licensing fees paid. They added thousands of dollars to an issue's cost, an unavoidable pain in the neck that cut deeply into profits.

His office, as always, was a mess. Littering the floor were piles of newspapers, some of them more than a year old. The file cabinets were covered with junk, having been filled to overflowing soon after the magazine had moved into the building a couple of years earlier.

At least a dozen Styrofoam cups could be seen scattered about. Each one marked a spot where Angus had stopped to talk on the phone. Two were by the window. One sat on his mini-fridge. And three were clustered near a huge dictionary on the edge of his desk. Angus didn't even notice them as he took a gulp from yet another cup and barked into the phone.

"Okay, Delafield, tell me again. And this time it'd better make sense. Exactly why is it that you're not going to get your story in on time? And why do I have to pay someone else to write a 10,000-word article to fill the pages I assigned to you—pages that *you* begged and pleaded for, by the way?"

Back at his apartment, Frank cradled the phone receiver in the crook of his neck and kept packing. "Because you trust me, that's why."

Angus stepped around two piles of old *Fortean Times* magazines and flopped into his chair. "Not good enough. But I'll give you one more chance before I call Jack in San Diego and tell him I have a job opening."

"Very funny." Frank crossed from his bedroom closet to a large suitcase sitting on the living room couch. "You know as well as I do that our dear friend from *The Journal* can't write a decent article longer than 5000 words."

"Oh, c'mon, Frank. Give me a break."

"Look, just tell Sarah to put her piece about haunted houses on hold. Then have her throw together something about Santeria or voodoo. Just make sure you add in a few photos of a chicken being sacrificed, or better yet, a goat. That kind of stuff always makes for good filler."

"Okay, okay, you win. But you still haven't told me what you're doing, where you're going, or when I can expect to see your next series installment. Why are you doing this to me—especially now? It's been a madhouse around here since yesterday."

"Uh…yeah," Frank replied, hesitating.

Angus squinted. "Delafield, tell me that you *do* know what's going on. And by the way, now that I think about it, where were you yesterday? I was calling you all afternoon."

Frank stopped packing to look at his watch, then sat down. "Angus," he said tentatively. "I think I know who did it."

Angus froze midway through a sip of lukewarm coffee, then slowly brought the cup down from his mouth. "What do you mean, you know who did it?" He swiveled around in his chair and lowered his voice. "You…you know who's responsible for the bombings?"

"Well, not exactly. But I think I have a fairly good idea who might have been behind the L.A. attack. Remember that Yahweh's Holy Temple group I told you about?"

"Yes," Angus replied as he stood up and crossed to close his office door.

"Well, I think I may have seen one of its members go into the museum just before it blew up."

Angus couldn't believe his ears. "You were there?"

"Yeah. I was there. That's why you couldn't reach me."

"Are you alright?" Angus asked, his heavy brow furrowed with concern.

"I'm fine. I'll tell you about it later. Right now I need to drop by the police station, then head up to Rosamond to check out a hunch. Just believe me when I say that you're going to get a fantastic story out of this."

"Now wait a minute, Delafield. You're not thinking of trying to get into that crazy compound up there, are you? Because the last thing I need on my hands is a dead journalist. Those people are nuts. Just let whoever is supposed to handle this type of investigation handle it. I want you to just stick to doing your job."

Frank closed his suitcase. "I *am* doing my job, Angus. It'll be the perfect wrap to my series. Don't worry. I'll be careful. I've gotta go."

Angus knew there was no way to talk his best reporter out of going after a once-in-a-lifetime story. "I'll leave it up to you, Delafield. But I don't want you taking any chances. Keep me in the loop."

"Yeah, no problem. I'll call you later." Frank picked up his suitcase and headed for the door. He still had to get a rental car, visit the L.A.P.D., get a new cell phone, and somehow make it to a Rosamond Motel 6 by nightfall. He was glad to finally be on his way, or so he thought, until he opened the door.

"Going somewhere?" asked the man on the other side, who was just about to knock.

Frank backed up a bit and put down his suitcase. "Can I...help you?" he asked.

"Are you Frank Delafield?"

"Who's asking?"

"I'm Special Agent Ed Stark. This is Special Agent Christine Carlyle. We're with the Secret Service, and we'd like to ask you a few questions."

"Well, I'm kind of in a hurry and—"

Agent Carlyle interrupted him. "It won't take long. If you could just give us a few minutes, we'd appreciate it."

Frank looked at Carlyle and paused without answering. For a moment he thought she looked very much like someone he used to know, but then decided it was only the dim light playing tricks on his tired eyes.

"Well," he replied, "sure...okay."

The two agents entered the apartment and immediately began scanning their surroundings, looking for any clues as to why Frank Delafield had just happened to make an emergency phone call about the Museum of Tolerance seconds before the explosion.

"Mr. Delafield," Stark began. "Let's talk about the 9-1-1 call you made yesterday afternoon."

10

*Thou shalt not be a victim. Thou shalt not be a perpetrator.
Above all, thou shalt not be a bystander.*

HOLOCAUST MUSEUM, WASHINGTON, D.C.

★ ★ ★

The few minutes Agent Carlyle said it would take to question the journalist gradually turned into a half-hour meeting that covered his occupation, his whereabouts the day before the attack, and his theories on who could have been behind the coordinated bombings. Frank didn't mind, since he'd planned to go to the police anyway. But things changed when it seemed the agents were beginning to suggest he knew more than he was willing to tell them.

"So, let me get this straight," Stark said as he continued taking notes. "You saw this guy several minutes before he entered the museum, but instead of calling the police right away, you just followed him?"

This particular question had been asked three times, and Frank was growing annoyed. "No. I didn't say that. I *said* I was having lunch when I noticed him. I followed him because I was trying to catch up to him to ask for an interview. And that's the last time I'm going to explain that."

Carlyle spoke up. "Look, Mr. Delafield, there's no reason to get upset. We just want to make sure we get all the facts so we

49

can do our jobs and find the people who did this, and stop them from doing it again."

"You really expect me to believe you don't already have some idea of who did this?"

"We're not here to discuss that with you," replied Stark.

"Oh, I realize that," Frank said as got out of his chair. "You never discuss anything with the public. I mean, hey, you didn't bother discussing the Oklahoma City bombing with anyone even though you were following McVeigh on the morning of the blast. You didn't discuss knowing about 9/11 either, although it was very nice of you to warn politicians not to fly in commercial airplanes that day. And you didn't discuss knowing about terrorists contaminating flu vaccines in 2004—did you?"

Stark and Carlyle stared thoughtfully at the reporter. He might not have been completely correct, but he wasn't far from the truth. He'd obviously uncovered a fair amount of information the general public had overlooked. What they didn't understand was why he hadn't written any articles on these events. They couldn't have known that Angus had stopped him, telling Frank that the stories would simply be too controversial.

Stark tried to stay calm as he responded. "Look, if we had had enough information to actually stop these attacks, we would have done something about it." But even as he spoke, he contemplated darkly to himself whether those words were true. He shook off his doubts, however, and pressed on. "We can stop these people if we receive cooperation from the public."

"Now I've heard everything," Frank smirked. "Even if you don't know who did this yet, do you expect me to believe that once you do know, you'll actually be able to catch them? On second thought, you probably *could* catch them—if all of your departments simply started working together. But you're all too busy cutting each other's throats to ever get anything done. The CIA has no idea what the FBI is doing. The FBI doesn't know what the Secret Service is doing. And none of you have a clue as to what your dirty undercover operatives are doing. C'mon, you guys can't even stop spammers from e-mailing Viagra ads to millions of Americans every day."

Stark frowned. "Spammers are very sophisticated in their knowledge of Internet usage and electronic subterfuge."

"Oh, I see," Frank nodded. "You mean like...terrorists?"

Carlyle and Stark shot each other a look. Neither one spoke.

"Yeah, that's what I thought," scoffed Frank. "And yet somehow you guys seem to have no problem tracking down ten-year-olds who upload a bunch of music files to their little cyber-pals. Why is that?"

"We're not here to talk to you about any of that," Carlyle countered bluntly. "You need to start giving us some answers."

"Hey, I'm just trying to figure out how in the world you think you're going to be able to identify, let alone stop, terrorists when the only bad guys you've been catching over the last few years can't even vote."

Stark finally lost his patience. "Mr. Delafield, would you like to be taken into custody?"

"On what charge?"

"How about obstruction of a federal investigation and failure to disclose information relating to national security?"

Frank looked at Carlyle in disbelief. "He's kidding, right?"

"Keep it up and you'll find out," she responded.

"It's your choice, Mr. Delafield," added Stark.

Frank laughed and stood his ground. "My lawyer would have me out so fast that your Donald Trump hairdo would be flapping in the wind," he threatened Stark.

The senior agent leaned in close to Frank. "Who said anything about a lawyer? Under the Counterterrorism Protection Act, we can take you in and deny you a lawyer for thirty days."

Carlyle interrupted. "Mr. Delafield, as long as you keep us informed of your whereabouts, there won't be any problems."

"Fine," Frank said as he picked up his suitcase and walked toward the door. Neither agent made a move to follow him.

"Would you mind telling us where you plan on going?" asked Stark.

Frank stopped and turned around slowly as he swung the door open for the agents. "Well, not that it's any of your business, especially since I'm not under arrest, but I'm going to Rosamond, okay? I still have an article to finish, and I think I'll find out what I need to know up there."

"That's about seventy-five miles south of Bakersfield, isn't it?" Stark observed as he slid his notepad back into his pocket.

"That's right. It's next to Edwards Air Force Base."

Stark and his partner rose from their chairs to leave. "You wouldn't happen to already have a contact up there, would you?"

"No, sorry, I don't," Frank bristled. "But even if I did, I wouldn't tell you who it was."

Stark asked one more question as Frank slammed and locked the door behind them. "You wouldn't mind if we gave you a call sometime in the next few weeks, would you?"

"Well, actually, I would," Frank snapped as he walked away. "But I have a feeling that doesn't matter. I don't have a cell phone yet, but when I do, I'll call your office and give you the number, just so you know I'm not trying to escape." He thumped down the stairs to the street.

After a moment, Carlyle exhaled sharply. "What do you think?" she asked her partner.

"Well, I think we have an extra investigator on this case... whether we like it or not."

Carlyle shook her head. "You know we can't ask a civilian for help with any investigation."

Stark grinned. "You're right. We haven't asked him to do anything. But just watch. He'll do plenty."

11

Together we can reach the masses with the Truth—
exposing jewry as Satan's kids and the Children of Darkness they are.

ARYAN NATIONS INTERNET SITE

★★★

Seventy-one-year-old Karl Gruber enjoyed his Saturday-night barbecues almost as much as he loved his Saturday-morning sermons. He found it so uplifting to see his small flock come together on the Sabbath, first as a unified body of committed congregants seeking spiritual nourishment, and then again as friends having fun, fellowship, and food. It was psychologically and emotionally healthy, he believed, to set aside a little time for relaxation in the midst of a chaotic and demanding world.

Karl wanted only the best for his followers.

"How's it going, son?" he asked an unkempt teenager who sauntered past him.

"The food's awesome," the youth replied around a mouthful of potato salad.

"Good. Eat up. Plenty more where that came from." The venerable Gruber smiled as he leisurely approached the platform from which he would be speaking.

Tonight was a special occasion. And not just because Karl had splurged on ribs and steaks in place of the usual burgers and hot dogs. It had been an important week, during which the congregation had worked tirelessly to spread the gospel to anyone who would listen. They passed out dozens of leaflets, left flyers on hundreds of parked car windshields, and even engaged in online witnessing in chat rooms, message boards, and blogs. Karl wanted to reward everyone with a memorable evening.

So far things were running smoothly. People had eaten their fill and those who said they were going to show up had arrived safely. The moonless night had descended speedily, making the campgrounds especially dark. And a slight winter breeze was now beginning to blow through the picnic area. The setting was perfect for the barbecue's climactic conclusion. The special surprise was something Pastor Gruber used to do for his first congregation in Alabama, back in the 1960s.

Tonight is sure bringing back a lot of good memories, Karl thought to himself as he and his personal assistant, Erich Strom, stepped up to the platform. Strom, who had a knack for keeping his hand on the pulse of the people, always knew just what the crowd wanted, and usually needed, to hear.

At forty-two years of age Strom had been an essential church member for the last year and was an invaluable asset to the tightly knit community. Erich, in fact, was far more than just Gruber's personal assistant. A better title for him might have been professional PR man. He routinely talked to church members, got to know them, listened to their concerns, and asked for their opinions on church matters. He immersed himself in their lives, often answering questions, going so far as to sometimes play the role of peacemaker when disagreements arose. And of course, he always reported back to Gruber about any troublemakers, who were then dealt with quickly.

"Brothers and sisters," Strom began after taking the microphone from its stand. "Can I have your attention, please?"

The underpowered amplifier made Erich's voice sound uncharacteristically weak and nasal. But that didn't matter because members of Karl's church, Yahweh's Holy Temple, had learned long ago that such superficial things were unimportant. Only the substance of a person's words mattered, not what they sounded like when they spoke those words. This encapsulated one of Pastor Gruber's favorite one-liners: "Tell me the truth if you have any truth to tell. And I'll listen to you no matter what you sound like, what you look like, or what you smell like." It always brought a good chuckle from his audience.

"Can I have your attention?" Strom repeated once more, raising his voice.

This time the crowd quieted down as they realized that their beloved leaders were going to make some kind of announcement. Several church members moved closer to the rickety stage, while others stepped back to get a better view of what was coming. A few of them merely plopped themselves down on the grass, content to listen and watch while they devoured a second helping of apple pie. Everyone was very curious to see what was hidden behind the huge canvas sheet that covered the far side of the stage.

"I want to thank each one of you for coming here tonight. And I promise you that we are all in for a very special treat," he said motioning toward the canvas. "But first, I think we should give a hand to our Sacred Servants ministry for cooking up this fine food. We really appreciate it."

The gathering heartily agreed and enthusiastic applause erupted.

Strom looked out over the men and women who had come together, most of whom were between twenty and thirty-five years old, with a handful of late teens rounding out the crowd. He was older than all of them, and they treated him with the respect due his position as their elder. Strom also had a great deal of personal charisma and was strikingly handsome. He stood at an impressive six-feet-four-inches tall, with sculpted Nordic features complemented by hair so blond it was almost white.

"As I said, tonight we have a very special treat in store for you. I'll let Pastor Gruber take care of that part of the evening. But before we enjoy what he has planned, I want us to join hands and

say a quick prayer of thanks to Almighty God for the many bless-
ings he's bestowed upon us."

As one, the congregation grasped hands, closed their eyes,
and bowed their heads. Although the temperature was dropping
rapidly, each person present felt warmed by the flames of faith
that burned within their hearts. No one was complaining about
the cold. It was an honor to be part of this event.

"Heavenly Father," Strom began. "Yahweh. King of kings and
Lord of lords. You are the mighty I AM. The Creator of heaven
and earth who has made us to be who and what we are at this
point in time, at this place, in this great nation. We thank you,
Yahweh, for our identity as your chosen people. We thank you
for not making us Jews."

Several church members voiced their agreement. "Yes, God,"
one whispered. "That's right," another said.

Strom struck his hand toward the sky. "We thank you for not
making us n——rs. Thank you for not making us vile perverts,
or race-mixers, or mud people."

"Amen," one person yelled out.

Strom drove home his point again and again. "We humbly come
to you this night as your white, righteous, powerful, spirit-filled,
holy people. Thank you, God, for our Martyrs Day celebration.
It's been a great week full of hard work for your kingdom. And
so we offer up to you this final night of joy and thanksgiving for
what you've done for us in the past, and for what we are prepared
to do for you in the future. In Jesus' name we pray, amen."

"Amen," echoed the crowd.

"White Power," Strom shouted to them.

"White Power."

"Hail Victory!" he chanted.

"Hail Victory!"

Strom then gave the Nazi salute and resumed his introduc-
tion over the ongoing shouts, saying loudly into the microphone,
"And now, brothers and sisters, I give you the man who has made

all of this possible. Our friend. Our leader. Our teacher. And our beloved pastor...Karl Gruber."

The whole assembly exploded with cheers for Karl and applauded wildly as he stepped up and took the mic. He allowed the exuberance to continue, but only for a few seconds, not wanting to delay the surprise he had in store for his faithful friends and followers. "Alright, alright," he said with a smile on his face. "That's enough."

"We love you, Pastor," someone hollered from within the crowd.

"Well, I love all of you too," Karl humbly replied. "And I could talk about that for hours. About how great all of you are and about how proud I am of you for the work you did this last week. But before it gets too late, let me tell you about something very important. As most of you probably know, the Jew World Order was dealt a harsh blow recently when several of its Zionist Occupational Government strongholds were destroyed. Now, please understand me, I have no doubts that some unfortunate white brothers and sisters were in the wrong place at the wrong time yesterday. And we grieve for all of those innocents who lost their lives."

Gruber observed a moment of silence before going on with his main point.

"But for every dollar taken away from the Jew regime controlling Washington..." he said, pointing off toward the east, "for every lying Jew that was killed, and for every Jew-made brick that was brought down, we say, PRAISE ALMIGHTY GOD!"

"Amen," "Yes, Lord," "White Power," shouted the true believers.

"We are in the midst of a Racial Holy War," he added, stirring up his audience even more. Then he gave the familiar Aryan war cry: "RaHoWa!"

The crowd cheered. "RaHoWa!" they declared in answer to him.

Gruber nodded his head approvingly. "So tonight I thought it'd be appropriate to close out our most holy week with a symbol of all we stand for," he explained as he signaled a young man standing by the stage, who in turn yanked a release cord that drew back the large canvas sheet which had been attracting so much attention. Behind it was a huge wooden cross.

"Brothers and sisters, behold the cross of Christ." He turned to his right-hand man. "Erich, if you please."

Strom approached the cross, and from a bin located to the left he pulled a thick stick with one end wrapped in gasoline-soaked strips of cloth. He took a lighter out of his pocket and lit the end of the torch, then set the ten-foot cross ablaze. Reverential awe overcame the onlookers as the fire's orange glow illuminated every upturned face.

"This burning cross is the sign of our faith. Its flame is the light of Christ that guides us and warms us in the midst of a cold and darkened world. The cross itself is the instrument of death upon which we ourselves are crucified with Christ when we give our lives to him. Don't listen to what the world says, my brothers and sisters. This is NOT a symbol of hate! It is a symbol of freedom, truth, justice, purity, and power. The only ones who say otherwise are the ignorant, the blind, the rebellious, and the ungodly."

The congregation burst into applause.

"Now, we only have about an hour left, so for the rest of this evening I want us to enjoy each other's company and take a few moments to look at this cross; reflect a bit on what it means. And if you have any question you can come talk to me or Erich. We are at war, people. Never forget, my friends—WE ARE AT WAR."

"WHITE POWER," his followers cried.

Gruber answered, "HAIL VICTORY."

More cheers rang out as Gruber waved to his flock and left the stage. The crowd in turn splintered off into smaller groups to finish conversations, have a last bite to eat, and make a trip to the foot of the cross. But one man stood motionless in the shadows near a distant row of trees, intently watching the scene unfold.

He was finally approached after a few moments by a skinhead dressed in black pants and a dark-brown leather coat.

"Pretty cool cross, huh?" the skinhead boasted.

The man flinched. "Yeah…pretty cool," he answered uneasily.

"He's like a father to me. And he really knows what he's talking about. He's got that look in his eyes. You know, that special look in his eyes that the Führer had. You can just feel the power. Don't you think?"

"Oh, yeah, yeah, I think so definitely. The same look."

After a few awkward beats of silence, the skinhead spoke again. "Are you living here now, or are you just passing through?"

"I'm just passing through. I was invited." The man held up one of the flyers that had been passed out earlier in the day all over Rosamond, Mohave, and California City. "See?"

"Oh, sure. I gave a bunch of those out and talked to people too. Almost got in a fight. That was pretty fun. Filthy n——rs started giving us a hassle."

"That happens sometimes."

"Well…anyway, I'm gonna go back to the bunkhouse. I'm freezing. Glad you came out tonight. What's your name, by the way? I'm Beau Baker."

"I'm Frank. Just call me Frank."

The skinhead slapped Frank hard on the back before moving away. "Okay. See ya around, Frank." Then added, "Heil Hitler," as he disappeared into the darkness.

"Uh…right," Frank stuttered. "White…Power."

Alone once more, Frank let out a long breath, then wiped the perspiration off his forehead. Despite the cold, he was sweating like he'd just run a marathon. But the meeting was breaking up now, so Frank knew it was time for him to go. And truth be told, he couldn't wait to get back to his motel.

12

*The unity of freedom has never relied on
the uniformity of opinion.*

JOHN F. KENNEDY (1917–1963)

★★★

The city of Rosamond had for many years been advertised as the ideal place for a family to get started. Houses and property were dirt cheap compared to real estate elsewhere in Southern California. The air was clean. The high desert offered seasonal niceties that ranged from dry heat in the summer to the occasional snowfall in the winter. And the landscape was breathtaking, with its expansive and panoramic views of the Antelope Valley dotted with Joshua trees and sagebrush. Being only ninety miles from downtown L.A. also made it the perfect spot for long-distance commuters who worked for one of the many businesses in the City of Angels.

The locals called their hometown the "Gateway to Edwards Air Force Base." And although that description sounded grandiose, it was no exaggeration. The base entrance was straight out Rosamond Boulevard, where the street dead-ended. That was just one of the things residents enjoyed boasting about to visitors.

But in the last few years the inhabitants of Rosamond had been bragging a lot less about their city, thanks to Yahweh's Holy Temple. Ever since the construction of Karl Gruber's compound several years back on some land just north of the city,

white supremacists had been causing trouble in and around Rosamond. There had certainly been racists in the area before Gruber.
But they tended to drift between Rosamond and nearby Mohave
or California City, sometimes as far north as Bakersfield. They
usually kept to themselves, and only once in a great while would
physically bully or verbally abuse some unfortunate Latino, black,
or Asian who crossed their path. But overall, the racist popula-
tion used to be insignificant.

Now, however, dozens of hardcore hatemongers were coming
to Gruber's enclave on a weekly basis. Some left. Some stayed.
No one knew exactly how many anti-Semites, Klansmen, and
neo-Nazis were living there, but it was a sizable number that was
growing steadily. The streets were no longer as safe as they used
to be at night. Racially motivated crimes were appearing more
often in local news stories and police reports. There had even been
several arrests made after a series of beatings were linked to some
members of Karl Gruber's congregation.

The offensive flyers that had been scattered around Rosamond
were the last straw, especially since their distribution had coin-
cided with the terrorist attacks. Rosamond's citizens wanted local
authorities to deal with Gruber and his congregation once and
for all. And since it was an election year, the area's politicians
decided to listen to their constituency and hold a special town-
council meeting on Tuesday night.

It had been several days since Frank's arrival in Rosamond and
his visit to Gruber's camp, but since that night he hadn't made
contact with anyone of interest. So he decided to show up early
at the public assembly hall in hopes of landing some interviews
with the various lawmakers who were contemplating a resolu-
tion against public displays of racism, or as one official described
them, visible examples of "hate conduct."

Unfortunately, a journalist was the last person that anyone
on the Rosamond Municipal Advisory Council wanted to talk
to. So instead of getting a recorder full of juicy quotes from key

council-persons, Frank was forced to settle for simply jotting down random observations about the situation that were being voiced by assorted ranchers and businessmen concerned enough to attend the gathering.

It seemed like just another colossal waste of time, until one older gentleman stood in front of the public microphone and addressed the council. The other residents who had preceded him only ranted and raved. But this man spoke in a quiet voice that was both calm and rational. The assembly hall was suddenly more attentive than it had been, as the once raucous mob of concerned citizens packed into the room fell silent.

"All of you know me," he began. "And you can trust me. I think I've proven that over the years. You also know I understand Gruber and his followers. How they think. How they feel about their beliefs. Please, listen to me when I say that they are indeed a danger to this community. They'll take over this city unless we make it impossible for them to freely terrorize and intimidate. So I ask that you enact, as soon as possible, some type of regulation that will bring severe repercussions to anyone who resorts to using racist threats—physical or verbal—within a twenty-five-mile radius of our community. Thank you."

The old man returned to his seat amid thunderous applause.

"Thank you, Reverend," one of the councilmen said. "We will, of course, take your words under special consideration." The official then looked down at his roster, and without delay moved forward with the proceedings. "Next, we have Mrs. Darlene Prather. Sophomore English teacher at Rosamond high school. Mrs. Prather, you may approach the microphone."

Frank, sitting on the far other side of the room from the podium, leaned over to the lady next to him. "Excuse me," he whispered. "Could you tell me the name of that older gentleman who just spoke. I'm a reporter and I'd really like to interview him for a story I'm doing."

The young woman shifted the baby in her arms, looked across

the seating area, and nodded her head in the Reverend's direction. "That's Bill Schmidt. He's the senior pastor of Christ's Chapel."

"Where's that?"

"On the other side of town. Just head out east on Rosamond Boulevard until you see the Denny's billboard. Go another hundred yards and you'll find the church on your right. His house is on the property too. You might want to stop by during the week if you want to talk to him. He's way too busy on weekends."

Frank continued watching the pastor, who remained seated only for another few moments before leaving with a young man.

"Who's that with him?" Frank asked.

"Oh, that's his grandson, Luke. He works with him at the church as an assistant pastor and worship leader. He's a great guy. Very mature for his age. Very kind too."

Frank stayed at the meeting for only another half hour, then decided to call it a night. It was getting late and he hadn't slept well since arriving in town. Each day brought him one day closer to Christmas, his least favorite holiday. So he decided to head back to his hotel, order a plate of spaghetti from room service, and down a few glasses of the house red.

The next day would bring yet another early morning, and he had to get some rest. Maybe the wine would help. But he wouldn't let the drinking get out of hand again. That had happened three years ago at this same time of year. *But things were different then,* he told himself as he climbed in his rental car and drove away.

13

★ ★ ★

The Reichsmarschall left the town-council meeting with no doubt in his mind that Yahweh's warriors would soon endure persecution at the hands of the city's Jewish-controlled regime. Although initially angered by the hypocrisy and lies that he'd been forced to listen to, the Reichsmarschall eventually felt a mixture of anticipation and excitement. This turn of events had actually inspired him to step up the war effort.

Any attempt by Rosamond's residents to subdue God's soldiers of righteousness would prove futile and only expose them for the fools they were, especially the accursed heretic, Schmidt. The pastor had gone astray after weakness and fear painted a yellow stripe of cowardice down his back. He had been a thorn in the Reichsmarschall's side for many years.

"Traitor," the Reichsmarschall muttered through clenched teeth. "Death for him would be too merciful. I want to see him suffer; slowly suffer as he has made me suffer."

But the Traitor's fate would have to be decided later. The Reichsmarschall's immediate concern was coming up with a new attack plan. So after arriving back home he retired to his study to formulate a course of action. A short three hours later, several of his most trusted soldiers followed him into the War Room. Only a handful of men, about a dozen, had been summoned. The most elite warriors from the martyr squads.

"Another move against our enemies is necessary," the Reichsmarschall explained in a low and rasping voice. "Any volunteers?"

SinisterNazi objected. "Shouldn't we wait until the new year?"

The Reichsmarschall gave his fellow soldier a cold stare. "No. We cannot delay our second attack. We must keep the opposition off balance. No one expects us to strike so soon, especially during their blasphemous holiday season. Christmas, Hanukkah, Kwanzaa—every one of them are abominations that mock the one true faith. Can you not see that it is the best time to attack?"

"But the country's alert status is elevated," objected IronCross, still skeptical of the timing.

"Yes," the Reichsmarschall grinned. "But they will be guarding the wrong places, just like last time. Our enemies will be concerned with airports, rail stations, government buildings. Obvious targets. But what I've planned runs contrary to the conventional wisdom of our enemies. We're going to take this conflict in the direction *we* want it to go by injecting so much fear into the populace that the whole of society will be paralyzed. Our adversaries will cower before us, and the citizens of this nation will long for the freedom and security they once enjoyed. We'll win the majority to our side. That is when our new Führer will make himself known and usher in the Fourth Reich."

After a few moments of silence, Terrorist101 volunteered. "I am ready."

"Excellent, my brother. Great will be your reward in heaven. Your sacrifice will help bring this country to its knees and purge God's promised land of the devil's spawn. Who else is willing to go? This mission calls for three of you—representatives of the Father, Son, and Holy Ghost."

"I, too, will go," declared IronCross.

"And I," said SinisterNazi.

The Reichsmarschall held up his hand. "Not you. I'm sorry. I admire your courage, but your skills must be saved for when we make our final push to change the course of this country. I only wanted you present here as a witness, and to train you to take my place if I should ever fall. Someone else must go."

"Yes, Herr Reichsmarschall."

Within seconds, a replacement for SinisterNazi boldly stepped forward. "Then let it be me."

"Very well, Thor. It shall be you. Remain here with Iron-Cross and Terrorist101." He then faced the others. "The rest of you may leave, but do not speak of this to anyone. You know the penalty."

Those who hadn't volunteered exited the War Room, leaving the Reichsmarschall behind with the men who would soon be laying down their lives in battle. Like the others who had already died in the line of duty less than a week earlier, these three warriors had been with the movement for several years and proven themselves adept at following orders. Each of them had come from different groups loyal to the Reichsmarschall.

IronCross was a member of the Priests of Yahweh. Terrorist101 represented the White Armed Resistance, while Thor swore allegiance to the Aryan Soldat Front. The others, those whose time for martyrdom had not yet come, represented two additional groups: Hammerskins Are The Executioners and Das Wolf Pack.

These soldiers, as well as dozens more who had not been called to the War Room, collectively formed the Nordic Brotherhood—an ultraclandestine faction of handpicked zealots so secretive that hardly anyone outside its ranks even knew of its existence. Each member, including the Reichsmarschall, served under the supreme authority of Der Neue Führer und Reichskanzler (The New Leader and Chancellor of the Empire). He would be the one to usher in Yahweh's Kingdom of Righteousness.

For security reasons, of course, no rank-and-file soldier in the movement had ever seen Der Neue Führer. None of them had ever communicated directly with him, either, except the Reichsmarschall. But even this contact had been done using online access only. None of the elite martyrs, however, doubted the existence of Der Neue Führer, nor did they question whether or not he had infiltrated the Zionist Occupational Government. When the appropriate time came, he would seize power. The nation would then be back in the hands of those to whom it had originally been given—whites. The Jew menace would be stopped. Nonwhites would be removed from America's holy ground. The Fourth Reich would reign for a thousand years.

The Reichsmarschall reminded IronCross, Terrorist101, and Thor of these inspirational events to come, encouraging them with descriptions of what America would be like after becoming a glorious white republic. He promised that they would see it all from their new abode in heaven, or as the ancient Vikings called it, Valhalla, the home of the gods. "Rejoice, brothers," he assured them. "Immortality will be yours in this world and in the world to come. Bless you in the name of the Father, Son, and Holy Ghost."

At this point, orders were issued to the three would-be martyrs, including what weapons to use, the date and time of the assaults, and of course, the location of the war targets. Although the Reichsmarschall's plan would again result in many victims, a high number of dead and wounded were not his primary goals for the operation. This time the coming acts of self-sacrifice would send a threefold message: *We are unpredictable. We are untraceable. We are unstoppable.* The Reichsmarschall believed that rampant fear would do far more for the cause than hundreds, or even thousands, of casualties.

And the Reichsmarschall was right.

14

We are never deceived; we deceive ourselves.

JOHANN WOLFGANG VON GOETHE (1749–1832)

★★★

Der Neue Führer sat impatiently in front of his computer screen, waiting for the Reichsmarschall to contact him using their special password-protected channel. *I told him 0900 hours sharp,* he griped to himself. *This is the second time he's made me wait.*

But such a minor infraction would have to be overlooked. The Reichsmarschall was a loyal devotee skilled at not only motivating, but also commanding the troops. Although still untrained in the finer points of war and political maneuverings, his zeal made up for his inexperience. He was a natural born leader.

More importantly, Der Neue Führer found him easy to manipulate. "I need your help," he'd explained to his protégé ten years earlier. "You understand the world as it is. I understand the world as it was. Together we can make the world as it should be."

Thanks to the steely leadership of both the Reichsmarschall and Der Neue Führer, a great deal had happened since that conversation. First, the Nordic Brotherhood was formed. Next, those who were most devoted to bringing down ZOG, the Zionist Occupational Government, were convinced that the time for a daring onslaught against the enemy had arrived. Then, the final obstacle to establishing the Fourth Reich—having no one in a position of political power to take over the nation—had been overcome by Der Neue Führer himself. His dreams of a white-ruled America would soon be a reality. And he'd be its first leader.

Der Neue Führer came from a long and proud line of politicians. His great-great-grandfather had served in the House of Representatives prior to the Civil War, but lost his seat when North Carolina seceded. Decades later, Der Neue Führer's great-grandfather became one of the nation's youngest senators. Then his grandfather, Wallace Koehler, followed the family tradition most famously, becoming involved in politics after making a name for himself during World War I.

Koehler was a brilliant field commander who had fought bravely in the trenches of France, remaining with his men until the war ended, despite having been wounded several times. By the late 1920s he was already being affectionately and respectfully called "The Old Soldier," even though he was only in his mid-fifties.

He was the perfect candidate for a behind-the-scenes ambassador to Germany, a government-sanctioned job created to analyze the feasibility of new business ventures in post–World War I Europe. Koehler's job was to use diplomatic means to secure guarantees from German leaders that American investments would be protected, and also find financially lucrative avenues of commerce that U.S. corporations could exploit. He assumed this position in 1925, the year Adolf Hitler published *Mein Kampf.*

The Old Soldier agreed with many things in Hitler's book. He believed, as Hitler did, that humans could indeed be divided into lower and higher categories based on features alone. The superior class (spiritually, intellectually, and culturally) was the fair-skinned, blue-eyed, blond-haired Germanic peoples—the Aryans, the Master Race, the fountainhead of classic art, advanced scientific research, and even the finest music.

In *Mein Kampf,* Hitler explained how the Nazi philosophy denied the equality of races, recognizing the higher or lesser value of each race, while promoting "the victory of the better and stronger," as well as "the subordination of the inferior and weaker in accordance with the eternal will that dominates the universe."

Koehler, too, believed these things. Such views, in fact, were common. But what Hitler had to say about the Jews was new to The Old Soldier. He'd never thought too much about this particular group of people. At first the accusations against them seemed preposterous. The more he read, however, the more he realized that this brave man from Germany was indeed exposing an insidious menace. It made perfect sense that there would be some driving force behind the evil in the world. Why not the Jews?

After all, Koehler reasoned, the Jews had murdered Christ. Was it so unreasonable to think they might also be guilty of the crimes Hitler accused them of? The global conspiracy outlined in *Mein Kampf* presented a viable theory, in Koehler's opinion; one that explained the unprecedented surge in hostilities throughout the world. If the Jews controlled the banks and media, which seemed plausible, and if they were behind the birth of Marxism, which again seemed likely, then they could indeed be promoting the international social disharmony threatening world peace.

Koehler himself witnessed the deplorable condition into which Germany had fallen. The people were starving to death. Children were being abandoned in the gutter by their parents, hoping that perhaps someone more fortunate might rescue them. Rival political parties—Communists, Socialists, and Nazis—were roaming the streets of Munich in gangs and fighting each other. The economy lay in ruins with a currency decimated by inflation. By 1923 Germans were already facing an exchange rate of one hundred million Reichsmarks to the U.S. dollar. Their money was essentially worthless.

Koehler decided that something had to be done, and embraced Hitler's noble goal to restore Germany's honor. He subsequently set himself up as the U.S. banking operative for the Nazis by entering into a business partnership with the German industrialist Gerhard Thyssen, who had personally funded Hitler's meteoric rise to power. He also fraternized with some of the most nefarious Nazis, including Joseph Goebbels, Hitler's Minister of Propaganda, and Rudolf Hess, Hitler's Deputy Führer.

From 1926 to 1943, even after the United States had entered WWII, Koehler ran numerous enterprises that raised millions of dollars for the German war machine. He also set up the United Banking Conglomerate (UBC) with several prosperous American business associates sympathetic to Nazism. This institution funneled untold millions of dollars in assets into Germany from outside companies controlled by Thyssen. UBC bought, sold, and shipped gold, steel, machine parts, coal, works of art, and even U.S. Treasury bonds. In other words, UBC was a Nazi money-laundering front.

The truth, which was leaked to the press in 1940, broke as a major front-page story a year later in the *Washington Post-Tribune.* "Hitler's Guardian Angel," the headline read. Koehler denied nothing. In fact, instead of ceasing operations, he simply attempted to better conceal his activities by changing the company names and redirecting cash to dozens of Swiss bank accounts. Eventually, however, all of the corporations were traced and their assets seized under the Trading with the Enemy Act.

But no further legal action was taken against Koehler, who by then had gained many important friends in key government positions. Moreover, he had received so many financial kickbacks from his business dealings that for the rest of his life he remained a multimillionaire ten times over. He could, and did, buy whatever was needed to promote the agenda that he never abandoned, even after the fatal collapse of Nazi Germany.

First, Koehler bought off every magazine and newspaper that might further publicize his treasonous activities. Then, he used substantial campaign contributions to purchase a bevy of high-powered politicians, including senators, representatives, and judges, and he even had the audacity to run for Congress following the war. Amazingly, he won a Senate seat, as did his son, Arlen Koehler, who after winning, legally changed his surname. This controversial decision was announced at a press conference, where the younger Senator Koehler explained how he wanted to stand on his own political feet. He didn't want any favoritism shown to him merely because of the fame and public adulation that had become attached to the name of the honorable Senator Wallace Koehler.

There was another reason for the surname change. Wallace hoped that either his own son, Arlen, or perhaps even his young grandson, who was still but a child, might one day usher in the Fourth Reich as Der Neue Führer. And it was critically important that until that time arrived, the entire family be disassociated from any past connections to both Hitler's regime and the war. It was a brilliant move that ended up working better than either Arlen or Wallace could have imagined. No one suspected anything.

Leaning back heavily in his plush office chair, Der Neue Führer pondered the paths of his father, Arlen, and his grandfather, Wallace. They were great men who had taught him many things about the world. If they were alive, he knew they'd be proud of him, especially when he took over the nation. Of course, the word "president" by then would no longer have any meaning. True, he might be forced to wear the label for at least a few years, a charade for the benefit of the public, but that would only last until the radical makeover of America was complete. Then, after that glorious transition, he would proudly tell the world that he was Der Neue Führer und Reichskanzler.

Der Neue Führer looked up from reading *Mein Kampf* at 0945 hours in response to his computer chiming three times, signaling the arrival of a message. PASSWORD VERIFICATION DETECTED, read the menu on the monitor screen. "Finally," he sighed with relief, as he punched the ACCEPT MESSAGE command key.

15

★★★

Luke Schmidt was exhausted and would've stayed in bed much longer if the heated discussion downstairs hadn't jarred him out of a deep and restful sleep. One of the voices belonged to his grandfather, Pastor Bill Schmidt, but he didn't recognize the man and the woman with whom his grandfather was talking, or rather, arguing.

What now? he groaned, rolling over and throwing back the blanket.

Although he and his grandfather had left the town meeting long before its conclusion, both of them ended up staying awake for hours after they'd arrived home. Pastor Schmidt needed to put the final touches on his Sunday sermon, while Luke had to visit his private office/studio behind the house to take care of some church business and other matters.

Many duties belonged to him as assistant pastor of Christ's Chapel, a position that he'd been filling for just over four years, beginning the day after he turned twenty-one. Luke was young, but he could deliver a Bible study as competently as any local preacher and knew his Scriptures as thoroughly as some seminary graduates. He was a fine counselor as well. Those in the congregation who were going through some personal crisis could always go to Luke for thoughtful advice.

The church loved him, due in no small part to the fact that many of its longtime members had watched the grandson of their pastor go from being a confused child to a spiritual inspiration within the community. His short-cropped hair, polite manner, and conservative appearance made older attendees at ease in his presence, while at the same time, his youthfulness, casual demeanor, and knowledge of pop culture made him the perfect bridge to Rosamond's GenXers and GenNexters.

Like most people his age, Luke excelled at working with computers—something his grandfather had still not mastered. Pastor Schmidt was part of the B.C.—before computers—generation. Only after a full year of persistent and persuasive arguing about the value of the Internet was Luke able to convince his grandfather that the senior pastor of a church *needed* to have an e-mail address and that every church, even one as tiny as Christ's Chapel, was expected to have a Web site.

Pastor Schmidt grudgingly agreed, but placed on his grandson the burden of finding a Web host and someone to build the church's Web site. These stipulations, however, didn't stall Luke's momentum in the least, because by the time his grandfather had resolved to enter the twenty-first century, he'd already found a Web host and begun building his own version of what would become the church's Web site.

Creating a Web site wasn't difficult for him. He'd been venturing into deep cyberspace for hours every day since his twelfth birthday. It all started when he received a high-end PC and a DSL-connection combo package as a present from a concerned teacher. His new computer, along with the extended time he spent surfing the Internet, finally brought to an end the severe depression that had plagued him since his father's death two years earlier.

Luke had become a pro at using the Internet and related

technologies, especially Teamspeak, an audio program used for real-time voice communication during Internet-based video games such as Eve Online, Battlefield 2, and Return to Castle Wolfenstein—his favorites.

Luke continued to struggle emotionally with the radical changes that had occurred in his life. In fact, one of the very reasons his grandfather started Christ's Chapel when Luke was fourteen was to get him involved with bringing some love and light to the world. Pastor Schmidt thought that such activities might help the boy heal psychologically and spiritually.

So the fledgling church was opened on an Easter weekend. But the event wasn't a very joyous one for Luke, who had no idea why everyone was so happy. There certainly wasn't anything to celebrate, at least in his opinion, especially since his mother had decided by then that raising him was no longer something she wanted to be bothered with. So she moved to Alabama or Mississippi. At least that's what he overheard his grandfather tell a police officer who'd stopped by the house. Alabama or Mississippi. Or maybe it was Georgia. Luke wasn't sure. And he couldn't comprehend at the time why his grandfather seemed so calm about her leaving. Eventually, of course, as Luke grew older, he understood the problem. It all made perfect sense.

Luke threw on his jeans as he continued listening to the disagreement going on in the living room. He could only make out a few words here and there—

"...told you no...without a warrant," his grandfather remarked.

The other man sounded like he was trying to explain, "Look, we just...since you were...and give us..."

"Next week...But we've already..." the woman added.

Although Luke hoped his gut feeling was wrong, he suspected that whatever was going on had something to do with the recent events in Rosamond. He tried to keep an eye on his grandfather, so he decided he'd take care of the visitors himself by basically showing them the door, whoever they were. He just prayed he could keep his cool while doing so.

"Is everything okay?" he asked as he came down the stairs.

Luke's grandfather and the two visitors stopped talking immediately and turned toward him. "Yes," replied Pastor Schmidt tersely. "Our guests were just leaving."

Luke would've liked very much to just kick the two strangers out of his house as soon as he entered the living room. At the same time, however, he didn't want to see the situation escalate. His grandfather was already worked up. "If there's a problem, maybe I can help," he said firmly, this time taking a step closer.

The man now facing him hesitated briefly as he made up his mind about what to do. "No. No problems here. You're Luke, aren't you?"

"That's right," Pastor Schmidt interjected, as he walked over and put his arm on Luke's shoulder. "He's also my assistant pastor and the worship leader at the church."

"Well, it's nice to meet you, Luke. I'm Special Agent Stark and this is Special Agent Carlyle."

Luke gave a half smile. "Hi. Nice to meet you. What's going on?"

Stark grinned nonchalantly. "Oh, nothing to worry about. We just had a few questions for your grandfather. That's all."

Carlyle stepped forward and handed a business card to Pastor Schmidt. "If you change your mind or think of anything you might want to tell us, feel free to call—anytime," she told him.

Schmidt snatched the card from Carlyle, his hand quivering slightly. "Fine," he snapped. "Now, I think you'd better go."

The two agents crossed the room, unhurried by Schmidt's tone. "We'll be in touch," Stark promised, as he opened the door for his partner, who walked out first. The agent then stared directly into Bill Schmidt's eyes. "By the way, it was good to see you again, *Wilhelm*."

16

★ ★ ★

Bill Schmidt stood alone in the kitchen of his modest two-bedroom home and stared out the window at Christ's Chapel. The worship center was fifty yards away, surrounded by plenty of dirt-lot parking for those who came to hear Bill's Sunday-morning sermons and Luke's Wednesday-night Bible studies.

The property had no landscaping to speak of, except for a few cactus scattered here and there around the grounds. But the bareness of his half-acre parcel of land actually complemented the chapel, which was unadorned compared to other churches in the area. It was clean, sturdy, and functional.

That was all Schmidt cared about, although at times he wished a different paint had been used on the building. The cheap white stuff he'd bought at a going-out-of-business sale had started cracking and peeling almost as soon as it had dried. It made him wince every he looked close enough to notice.

The church, constructed by local residents who'd volunteered their time and energy as a "love thy neighbor" gesture of service, had yet to be filled to its capacity of two hundred. But Bill was satisfied with teaching his little flock, thankful to be doing something good with his life, maybe as a way of making up for all the pain he had caused so many people in his younger days.

His tiny house, also built by community volunteers, looked remarkably similar to the church, but with a porch and a second story added. It was square and plain, having only two points of modernity: air conditioning and central heating. These luxuries made the place bearable in the summer and inhabitable in the winter. It was the ideal setup for Bill and Luke, neither of whom needed much in the way of creature comforts. They had the house, the church, and the property. And Luke, of course, had his office/studio out back. Bill often asked him, "What more do we need to accomplish the Lord's work?" The answer, of course, was nothing.

A grateful heart and a contented soul were the most precious things he wanted to pass on to his grandson. And after that, a legacy of faith, hope, and love. But now, due to the sudden appearance of Carlyle and Stark, Schmidt would have to wait a bit longer for his ugly past to go away. *Why won't they leave me alone?* the pastor brooded, as he turned from the window and walked over to the small dinette shoved up against the wall.

He sighed heavily and plopped himself down into one of the three wooden chairs at the table, his shoulders sagging, his eyes filled with regret. The last thing he wanted to do was dredge up memories and open up old wounds by dealing yet again with law-enforcement officers, especially Stark. Schmidt didn't blame the veteran Secret Service man for harboring mistrust, probably even hatred, toward him. In fact, he was surprised Stark hadn't taken a swing at him. But the agent's parting shot was a good one. No one had called him Wilhelm in a long time, and it hurt to hear the name spoken again. He wondered if Stark knew just how deeply his stab had cut.

It was coming up on fifteen years since the two men had first encountered each other at a Bakersfield Klan rally. The riotous event had almost ripped the community apart. Stark was still in the FBI. William Schmidt was a neo-Nazi recruiter, agitator, and all-around troublemaker. The FBI showed up at the rally to scrutinize the situation, take down names, and snap a few photos. Schmidt was doing what he did best—inciting the masses.

He was known as Wilhelm back then, in honor of Kaiser Wilhelm II, the militaristic German emperor who'd led his country into World War I. Schmidt cofounded and helped run the Aryan War Heroes, a gang of radical racists known for their willingness to commit murder for hire, extortion, armed robbery, and other serious crimes—whatever needed to be done to advance what they called their Radical Religious Reformation. The group's goals mirrored those of all Christian Identity adherents: destroy the Jews, rid the U.S. of blacks and other people of color, prevent race-mixing, and topple the Zionist Occupational Government controlling America.

But unlike the majority of Christian Identity believers, the Aryan War Heroes did more than just talk about establishing a white theocracy. They actively sought to bring about a new world through direct confrontations with the enemy, much like The Order and Bob Matthews had done many years earlier. Schmidt and his right-hand man, Karl Gruber, were the brains of the organization. They coordinated vandalism of Jewish synagogues, organized public protests against minorities, and even planned a string of robberies that netted the group nearly two million dollars.

Eddie Stark and his partner at the time, Anthony Torino, were assigned the task of monitoring Schmidt and Gruber in hopes of finding out how their directives were being relayed to followers located throughout Southern California. The two lawmen eventually discovered that commands were being sent out via UPS and FedEx drivers who were part of the group. These drivers would make their daily deliveries on routes that took them hundreds of miles in every direction. They would simply take a short detour during the course of a work day, pass along the orders to someone waiting for them at a designated contact spot, then continue along as usual.

The puzzle pieces fell together after Torino started mapping out the distances from various crimes that had been committed. He recognized a snakelike pattern that weaved through the city, just like a delivery route. It reminded him of the regular stops he'd made for a catering company during the years he worked his way through college. No one else saw the pattern, but Stark trusted his partner, so together they tracked down all the newly hired employees of major driving companies in that area.

After months of investigation, they not only identified several workers involved with the Aryan War Heroes, but intercepted one of the communications: "Los Angeles Federal Credit Union, Branch #127, 3:00 a.m., July 17." Schmidt would later tell authorities that these instructions had been sent out by Gruber, but that the operation had been set up without the approval of Schmidt, who was already beginning to have doubts about the cause and feeling guilty about the mayhem he'd been creating. He was already thinking about getting out of the movement altogether.

Schmidt also sensed that the law was closing in on them and told Gruber a bank robbery would be too risky. But Gruber didn't listen. He was headstrong and thought that Schmidt was beginning to go soft. So he planned the operation by himself and convinced a few of the group's most dedicated members, including Schmidt's own son, David, to proceed with the robbery. Their projected haul was $4.5 million.

They entered the bank using homemade sticks of dynamite, expecting to blow the safe and be out within seven minutes, with two minutes to spare before police arrived. But the L.A.P.D., the FBI, and two Los Angeles S.W.A.T. teams were waiting for Gruber's foot soldiers to show up and watched the whole scene from less than a block away. When the surprised band of Aryan War Heroes emerged from the bank, a gun battle erupted between them and law-enforcement agents who found themselves up against the automatic weapons carried by the robbers.

The shootout lasted nearly two hours, ending only after the

last surviving gunman threw his AK-47 into the street and raised his hands. Stark and Torino were in the thick of the action, successfully dodging high-caliber, armor-piercing rounds, until one unfortunate shot penetrated the police cruiser they were using as a shield. The bullet missed Stark but struck Torino in the heart. He was dead before he hit the ground. The thirty-year-old FBI agent left behind a wife and two daughters, ages three and four. Wilhelm's son, David, died that night too. He was twenty-eight, with an on-again-off-again girlfriend, by whom he had had a son, Luke, who was ten years old.

After a lengthy trial that escalated into a media circus, Gruber and Schmidt got off easy. Both men had covered their tracks so well that nothing substantial could be pinned directly on them, though it was obvious they were somehow connected to the attempted bank heist. In the end, Schmidt got out of jail after serving only a few months for minor offenses: inciting violence, possession of stolen property, and obstruction of justice. He had plea-bargained his way down to the lightest charges possible.

In return, Schmidt not only helped convict Gruber of similar crimes, but revealed to investigators where they could find a cache of automatic weapons in Gruber's home. That cleared the way for a possession-of-illegal-weapons indictment, a far more serious charge that put Gruber behind bars for two years. It was also Schmidt who'd divulged the names and whereabouts of other Aryan War Heroes, all of whom were arrested, tried, and convicted.

Gruber never forgave Schmidt, who changed his name back to William after finding God in the words of a prison preacher. The nondenominational minister had encouraged him to repent of his sins and accept Jesus as Lord and Savior. He did just that, and when he got out of jail several months later, told people at the church he started attending to just call him Bill. That was the name that had now stuck with him, to the present.

Schmidt didn't receive any forgiveness from Stark, either. The

FBI agent didn't buy the whole spiritual conversion line he'd heard so many times before from inmates seeking to win sympathy from juries and parole boards. Besides, his best friend and partner was dead. That was the only thing he could see. "Don't give me that God stuff," he'd railed after hearing about Schmidt's conversion. "Jesus isn't the one who's gotta give an answer to Tony's little girls when they ask why Daddy isn't coming home!"

God, I'm so sorry, mumbled Schmidt as he stared down at the worn newspaper clippings. "FBI Agent and Four Suspects Dead," read the headline. *You know how sorry I am. But please, I'm so tired of this. I just want to go on.*

The Bible sitting on the kitchen table was open to Galatians 6:9: "Let us not become weary in doing good, for at the proper time we will reap a harvest, if we do not give up." Schmidt closed it, wanting to do the very opposite of what it said. He had no desire to talk to any law-enforcement personnel. No desire to help. To them he was still just Wilhelm.

Three sharp raps on the door startled Bill out of his thoughts. "Luke, can you get that?" But there was no response from upstairs. The pastor had forgotten he'd sent Luke out on an errand. "Just a second," Schmidt shouted as he got up to go see who it was. Along the way, he gently folded the newspaper clippings back along their edges pressed sharp by years of storage and tucked them into an envelope.

"Can I help you?" the pastor asked pointedly after opening the door.

"Excuse me. My name's Frank Delafield. Might I have a few minutes of your time?"

The man looked just like a federal agent. He was clean-cut, just about the right height and build, and was wearing a dark suit. "Look, I've had it with you people. Unless you have a warrant I'm not going to talk to you. I told that to Stark and Carlyle. I don't care who you are—CIA, FBI, NSA—whatever. Just leave me alone or you'll be hearing from my lawyer."

Frank stepped back. "I'm sorry. I think you might have me confused with someone else. I'm a journalist. I only wanted to interview you for a story I'm doing on white supremacists and their possible connection to recent events." He rummaged in his pocket and handed Schmidt a card.

Schmidt peered down at it. "Delafield," he muttered. "Frank Delafield...hey, I know you."

"You do?"

Schmidt nodded. "You're the one who's been writing those magazine articles on Christian Identity."

Frank chuckled. "Yeah, that'd be me."

"Hate the magazine, but your articles are good."

"Thanks. I still have a final installment to finish for the series and thought maybe you could provide me with some information. I saw you at the town meeting and you seem to really know what you're talking about. I promise it won't take long."

"Oh, I know what I'm talking about, alright," Schmidt replied. "I'm sure I could tell you a lot of things that your readers would find very interesting. C'mon in."

17

Courage is being scared to death…and saddling up anyway.

JOHN WAYNE (1907–1979)

★★★

Mike Coletti telephoned Stark at 9:00 p.m. sharp, right on time, just like always. He was one of the agency's best men, intelligent and resourceful, with a black belt in Tae Kwon Do and a ninety-eight percent proficiency rating in firearms. He played his undercover roles better than anyone, paying special attention to details overlooked by others.

He'd masqueraded as an underworld hit man, a heroin supplier, a smuggler of undocumented immigrants. Coletti found no job too dangerous. No matter what kind of organization he infiltrated, even the most hard-core members quickly accepted him with little suspicion.

That was one of Coletti's specialties. He could gain the trust of others by using a chameleon like ability to mirror their attitudes, beliefs, and outward appearance. Sometimes he put on such a good show that he was asked to take on duties normally reserved for leaders of the organization he was infiltrating, which was why he was selected to investigate Karl Gruber's compound.

The phone rang only once. "Stark here."

"This is Coletti."

"Always good to hear from you, Mike. You okay?"

"No problems on this end. But you guys are going to have to keep your eyes open over the next few days. Sounds like another strike is being planned, or maybe it's already been planned. I'm not sure. Just be ready."

"Gruber?"

"No, I don't think so. I'm starting to believe he's completely out of the loop. There's someone called the Reichsmarschall. I have no idea who he is. I suppose it could be Gruber, but I don't think so. Whoever he is, he's the one coordinating everything. I've also confirmed that there is a War Room, no doubt about that. I overheard a couple of soldiers in the Brotherhood talking about having been there a few nights ago, but I still can't find it. They kept laughing about it, saying how the War Room was so obvious."

"They didn't say any more?"

"No. Unfortunately not," he said, looking behind him to make sure no one was watching.

Stark shifted the receiver in his hand, and picked up a pen. "Any names for me this week?"

"Yeah, a few, sort of. But they're not really names. More like nicknames or code names. I'm not sure."

"Go ahead," said Stark.

"I only have two: 'Terrorist101' and 'IronCross.' A few of the guys around here, as well as some members of the other groups I've been hearing about, are starting to mention these kinds of names more frequently. One of the guys I overheard, for example, called his buddy 'SinisterNazi.' Maybe they're e-mail addresses."

"Okay. I'll start trying to run a check on the names to see if anything turns up under aliases or e-mails. Any information on possible targets or dates?"

"I wish," he huffed in frustration. "I suppose something could go down on Christmas. Everyone here's always complaining about it, saying how they wish the pagans would get what they deserve. And these guys the other night mentioned something about a holiday."

"Thanks, Mike. Anything else?"

"Hold on," Coletti stopped abruptly.

Muffled talking on the other end of the line replaced the sound of Coletti's calm voice. It sounded like another member was telling him something about Gruber. Finally, after a few minutes, the undercover agent pulled the cell phone back out from his pocket, and was again able to speak freely. "Sorry about that," he continued.

Stark began to breathe again. "What was that about?"

Coletti paused. "Nothing to worry about, but I have to go. Gruber's called one of his spur-of-the-moment inspirational meetings. Whenever he needs a dose of hero worship he calls a get-together so everyone can listen to him drone on about the glory of the Aryan people and how the day is coming soon when Yahweh will reign."

"Hang in there, Mike," Stark urged, hearing the fatigue in his friend's voice. "We're getting close, thanks to you. Hey, I'll recommend you get a raise."

Coletti smiled. "Sounds good. I'll talk to you later," he said, and then hung up.

Stark flipped his own cell phone closed and got up from the desk in the far corner of his hotel room. It had been over two weeks since he and Carlyle had traveled to Rosamond, but their leads were still few and far between. He'd hoped that maybe, just maybe, Schmidt would offer to help. *That was a mistake,* Stark told himself as he pulled out a five-inch file on Wilhelm and threw it on the coffee table.

It was all in there, from his first misdemeanor to his plea-bargaining deal. Everything was covered in minute detail, except for how his actions forever destroyed the Torino family. Stark had tried to keep in touch with his partner's widow for a while, even feeling as if he should help her and the girls out financially. But staying close to them only intensified his guilt. It was just too much to bear. So after a few months, his weekly visits turned into once-a-month phone calls, which eventually became yearly Christmas cards that he one day decided to stop sending.

Stark took off his shirt and clicked on the television before flopping down on the bed. Nothing on as usual. He had clicked the channel changer a dozen times or so, when the phone rang.

"Hello," he said as he hit the mute button.

"Evenin', Stark. I thought you'd still be awake."

"And I thought you'd be out of here by now. Weren't you on your way back to Maryland for Christmas?"

Carlyle sighed. "Yeah, well, the whole East Coast is shut down. I made it as far as the LAX terminal. The blizzard back East is supposed to last at least another two days, maybe more. The airlines told everyone they'd better make new plans."

"Sorry, Chris," Stark replied as he shut the TV off. "I know you were looking forward to seeing your parents."

"That's alright, California's nice. Might as well make the best of things."

"True."

"Hey, only two days before Christmas. So why don't you meet me in the lobby and I'll buy us a few rounds of yuletide cheer down here in…" she paused to look over at the hotel bar, "Cactus Jack's."

"Sounds good to me. I'll be down in about fifteen minutes."

"That's fine. It'll give me some time to check back into a room and throw my stuff inside."

"And Chris?" Stark added.

"Uh-huh?"

"Do me a favor and leave your sidearm in a drawer. You don't need to take it everywhere you go."

"Sure, sure," Carlyle chuckled. "By the way, did Coletti call?"

"Yeah, I just got off the phone with him," Stark answered. "I'll tell you what he said while we drown our sorrows in the bar."

"Okay. See you in a few minutes."

18

The world is full of suffering.
It is also full of overcoming it.

HELEN KELLER (1880–1968)

★ ★ ★

Frank got up early on December 25, long before the sun peeked out from behind the mountains that rose majestically in the distance. He didn't have any gifts to open, or to give. Nor did he have any special dinner plans or a party to get ready for. The alarm had been set to 5:00 a.m. so he could finish transcribing his conversation with Bill Schmidt. He figured he could wrap that up by lunch. Then, proofreading and editing the interview would take most of the afternoon, probably until supper. In the evening, he'd work on hammering out his next article.

"Where's that breakfast I ordered last night?" Frank mumbled as he shuffled out of the bathroom. His laptop was already waiting for him, flipped open on the desk, hard drive spinning, with the document "Schmidt Interview" on the screen. He'd hit the start button of his computer right after climbing out of bed. Frank was the ultimate multitasker, especially when he was excited about a project, and this one was becoming exceptionally interesting.

A knock at the door told Frank that what he'd been waiting for had finally arrived. "Room service," a man called out from the hallway.

"Just a second." Frank quickly threw on a robe and crossed to the door. "C'mon in." It was all there: pancakes, scrambled eggs, bacon, sausage. A side order of fresh fruit, orange juice, toast, and a large pot of steaming coffee.

"That's $38.86," the man politely noted. "Just sign here."

Frank found it hard to believe he was paying almost forty bucks for what he could normally get at Denny's for only five-ninety-nine. But at least he now had everything he needed to get started. "Thanks," the reporter said, as he handed the man a ten-buck tip. "And, uh, Merry Christmas."

The man looked down and smiled. "Thank you very much, sir. Merry Christmas to you too."

A lot of people at the office thought Frank didn't like Christmas, but he did like it, at least as a concept. He just hated the commercialism of the season, what it had become, the sense of obligation he felt every year to buy something for everyone—or as he often put it, *anything for anyone*. He also saw no reason to bring religion into the picture. The holiday, after all, was originally a pagan celebration. So why not just keep it as a nice time of year for people to come together, enjoy each other's company, appreciate friends and family, and be grateful for what good things there are to be had in this world?

It wasn't that he minded religion. Not at all. He just wasn't into "faith." Whether or not other people found comfort in religion was their business—as long as they didn't use their beliefs to attack or harm others. "Religion is like fire," Frank often told his fellow journalists. "A useful thing in the hands of most people, but terribly harmful when used by somebody bent on doing a little damage."

He rarely took a second look at run-of-the-mill religious news like church growth trends or papal elections. Common stories put him to sleep. So he eschewed anything handled by the mass media. Aside from a quick look into the embarrassing closets of the Vatican, Delafield had confined his focus to the seriously offbeat, the odd, even the comical (but only to those with a twisted sense of humor).

He liked investigating the faith of others, mostly because it enabled him to vicariously experience the highs and lows of the metaphysical. He'd set aside his own spirituality long ago because of what had happened to his wife, Blair. Without a word of warning, she'd been taken from him, which convinced him that there was no God. There couldn't be. No God would inflict so much pain on someone who had lived his life as a fairly decent person.

Just eight months into their marriage, Blair had decided to go to the supermarket for a carton of butter pecan Häagen-Dazs. That wasn't unusual. She craved ice cream at the most inconvenient times, but it was one of those things about his college sweetheart that made him love her even more. Frank wanted her to stay home and finish the movie they were watching.

"C'mon, babe," he pleaded. "We only have another half hour left. And it's raining."

"I'll be right back," Blair promised, kissing him on the cheek. "A little rain never hurt anyone."

But less than a mile from home, a drunk driver had proved her wrong. No squeal of tires. No horn. No indication whatsoever that an affluent, martini-loving lawyer had blown through a stoplight on her left. The intoxicated attorney slammed his shiny new $65,000 Mercedes into Blair's Toyota at seventy miles an hour. Frank never got a chance to say goodbye.

The inebriated litigator also died in the crash. But that gave no solace to Frank, who didn't even begin recovering emotionally until more than a year later. He was just about to go over the edge when, in a last-ditch effort to regain his sanity, he wrapped his mind around one pain-numbing, seventy-five-hour workweek after another.

Frank eventually secured a position with Angus Reid's *Bizarre Times International*. The position was hardly lucrative, but it paid the bills, which meant that he would continue to afford a place to sleep at night, plenty of food, clean clothes, and a reason to get up every day. He didn't need or want anything beyond that. Not anymore. Not since Blair had taken all of his dreams with her when she left.

Angus immediately appreciated the talent he'd found in Frank. Thanks to his new reporter, *BTI*'s circulation had shot up three hundred percent in the four years since his first series: "Welcome Space Brothers: Understanding the Unarians." Angus was ecstatic about that one. "Delafield, you're a natural," he exclaimed. "You interested in a regular feature of your own?"

And so began Frank's regular column. A few more articles soon solidified his popularity among readers. Letters to the editor poured into the mailroom. *I really like those religion stories…a refreshing twist on your regular content…I couldn't believe what you wrote…enlightening piece on the Ghost Hunter…will be waiting to see your final installment on the psychic who says she can talk to dogs and angels.*

The public devoured Frank's bimonthly reports, probably because each one made them feel so much better about themselves; made them glad they weren't involved with some nutty cult or madman; made them thankful that when such-and-such a group came knocking at *their* door, they were smart enough to turn down the TV and hide behind the curtains instead of saying, "Come on in!"

Interestingly, ex-members of the religious groups he covered were his most ardent fans. "Thanks," they'd say, "for telling the truth." And that's what made Delafield unlike other tabloid journalists. All of his stories were true. He didn't invent or embellish any part of the spellbinding narratives he put together. He didn't have to. There was no way to improve on reality, which was sufficiently nutty enough to capture people's interest.

Frank wondered if his last piece on religious racism would help anyone. Schmidt, it seemed, was already grateful. The broken man had spoken to him for three-and-a-half hours about his past, why he got involved with racists, what he did during his many years as a neo-Ñazi, why he left the movement. None of Frank's other interviews had ever lasted as long. And no other person had ever spoken to him with so much depth of emotion about a subject. It was too bad that Schmidt had had to lose his son to see the light.

After taking several scalding gulps of java and sinking his teeth into some buttered toast, Frank threw on CNN for background noise, looked at his laptop screen, and began typing.

19

★★★

One of the busiest shopping days of the year, December 26, started out as expected, with millions of consumers rushing out to congested megamalls, their patience spent and nerves frazzled. Buying the perfect Christmas present, of course, was no longer the goal. Different objectives on revised to-do lists now weighed heavily on their minds: *Exchange Auntie Lulu's dress for one that fits. Return the tie from cousin Tony for a store credit. Trade in Mom's gift certificate for cash.*

The long lines and crowded parking lots didn't make for a pleasant experience. But fortunately, *ONE-DAY SALE* and *60% OFF* signs decorated just about every department-store window and product display. Bargains, it seemed, were plentiful, thanks to corporate executives who were offering deep discounts on their overstock of odd-sized fashions and recently damaged goods— a belated holiday gift of sorts for anyone brave enough to leave home, especially in light of the Homeland Security Advisory System's ongoing terrorism threat level: *red.*

Near Iowa City, Iowa, the Coral Ridge Mall was packed. Its doors had opened at six a.m., which explained why, by nine o'clock, caravans of cars were flowing from its many entrances toward the mall like streamers hanging from a piñata. Most visitors were not only looking forward to taking care of a few errands, but also having some fun at the mall's regulation-sized ice-skating rink, children's museum, and movie house, complete with ten theaters that screened only the latest films.

Less than a three-hour drive away, just outside Chicago, the Woodfield Mall in Schaumburg was even more crowded. Nearly every one of its 13,000 parking spaces was taken up by shoppers eager to finish their year-end tasks and then enjoy some snacks at the mall's renowned eateries. The 2.7-million-square-foot shopping center was well-known for selling some of the best hot pretzels and Chicago-style pizza anywhere in the suburbs.

Four hundred miles to the northwest, there was the world-famous Mall of America in Bloomington, Minnesota, the largest mall in the country, a combination shopping center and indoor amusement park sprawled over 4.3 miles of storefronts. On the day after Christmas the MOA could always be relied upon as the perfect place to take the whole family. Its attractions never failed to enthrall even the youngest kids: a roller coaster called the Timberland Twister; a walk-through dinosaur museum that included sixty life-sized creatures from prehistoric era, and an underwater sea aquarium with over 4500 sea creatures featuring not only a virtual submarine ride but also a shark encounter.

The attacks planned by the Reichsmarschall did not take long to carry out. They began at 1:00 p.m. sharp, Central Standard Time, in Iowa, Illinois, and Minnesota. All three martyrs reached their targets with plenty of time to spare, were committed to fulfilling their assignments, and were clear on their leader's instructions to leave the same message—a message that would let everyone in America know they were in a war.

IronCross arrived at Coral Ridge Mall by noon so he could thoroughly scope out the area. Within forty-five minutes he had decided that the entrance between the Iowa Children's Museum and the ice arena, and located across from the movie theater, would be the best place for him to begin his assault. It was the most crowded entrance he could find.

Thor also reached his destination, the Woodfield Mall, at around twelve o'clock. He came in through the entrance on the first floor next to Sears, where he waited on a bench for almost an hour by the Rainforest Café. He watched the tropical birds and fish on display in the restaurant, captivated by their intricate beauty. He also liked the giant mechanical butterflies clinging to the walls, and the stuffed gorilla that moved its arms up and down, turning its head back and forth. By 12:50, Thor had decided not to hurt anyone or anything in that particular spot. So he walked several hundred feet in the opposite direction, toward the center of the mall, far from the Rainforest Café, stopping adjacent to the main kiosk, then sat down near the mall's cascading water fountain.

Meanwhile, in Bloomington, Minnesota, at the Mall of America, Terrorist101 continued his purposeful march toward the south food court, which was strategically built on the third floor, between Macy's and Bloomingdale's, the most frequented department stores in the complex. It was packed with hungry shoppers, some queuing up to order, others already wolfing down whatever they had been looking forward to eating.

He first noticed the Bubba Gump Shrimp Co. after rounding the corner of The Photo Memory Store. Next, McDonald's caught his eye, followed by Hot Dog on a Stick, Sbarro, and Panda Express. He looked at his watch—12:57—sat down near the outer edge of the food court at an empty table, then slowly reached into the large black satchel he'd been carrying and pulled out a one-gallon jug filled with liquid.

No one had paid much attention to the bag, nor had anyone suspected anything out of the ordinary about the industrial sprayer on Terrorist101's back. He just looked like another maintenance worker hired by the mall to water the plants or spray for bugs. But there was no insecticide in the four-gallon backpack sprayer that he cautiously slid off his back and put on the floor. The unit contained three chemicals—phosphorous pentasulfide, diisopropylamine, and methyl phosphonyl chloride—separated into different compartments by thin walls of nonporous plastic. The one-gallon carton, which he carefully opened, held ethylene oxide along with a few other choice ingredients readily obtainable from any chemical retailer. He poured this final solution into the sprayer after removing a secure cap that had been locked down on top of the unit.

After replacing the cap, Terrorist101 hit the on/off switch, which first broke the fragile partitions that had been placed between each chemical, then activated the internal jet agitator, which in turn mixed the liquids. They combined rapidly to make an odorless, lightly golden mixture known by its chemical name as O-ethyl S-2-diisopropylaminoethyl methylphosphonothiolate, or in layman's terms, VX nerve gas—one of the most lethal weapons of mass destruction ever created.

This concoction, to be more precise, was VX-G, a new variant of the conventional VX gas invented in England in 1952. Although it retained the same high-grade motor oil consistency of its predecessor, VX-G was slightly less viscous, and therefore, it translated more easily into a fine mist that could be spread farther and faster than VX. And unlike regular VX, VX-G caused symptoms of exposure to appear within seconds, no matter how it was absorbed into the body. Moreover, the common antidote for VX poisoning, atropine injected directly into the heart, was ineffective against VX-G.

After blending the ingredients for three minutes, Terrorist101 stood up and faced the food court, the wand of his sprayer pointed high overhead, directly toward the crowd of unsuspecting victims. He bumped a stroller as he backed up, and the child's mother didn't know what in the world the custodian was doing. He didn't even say "Excuse me" or "I'm sorry." The next thing the woman knew, both she and her baby, along with everyone else within a thirty-foot radius, were covered with moisture.

Millions of tiny droplets, many of them invisible, landed on dozens of shoppers, then on hundreds of them. Terrorist101 quickened his pace backward, trying to avoid physical contact with the VX-G, while at the same time hoping not to inhale even a microscopic amount of it. Everyone else, however, immediately received massive doses of the nerve agent. Some breathed it deep into their lungs, others put a contaminated forkful of penne pasta or shrimp-fried rice into their mouths, not yet realizing what was going on. It ended up in the eyes of several people closest to the sprayer, and nearly every victim felt the gooey fluid land on their skin, where it seeped instantly into their pores.

Terrorist101 saw the results of his handiwork less than four seconds after releasing the spray. Children and babies reacted immediately, writhing and jerking in agony as intense muscle spasms racked their bodies. Mothers and fathers, along with other adults and teenagers standing nearby, could only let out momentary gasps of horror before they, too, started suffering the effects of nerve-agent exposure. A runny nose at first, followed rapidly by explosive vomiting, bleeding from the eyes, choking, involuntary urination and defecation, respiratory shutdown, then violent convulsions so intense that arms, legs, and backs could be heard breaking as a result of the muscular contractions. Then, mercifully, heart failure. Total time elapsed between initiation of symptoms and death—one minute.

The hideous scene that unfolded with lightning speed came as a shock to everyone, even Terrorist101, who had no real idea what the effects of the VX-G would be. He thought people would merely stagger around a bit, then just faint, never to wake up again. No one had prepared him for what he witnessed. He froze in his tracks, staring blankly at the dead and dying, his hand squeezed tightly around the lever of the sprayer. Many people tried to run, but collapsed after taking only a few steps, gagging on mucous being expelled from their lungs. The sound of bones breaking in the numerous bodies convulsing before him was now growing louder as more victims fell to the ground.

Tightening his resolve, Terrorist101 swung the unit's nozzle in the opposite direction, over the third floor's railing, and sent a light mist of destruction down on passersby who were looking up from the first and second floors, trying to see the cause of the loud commotion. VX-G landed in their eyes, mouths, and noses, instantly sending them into death throes. The nerve agent moved like an unstoppable wave through the mall as other shoppers not yet exposed to the liquid were touched either by it, or by those who had the oily substance clinging to their clothes and hands. People trying to help the helpless became victims themselves.

The microdroplets, after only a few minutes, were sucked into the air-conditioning vents and distributed throughout the mall. By that time, Terrorist101 was himself dead, clutching a note in his hand that read "RaHoWa." His watch, which had smashed against a concrete pillar during the convulsions he endured before dying, was stopped at 1:06. Mission complete.

By then, in Schaumburg's Woodfield Mall, Thor had also completed his job, and he lay dead of a self-inflicted gunshot wound administered by a Model 500 Smith & Wesson handgun he'd placed in his mouth. The .50 caliber, hollow-point round blew the entire back and top of his head off. He'd committed suicide soon after lobbing his last grenade at a group of fleeing teenagers.

A total of thirty-two grenades had been thrown by Thor as he walked along the mall's first floor, pitching them backward over his shoulder, slinging them to his right and left into stores, and heaving them straight forward, as far as he could, like a professional baseball player trying to throw out a runner at home plate from center field. He died at 1:04 p.m., but not before using an aerosol can of black paint to write the word "RaHoWa" on the floor where he died.

IronCross, at the Coral Ridge Mall in Iowa, outlived both of his fellow soldiers, although not by much. The weapons assigned to him were two M11 automatic machine guns, one for each hand. They weren't difficult to carry at three-and-a-half pounds each, easily concealable at less than ten inches long, and had a rate of fire capable of dealing considerable death and damage at close range: sixteen hundred rounds per minute.

His attack started outside the mall when he pulled the M11s from two extra deep pockets sewn onto his baggy pants. He shot everyone standing in line to buy tickets at the Cineplex, then moved leisurely toward the mall doors, firing short bursts at anyone running in the opposite direction. Two fifty-round magazines had been spent by the time he hit the main entrance, where he popped out the empty clips and reloaded.

Once inside, he walked the length of the mall, unhurriedly shooting at anything that moved until it was again time to reload, which he did a total of ten times. Almost fifteen minutes had elapsed when he turned around to see an empty shopping center littered with bloody corpses and twitching bodies desperately holding on to precious life.

IronCross's ears rang loudly from the machine-gun blasts, but he could still hear crying mixed with screams, perhaps from the lucky few who'd run fast enough to get into a store and hide. In the distance, the sound of police sirens grew louder and louder. He dropped his guns and pulled out a small digital recorder with enough battery power to broadcast an audio message to the world for at least six hours.

He hit the play button as he sat down and bit into a cyanide capsule. The martyr fell back, dead in seconds, although his voice continued to echo throughout the mall, a greeting for the S.W.A.T. team when it arrived, repeating the same word over and over in a cold, lifeless monotone: "RaHoWa…RaHoWa… RaHoWa…"

20

★★★

Blair Delafield led Frank down the hallway of their new apartment, her left hand holding his arm, her right hand shielding his eyes. "Don't peek," she warned. "Don't you dare peek."

Frank laughed. "I won't, I promise."

"Okay," she said after they'd come to a complete stop. "Are you ready?"

"Yes, I'm ready," Frank answered with a huge smile on his face.

"Ta-Da!" exulted his wife, pulling her hands away.

Frank slowly opened one eye, then the other, looking around at the vibrantly painted walls. They were a pop-culture addict's dream come true, intensely bright, almost to the point of being luminescent, pomegranate red and sunflower yellow, up against a shade on the ceiling that, although Frank couldn't actually identify it by name, looked like a cross between the bluest sky he'd ever seen during a California summer and the dazzling turquoise eyes of Minxie, his sister's Persian kitty.

"Wow!" exclaimed Frank.

Blair tried to hide her excitement but couldn't stifle a childlike giggle as she bounced up and down ever so slightly. "Well?" she asked. "Do you love it?"

Frank grinned and nodded, still staring in disbelief at the garish color scheme reminiscent of an Andy Warhol poster, amazed at what the center of his life had accomplished using her creativity, imagination, and boundless energy. "Oh, yeah," he answered. "I *love* it."

Blair clasped her hands together under her chin, trying to maintain at least a modicum of composure. "Do you, really?"

"Oh, babe, I really do," he replied, slowly walking up to one of the walls to take a closer look at what seemed to be a bit of texturing.

"Wait, sweetie, don't touch it—it might still be wet. I just finished it a couple of hours ago."

Frank turned around and looked at his bride of six months, who was beaming from ear to ear. "I'm so proud of you. It looks awesome. Absolutely awesome!"

"Hurray!" Blair shouted as she threw her hands up into the air and ran over to him. "All because I adore you," she whispered, wrapping her arms around his neck and pulling him close.

"I adore you too," Frank responded. Then he kissed her. "And you know what?"

"What?"

"Everyone's gonna get a real kick out of it when they come over tomorrow night for the party. They're gonna feel like they walked into a Bugs Bunny cartoon."

Blair pulled back. "Ooh, that reminds me," she enthused, then walked over to the kitchen. "Speaking of the party, look at what I bought today at Beverages & More." She opened the refrigerator and pulled out a bottle of Moët & Chandon champagne.

Frank was just about to tell his wife how impressed he was with her selection, but stopped suddenly when a pair of ice-encrusted hands with claws at the fingertips reached out from the freezer and began choking her, viciously tugging at her hair and trying to drag her inside.

"Frank!" she screamed in terror. "Frank!"

He ran toward her, dazed by the bizarre scene, but knowing he had to save her. The hallway, however, was lengthening, at first by only a few feet per second, then by several yards with each passing moment. The harder he tried to reach her, the more sluggish his movements became, until finally, forward progress of any kind was impossible. It was as if his legs were stuck in cement. "Blair!" he shouted.

Suddenly, the lights in the kitchen began to flicker on and off, sending sparks and electrical discharges into the air. Beneath the blinking lamps he could still see his wife fighting her losing battle with the awful creature inside the refrigerator, its spiked and scaly torso now visible, coiled around her struggling body like a monstrous python, pulling her closer and closer to some netherworld region.

After a few more moments he could barely see the top half of Blair, thrashing about on the floor, arms frantically trying to grab onto something...anything. "Frank! It's hurting me. Frank! *Help me!*"

But Frank couldn't help. Although his mind was telling him to move, not a single muscle was responding. He was paralyzed, utterly powerless to stop the inevitable, unable to do anything but watch his wife disappear into what had just become a glowing rectangle of pulsating orange light. Her pleas grew more muffled as the brightly painted walls that she had so lovingly worked on turned into a dull gray, then faded away, until nothing was left but blackness all around.

"Blair, hang on," Frank sobbed. "Please hang on." Tears streamed down his face.

Soon, the only part of Blair that remained underneath the gloomy kitchen lights was a quivering fist pounding on the floor. *Bang bang bang.*

"Frank!" she continued to yell, but more and more faintly. "Frank!"

Bang bang…bang bang bang.

The journalist's eyes popped open as he sprang up in bed, sweating from every pore, goosebumps covering his body, breathing heavily. Someone was knocking on his room door.

Tap, tap, tap. "Frank! Frank!" *Tap, tap, tap.* "Hello?…Frank Delafield! Can you open up if you're in there, please."

"Ah…yeah, just a minute," he yelled, finally getting his bearings. He looked at the clock next to the bed. *11:45 a.m.… I can't believe I slept this late.*

He threw on his jeans and a T-shirt. "Hold on," he blurted out, then stumbled toward the door, opening it after fumbling with the deadbolt for several seconds. "Yes?" he asked. "What's going on?"

"Mr. Delafield, I'm Special Agent Christine Carlyle—"

"Sure, sure, I remember," interrupted Frank. "Look, I don't mean to be rude or anything, but what in the world are you doing here?"

Carlyle didn't miss a beat. "Sorry, I thought you'd be awake."

"Well, I usually am by now, but I overslept big-time."

"Then I assume you don't know what's going on?" the agent continued.

"No, I…I guess I don't. What do you mean?"

"May I come in?"

Frank paused for a moment, then hesitantly swung the door all the way open. "Sure," he said, still groggy.

Carlyle immediately crossed to the other side of the room, threw open the curtains, and grabbed the TV remote control. "You might want to sit down for this," she advised him, then flipped on MSNBC.

> "…Schaumburg, Illinois, and also Bloomington, Minnesota. But right now we're going back to our affiliate, KWQC, on the scene in Iowa City, Iowa. Jim, are you there?…Jim Mitchelson, can you hear me?"

"Yes...yes, Marcia, I can hear you, but just barely. It is utter chaos here with paramedics and police literally swarming all over the place, trying to assist the survivors of this attack, who are still reeling. So far, we have at least 62 confirmed dead and another 244, that's 244, seriously wounded, many of whom, it is predicted, will succumb to their injuries that, according to one police official I spoke with, and I quote, "were probably inflicted by high-caliber rounds from either a semi-automatic or fully automatic weapon."

"Jim, do they have a suspect? Is there any kind of pursuit going on at this point?"

"From what I understand, Marcia, the suspect has been found dead inside the mall. No other information is available. But police are assuring everyone, based on eyewitness accounts and a full sweep of the area, that there was only one gunman and that he is indeed dead. We do not know whether it was a suicide or whether he was shot by a security guard or police officer. It's just too soon to know those kinds of details."

"Thank you, Jim—we'll get back to you later for an update. Once again, for anyone who has recently joined us, regularly scheduled programming on all channels has been temporarily suspended by the Department of Homeland Security. America, for the second time this month, has been attacked by terrorists at multiple locations across the nation—to be more specific, throughout the country's Midwest region at three megamalls: the Coral Ridge Mall in Iowa City, Iowa; the Woodfield Mall in Schaumburg, Illinois; and the Mall of America in Bloomington, Minnesota. The death toll so far, as well as the number of injured, appears to be substantial and is continuing to rise since the coordinated attacks took place at 1:00 p.m. Central Time at each of the locations.

"In Iowa City, as you just heard, 62 dead and 244 wounded

from what may have been an attack by someone using an automatic or semi-automatic weapon.

"In Schaumburg, we have reports of 28 dead and 116...no, I'm sorry, make that 118 wounded. Several eyewitnesses at that location say they saw and heard dozens of explosions occurring along the complex's main inner walkway. Some describe what might have been hand grenades being thrown by a lone male, approximately five-foot-nine, one-hundred-eighty-five pounds, with blond hair and a thin build.

"And in Bloomington, Minnesota, unfortunately, we have very little information for you. The news teams in that area are not being allowed any closer than 30 miles from the mall, and residents within that same radius are being evacuated, leading to speculation that some kind of chemical or biological weapon may have been used. Although we are not getting any confirmation on that theory, the possibility of such a weapon is high given the fact that emergency response personnel in full Hazmat suits, complete with gas masks, were seen speeding toward the location, along with teams from the Centers for Disease Control and the military's elite Chemical–Biological Incident Response Force..."

Carlyle muted the television. "Those numbers, of course, are going to go a lot higher, especially in Bloomington, where the terrorist released VX-G."

"VX-G? That's a nerve agent, isn't it?"

Carlyle nodded. "Pretty much the worst kind out there. The good news is that it won't spread beyond the mall, or rather, not any further than the fastest victim ran with it on his or her clothes. Wherever he or she collapsed, that's where it stopped. We'll have to quarantine the area for about six months, but we should be able to clean it up. It's a political and economic nightmare, though."

Frank gazed at the floor, stunned by what he was hearing, then looked up. "So what's the bad news?"

"The bad news is something we're not likely to share with the public for quite some time: Trace elements of inert compounds already showing up in the ground near the mall indicate that the grade of VX-G used by the terrorist was very pure—we're talking U.S. military pure. And if that's not bad enough, we've already confirmed by using an automated camera drone sent inside the mall that at least seven to eight thousand people in there are dead. And another two thousand or so are lying dead outside in the parking lots."

Frank couldn't believe what he was hearing. "You're telling me that ten thousand people were killed today, at a single location, by one person?"

"I'm telling you that ten thousand people were killed today, at a single location, by one person—*in less than fifteen minutes.*" Carlyle threw the channel changer on the desk and waited for Frank's response.

"So here's the million-dollar question," he began. "Why are you telling me?"

"Because I'm hoping that if I share some information with you, you'll share some information with me."

"What information?"

"You talked to Schmidt a few days ago, right?"

"How did you know about that?" Frank barked, unable to decide whether he should be angry or worried.

"That's not important. What's important is figuring out a way to stop these terrorists. You're more than welcome to come over to the Hilton with me where we can discuss things more thoroughly. Stark is there with some other agents. You don't have to come. It's up to you. But if you want to stay on top of things, then it would probably be in your best interest to see what Stark has to say. I guarantee you that you'll get far more accurate and up-to-the-minute info from us than you'll ever get from CNN."

"Okay. Give me ten minutes. I'll meet you downstairs," he said, already starting to pack his laptop.

"Good enough." Carlyle moved to the door and opened it. "By the way, we have an extra room at the Hilton on the floor beneath us, if you're interested in staying there. No charge. I'd be more than happy to send someone over to get the rest of your things."

"Thanks, that'd be great," he replied. Then, just as Carlyle was leaving, Frank suddenly had a disturbing thought. "Hey," he called to her.

The agent stopped short, her foot levering the door open.

"I'm not going to…you know…disappear or anything like that, never to be heard from again, am I?"

"Believe me, Mr. Delafield, you have nothing to worry about. If we'd wanted you to disappear, you would've already been gone by now."

Carlyle let the door slam shut, and as she strode down the hallway toward the elevators, allowed a small smile to play across her lips.

21

★ ★ ★

"We now take you to Washington, D.C., where President Beckett has arrived in the White House Press Room to make a brief statement."

"My fellow Americans, as many of you already know, our nation has suffered another terrible day of tragedy. At 1:00 p.m. Central Time, three large shopping centers— one in Iowa, one in Illinois, and one in Minnesota—were attacked by terrorists. I have been in emergency meetings with the governors of those states, as well as the vice president, the director of the FBI, and the Secretary of Homeland Security, and have ordered a full-scale investigation. I have also approved the formation of a special task force to be set up to determine if there is any connection between today's crimes against America and the terrorist acts committed earlier this month in Los Angeles, Seattle, Montgomery, New York, and Baltimore.

"Now let me be very clear. Terrorism in this country will not be tolerated. We are going to find the individuals who orchestrated these despicable acts of violence and bring them to justice. And now, if you would, please join me in a moment of silence..."

President Beckett lowered his head for a few seconds, then raised his eyes, gripped the edges of the podium, and resumed speaking in a low, steady voice: "May God bless the victims, their families, and America. Thank you."

22

There is nothing in the world like a
persuasive speech to fuddle the mental apparatus.

MARK TWAIN (1835-1910)

★ ★ ★

"God bless America," the Reichsmarschall hissed at the television, his teeth clenched. "God bless this Zionist Occupational Government?" he asked more loudly as the cameras stayed on Beckett leaving the podium. "I THINK NOT," the Reichsmarschall shouted, suddenly talking as if Beckett were actually walking away from him.

He shut off the TV, disgusted by the lies and seething with contempt for the president, Congress, the Supreme Court—everything connected to the Jewish regime controlling the nation. *Der Neue Führer will make things right again,* he promised himself. But how many more brave soldiers would have to die before the rise of the Fourth Reich? How many men and women would be forced to make the ultimate sacrifice? The Reichsmarschall also wondered how long the war would last. A year? Ten years? Would he live to see the glorious establishment of America as the white republic?

Except for these concerns, the Reichsmarschall wasn't really that anxious about his life or the future, not like he used to be. *God works in mysterious ways,* he thought, as the bright California sun streamed through his bedroom window. It was a modest living space, certainly small by modern home standards, but adequate for him as a place to both rest and work. He was grateful for the quarters, still mindful of the years spent not knowing where he might end up or what would become of him.

But Der Neue Führer had changed all of that, the Reichsmarschall recalled, while he dressed and readied himself for another busy afternoon. He had met Der Neue Führer while surfing the Internet as a teenager looking to find his place in the world. A miracle, he now believed, had taken place on the day he happened to visit the Internet chat room frequented by Der Neue Führer. The room, created by the Aryan Alliance, was for white people with questions about not only their heritage and lineage, but also the bondage into which they had been placed by God's enemies.

It wasn't the kind of place to which the Reichsmarschall would've normally gone, since he'd been told throughout his life that white supremacists were evil, hateful, twisted, and violent. But he was curious. So one day while online he casually searched "White Power," "Christian Identity," "Jews," "Adolf Hitler," "Aryan War Heroes," along with a plethora of other search strings that led him to thousands of Web sites that had repeatedly incited controversy: stormfront.org, kingdomidentity.com, biblebelievers .us.com, and skinheads.net.

The Reichsmarschall, however, chose none of these old-school Web sites with their shabby formatting and dated color schemes. Instead, as if some unseen hand was guiding his, he clicked on aryanalliance.info, which was Der Neue Führer's Internet base of operations. This recent addition to the list of white pride/white power sites featured a highly interactive graphical interface loaded with sights and sounds expertly chosen to attract the MTV generation.

Using cutting-edge technology, the Aryan Alliance's home page included a directory of links that took visitors to message board forums, informative articles laced with evocative .jpg images, .mpg videos, .wmv sound clips, and even cell-phone ring tones that ranged from recordings of patriotic German songs to a phrase taken from a 1933 speech delivered by Hitler: "Only when we ourselves raise up our German people, through our own labor, our own industry, our own determination, our own daring, and our own perseverance, only then shall we rise again."

The chat room was filled with people from all over the world. The Reichsmarschall, known back then as ShadowBoxer, met hundreds of other youths from England, Canada, Australia, Iceland, other places. One individual, however, stood out immediately from the rest of the group. He was a born leader. The rest were followers. He was known by his cryptic screen name, DNF, though hardly anyone knew what the letters meant.

To ShadowBoxer, Der Neue Führer really seemed to know what he was talking about, and spoke with great authority as well as conviction. He offered intelligent answers backed by convincing arguments and historical documentation not easily dismissed. Gradually, DNF cleared up the aimlessness and confusion that had been filling ShadowBoxer's head for as long as he could remember. White people were indeed God's chosen race. And his enemies, the Jews, Satan's spawn, were bent on destroying the Lord's people while simultaneously increasing their influence throughout the world.

The whole insidious plan, according to DNF, had been set forth by Jewish leaders during a secret meeting held in France during the late 1800s. The transcribed minutes were subsequently stolen, then secretly taken to Russia, where copies were made and distributed in 1905. This text, titled *The Protocols of the Learned Elders of Zion*, boldly outlined the Jewish conspiracy to overthrow free nations and subjugate humanity.

At first, ShadowBoxer doubted DNF's alarming assertions, but after reading the *Protocols* for himself, he had to accept what they openly revealed. Anyone looking at society with a discerning eye could see that the protocols, in fact, were being deftly implemented under the guise of "Liberty, Equality, and Fraternity" in an effort to obliterate the freedoms, values, and biblical beliefs of the *goyim,* the Gentiles.

The first protocol clarified that the very terms "Liberty, Equality, and Fraternity" had been sown like seeds of corruption in the mind of the *goyim* by the Jews as a way of instigating social changes that, in reality, could be used to eradicate "true freedom of the individual." The rest of the *Protocols,* ShadowBoxer saw, were just as straightforward and simple, but when they were combined into a single course of action, they became an almost unstoppable means by which society could be subtly conquered over time:

PROTOCOL I. Right Lies in Might: Political Maneuvering

PROTOCOL II. Economic Wars: The Foundation of Jewish Control

PROTOCOL III. Mob Power: Manipulating the Masses

PROTOCOL IV. The Cult of Gold: The Exaltation of Materialism

PROTOCOL V. Despotism: Creating a Strong Centralized Government

PROTOCOL VI. Business: The Monopolization of Trade and Industry

PROTOCOL VII. Fostering Wars: Turning Country Against Country

PROTOCOL VIII. Provisional Governments: Jewish Politicians in Office

PROTOCOL IX. Liberalism Re-Education: Indoctrinating the Youth

PROTOCOL X. Preparation: Creating Dissension, Unrest, and Fear

PROTOCOL XI. Totalitarianism: The Removal of Freedom Through Laws

PROTOCOL XII. Harnessing the Media: Controlling the Press

PROTOCOL XIII. Distraction: The Utilization of Controversy and Confusion

PROTOCOL XIV. Attack Religion: Replacing Religion with Philosophy

PROTOCOL XV. Thought Suppression: Silencing the Opposition

PROTOCOL XVI. Brainwashing: Alter Social Thinking via Higher Education

PROTOCOL XVII. Target Nonconformists: Identifying Dissidents

PROTOCOL XVIII. Social Cleansing: Arresting the Dissenters

PROTOCOL XIX. Ruling the People: Governing a Conquered Populace

PROTOCOL XX. Finances: Using the Economy to Destabilize Governments

PROTOCOL XXI. Loans and Credit: Establishing a Jewish Banking System

PROTOCOL XXII. The Power of Gold: Using Jewish Gold Reserves

PROTOCOL XXIII. Establishing Jewish Rule: Teaching the Goyim to Obey

PROTOCOL XXIV. Installing the Jewish King

"The extended explanatory texts attached to each protocol," DNF pointed out to his online pupils, "show unmistakable signs of being penned by a Jew. For instance, the frequent references to 'Gentiles' and the passing comments about 'our Jewish brothers.'"

Der Neue Führer further informed his cyberspace devotees that many respected men in the modern era had accepted the *Protocols* as authentic and did what they could to warn the public.

"A good example of just such a man is Henry Ford," DNF would teach. "Consider the 1921 interview with Ford published by the *New York World*. He made no secret of his support for the *Protocols*. When asked how he felt about them, the great industrialist matter-of-factly replied, 'They fit in with what is going on. They are sixteen years old and they have fitted the world situation up to this time. They fit now.'"

ShadowBoxer, of course, didn't just blindly believe DNF. He looked up information on the legendary automobile magnate, and sure enough, it was true. In fact, Ford not only accepted the *Protocols* as authentic, but went so far as to reprint them in serialized form in *The Dearborn Independent*, a widely distributed periodical published through Ford Motor Company. He then ran a series of lengthy articles titled "The International Jew: The World's Foremost Problem."

ShadowBoxer also discovered that Ford was a Nazi sympathizer who supported Hitler. A book he found in the library, *Who Financed Hitler*, which was not even written by a white supremacist, confirmed that "the Nazis got forty-thousand dollars from Ford to reprint anti-Jewish pamphlets in German translations, and an additional $300,000 was later sent to Hitler through a grandson of the ex-Kaiser who acted as an intermediary."

"That is true," DNF commented when his new student one day mentioned to him this rarely discussed piece of historical trivia. "And did you know," Der Neue Führer continued, "that in 1937 Ford actually opened up an automobile factory in Berlin that built armaments for the German military?"

"I had no idea," ShadowBoxer answered with astonishment.

"And in 1938, on his seventy-fifth birthday, Ford was awarded

the Grand Cross of the Supreme Order of the German Eagle—
the highest decoration that could be given to a non-German. Ford,
in fact, was only the fourth person in the world to ever receive
that honor, and it came with a certificate of personal congratulations from Hitler himself."

"So Henry Ford definitely supported Hitler?"

"Absolutely," DNF replied. "You have seen the proof yourself."

That was the beginning of what would gradually become a
close relationship between ShadowBoxer and DNF, who went
on to reveal himself as Der Neue Führer. "Curiosity may have
brought you to the Aryan Alliance," Der Neue Führer was fond of
saying to his young protégé, whom he later renamed the Reichsmarschall. "But after your first visit, it was not me who kept you
coming back, it was destiny."

The Reichsmarschall, now Der Neue Führer's second in
command, nonchalantly closed the door to his room, leisurely
walked through the house in which he was staying, and ventured
outside, relaxed and at peace, eager to start another day. *The war
is going well*, he thought. *Der Neue Führer will be pleased by the
events of this day.*

He then praised God for the success of all three missions.

23

*Any government that is big enough to give you
all you want is big enough to take it away.*

BARRY GOLDWATER (1909–1998)

★ ★ ★

The Hilton was crawling with a colorful assortment of federal agents—men in black wandering around the parking lot, a Hawaiian-shirted "tourist" reading a travel brochure upside-down near the lounge, a concierge's assistant who did nothing but fidget behind the information desk while keeping an eye on the front entrance, a maintenance worker who walked back and forth through the lobby with no tools, and a muscular janitor sweeping the same spot on the floor long after it was clean.

Frank noticed each of them as he strode with Carlyle toward the elevator that took them to the twenty-first floor, where the hotel's most spacious suite had been turned into a makeshift headquarters for the Department of Homeland Security; specifically, its Secret Service division. In fact, by the time Frank arrived, twelve agents had been using the luxury accommodations as a base of operations for nearly two weeks.

High-tech surveillance equipment was sitting everywhere, along with computers placed conveniently throughout the room, most of them next to stacks of files stuffed with rap sheets and mug shots. Empty pizza boxes were also strewn about, their grease-soaked lids weighted down by empty soda cans. The TV was on, but muted, its screen facing a bed stripped bare, a king-sized surface for hundreds of documents arranged in neat piles. Some stacks consisted of only a few pages. Others were several inches thick. And many of the papers were stamped CLASSI-FIED in red ink.

Everyone present had a sidearm holstered at either the small of their back or high on their side, just off the rib cage—out of the way for daily office work, but easily reached if needed. Four agents were talking on their cell phones, at least two others appeared to be intently surfing the Internet, and the rest were in a hushed meeting around a small table at the far side of the suite. *This looks like a scene out of a Robert Ludlum novel*, thought Frank, amused by how out-of-place he felt.

"Stark?" Carlyle called, as she led the journalist into the den.

The agent turned around, not surprised by Frank's presence at his partner's side.

Stark smiled. "Enjoying your stay in Rosamond?"

"You tell me," Frank answered sharply.

"What do you mean?"

Delafield looked at Carlyle, who immediately spoke up, "He knows we've been watching him. I also told him that we're aware of his conversation with Schmidt."

Stark didn't miss a beat. "Good," he said. "Then we're all on the same page. That'll make everything a lot easier."

Frank, however, didn't share the senior agent's take on the situation. "Well, to be honest, I'm not really accustomed to having the government spy on me. And now that I know you've been doing just that, it makes me kinda nervous."

Stark turned and walked over to the room's minibar, on top of which rested a well-used Mr. Coffee. "Would you like some, Frank?" he asked politely.

"I'll pass."

Stark looked at Agent Carlyle and motioned with his head

toward the living room. "Chris, would you mind giving me a few moments alone with Mr. Delafield?"

"You know, I've been meaning to do exactly that," she responded, already heading for the door. "It was nice to see you again, Frank."

He said nothing as she left.

"Mr. Delafield," Stark began. "I believe we want the same things. You want to know what's been going on and who the terrorists are. And we want to know what's been going on and who the terrorists are."

"So you have absolutely no idea who the terrorists are?"

Stark took a slow sip of coffee. "You sure you don't want some of this? Hazelnut-vanilla. I make sure to always take some with me wherever I go. You don't know what you're missing."

"I'd rather just have some answers."

"Well, that's what we want too, Frank—some answers. If you could tell us what Schmidt had to say, for example, that would greatly assist us."

"Why don't you ask him yourself?"

"We did. He won't talk to us. But he will talk to you. So if you could simply fill us in on anything of substance that he might've said, we'd appreciate the help."

Frank thought for a moment. "And in return, I get...?"

"You, Mr. Delafield, will get to publish the last installment of your story, complete with photocopies of government documents relating to the terrorists, interviews with high-ranking federal law enforcement officials, which I'll arrange for you, and perhaps even a few pictures of the terrorists who attacked our country earlier this month—pictures no one outside of my office has seen."

The offer was enticing, but one thing still bothered Frank. "And what if I refuse?"

Stark looked disappointed. "Well, if you refuse, then I'm afraid you won't have much of a story to tell your readers."

"I have plenty of material to finish my series," scoffed Frank.

"I don't doubt that, Mr. Delafield. But unfortunately, you won't be able to publish any of it after federal authorities, in the interest of national security, classify as top secret the information you received from Schmidt—along with anything else you might uncover that relates even superficially to this investigation."

Frank glared at Stark, whom he was liking less and less. But the agent was actually being rather nice about the whole thing. He could have had Frank arrested and held for thirty days under suspicion of withholding information relating to a terrorist act or acts.

"I guess I have no choice, then, do I?" Frank responded.

Stark grinned. "Of course you have a choice. You just don't like your options."

Frank could only hope to get a good story out of the deal. "Alright," he said. "You'll get your information. I just have to gather my notes from my suitcase as soon as it arrives here."

"No need to bother with all of that. I guess I forgot to mention that you're already checked in and your bags are in suite 2107. I'm sure Agent Carlyle won't mind accompanying you to your room and going over the information with you there. I think right now would be a good time."

"Looks like you've thought of everything," Frank observed. "How efficient."

"Now, let's be very clear about something before you go," Stark said, staring Frank directly in the eyes. "You are not helping federal agents with this investigation in any way. You weren't asked to do so by anyone. You're simply a good American who happens to have some information you feel might be helpful to your government. Are we straight on that?"

Frank nodded in mock solemnity, and placed his right hand over his heart. "Oh, sure, Agent Stark. I'm just an ordinary citizen doing my duty for my country..." he exhaled bitterly, "...or else."

24

In Washington, D.C., snowflakes the shape and size of cotton balls were floating through the air as evening fell. Gracefully, yet surprisingly fast, they glided toward the earth, swept ever nearer to their final resting places on the frozen ground by a Canadian wind blowing out of the north. The dark streets were empty, silent, and cold, having been deserted shortly after the terrorist attacks. Restaurants had closed early, along with shopping centers and movie theaters—a predictable response to the national state of emergency that had been issued by the government earlier in the day.

President Beckett, meanwhile, was wrapping up an arduous series of meetings with various national-security advisors, members of his cabinet, and high-ranking law-enforcement personnel including Vice President Martin Mayhew, Secretary of Defense James Gleason, FBI Director Craig Malone, FBI Deputy Director Grant Shaeffer, Secretary of Homeland Security Duncan Phelps, Secret Service Director Lance Vaughn, and CIA Director Mark Hellingsford.

By nine p.m., a number of decisions had been made that would affect the course of the conflict now taking place on American soil. "The United States," Beckett told his staff, "is not going to become yet another country wherein innocent citizens are forced to live in constant fear of being blown to bits or gunned down while having lunch in a café or riding the bus to work. I will *not* have it, gentlemen. The losses we've suffered so far are unacceptable. This administration will not go down in history as the one that was soft on terrorism."

Homeland Security Secretary Duncan Phelps ran his fingers over the classified intelligence file in front of him as he listened to Beckett, then suggested a response. "I believe it's time we made a few arrests, Mr. President."

"I agree one hundred percent," chimed in Vice President Mayhew, who leaned forward across the table for Phelps's file and slapped it open for a look. "At least it would show the American people we're making some headway against these killers."

"My department has the names and locations of several persons associated with numerous white-supremacist groups," continued Phelps. "We probably won't apprehend anyone directly responsible for this month's attacks, but there's a good chance that we'll get some useful information."

Mayhew pushed the file back over to Phelps. "It sounds like a solid plan to me, Mr. President."

"They'll never talk," opined Secret Service Director Lance Vaughn.

Phelps continued to stare steadfastly at Beckett, irritated by the interruption but otherwise unfazed. "They *will* talk, Mr. President, after a period of...persuasive interrogation. I can assure you of that." The secretary blinked dismissively at Vaughn. "I certainly haven't heard any better ideas being put on the table."

"Mr. President," Vaughn argued, "if arrests are made prematurely we will most likely alert the terrorist leaders as to how close we're getting to their organization's inner structure. And the manpower it would take to round up their underlings will pull necessary resources away from tracking down the terrorist hierarchy. The main organizers of these attacks are the ones we have to concentrate on. The intelligence we've gathered indicates that rank-and-file soldiers have no idea what their mission is until shortly before they attack. We've already discussed these matters at length. The War Room, wherever it exists, is the key to this particular terrorist network."

"I disagree," countered Phelps.

"You always disagree, Duncan," snapped Vaughn impatiently.

"Untrue, Lance. What I'm always doing, it seems, is figuring out how to make some headway despite your department of inept wannabe heroes."

"Please, Duncan," the president chided.

"Excuse me, sir. I meant no disrespect. But we've been going in circles for the last six months."

"Mr. President," Vaughn implored, pleading his case further. "When we began investigating the Nordic Brotherhood two years ago, we knew and accepted the fact that there might be casualties prior to capturing the organization's leaders. But it was a risk everyone agreed to take because the greater risk would be to not dismantle the network from the top. We've been monitoring the groups we believe are involved, gathering intelligence, and now we're close to actually identifying the centralized commanders. There are at least two: one called Der Neue Führer, and another named the Reichsmarschall. We also know that they meet with each other, and with their followers, in a place called the War Room, and that only certain individuals can get into it."

Beckett scowled as he turned away and walked toward the window. "And where has any of this information gotten us, Lance?" he asked, raising his voice. "Thousands dead, and a nation cowering in their homes. The public is losing their confidence in this administration, and I'll not let that continue."

"Mr. President, I warn you, if the terrorist commanders are not taken into custody, we could be facing even greater damage to this country—its economy, its people, its entire infrastructure. Our American way of life. God only knows what these leaders are planning even as we speak."

Beckett paused momentarily at the side of his desk before sitting down and facing those seated in the room. "I'm putting Duncan in charge of the investigation."

"Mr. President!" The Secret Service director balled his fists in frustration beneath the conference table.

"I'm sorry, Lance."

Vaughn protested. "The only reason Phelps even has his precious list of names and locations is because of *my* team and its work."

"That's enough," the president said, ending the debate. "And please forgive me, by the way, for making this additional announcement in front of everyone without first notifying you privately—but effective as of tomorrow, FBI Director Malone will be taking over your position as Director of the Secret Service. And Mr. Shaeffer, you will move from your position as FBI Deputy Director into Mr. Malone's role. Lance, I think it best that you go on administrative leave until I've decided where your services can best be utilized during this crisis."

No one looked at Vaughn, who was completely blindsided by the decision.

Beckett turned toward Shaeffer and Malone. "Congratulations, gentlemen. I have full confidence in both of you. Please meet with Mr. Phelps tomorrow at 7:00 a.m. to outline a plan of action. I'd like a report on my desk by noon. Everyone else, I'll see you back here in the morning at nine o'clock sharp so we can discuss in detail the security measures proposed this evening by Mr. Phelps. I want to thank all of you for working so hard today, and hope that you have a safe trip home. Get some sleep. We have a long week ahead of us. Thank you."

At this, the president's advisors stood up, gathered their scattered documents, notes, and other materials, and began to exit the room—some stopping briefly in the outer hallway to shake hands with the new directors of the FBI and Secret Service.

"Lance, I'd like a moment with you, please," the president said just before Vaughn reached the door.

He looked at President Beckett while the rest of the staff passed him on their way out, standing motionless and silent, until Brigadier General Forrest Cooper from the Department of Defense had shut the door, leaving the two men alone in the office.

"Why?" Vaughn asked, his face a mask of bewilderment. "Why? That's all I want to know."

"Because we need to get these people. You know that, Lance. I gave you the time you asked for, but nothing materialized."

"I'm not asking why you fired me, Mr. President. I'm asking you why you didn't *tell* me you were going to fire me before announcing it in front of everyone else. You made a fool out of me."

Beckett rose from his desk, clearly bothered by what he'd done to his longtime friend. He walked to the eighteenth-century cabinet where he kept an elegant crystal carafe filled with twenty-year-old cognac. The handcrafted decanter had been given to him during his first term by French prime minister André Boudreau. He poured himself a snifter of Louis XIII de Rémy-Martin, took a short swallow, then offered a glass to Vaughn, who declined.

"Lance, you know that was not my intention. I've always had the utmost respect for you. We've known each other far too long to start playing politics."

"Then just give me a straight answer."

Beckett took another sip of the imported liquor, allowing its warmth to slowly wash over his palate, blissfully distracted for a few seconds by its smooth taste and rich, leathery aroma. "It's been a difficult day, to say the least," he continued, his back still toward Vaughn. "I didn't have the opportunity."

"You didn't have the opportunity?" Vaughn asked incredulously. "I thought you said we were beyond playing politics."

The president turned sharply on his heels. "Look, Lance. I'm sorry if your feelings were hurt, but I've got a country to run; a country that's been attacked from *within* by domestic terrorists. Eight governors from some very powerful states are fit to be tied, three times that many Congressmen are ready to pull their support from several important bills that I've been trying to get approved since the start of my second term, and the entire nation is afraid to go outside. And here you are, bent out of shape because I couldn't find a few minutes between the dozen or so meetings I've had over the last eight hours to say, 'Oh, by the way, Lance, most of us are fairly certain that your War Room theory is ridiculous and, to be honest, your performance throughout this whole investigation has been substandard, so I'm going to have to fire you. See you in the meeting.'"

Beckett set the glass down and crossed back to his desk. "I did the best I could given the situation. If that's not good enough, then I can't help you."

Vaughn couldn't deny that Beckett's schedule that day had been absurdly tight. He also couldn't deny that he hadn't yet located the War Room. "You're right, sir," he admitted. "But ever since the first attacks, my men have been working 24/7. And my undercover operative truly believes he's getting close to finding the War Room. I'm asking you for just one more week. One more week."

The president rubbed his forehead, making the creases around his eyes more pronounced. They were deeper now and more numerous compared to when he'd taken office. He looked up, hands clasped together in front of him. "No, Lance. I'm sorry. You had your chance. Phelps will be calling the shots now."

Vaughn swallowed hard. "Very well, Mr. President," he replied stonily. "Good night, then." He turned to leave, but just as he was about to close the door, the president stopped him one last time.

"Lance?"

"Yes, Mr. President."

"I'd appreciate it if you'd be supportive of Phelps, perhaps make some kind of public statement, and also bring Malone up to speed on everything. Tell your people to be cooperative."

"Of course, Mr. President."

Beckett paused. "And...I *am* sorry."

"I understand, Mr. President," Vaughn uttered without emotion, then left the office, walking heavily downstairs and outside to his car, where he sat in silence for a few minutes before starting the engine. On the way home, he made one phone call.

"Stark, this is Vaughn."

"Yes, sir."

"Well," he began, as he pulled out onto the Beltway, "it looks like you're going to have a new boss tomorrow."

25

A religious service in Rosamond, California, on the Sunday morning after a terrorist attack against America was not somewhere Frank Delafield would've ever predicted he'd be. But that was exactly where he found himself less than forty-eight hours after his meeting with agents Stark and Carlyle at the Hilton. He was standing alone at the back of Pastor Schmidt's little chapel, wearing a suit and tie, speaking to no one, looking around nervously, and anxiously flipping back and forth through a two-page bulletin of church announcements. He felt uncomfortable beyond words.

"A man destined for hell in a crowd bound for heaven," he muttered while scanning the sanctuary for a spot to hide.

The folks who greeted him at the door were nice enough, although he noticed after entering the building that a few long stares in his direction were followed immediately by short whispers.

I shouldn't be here, he decided quickly, almost turning around to go wait outside in his car. But then he calmed down. He had no proof anyone was saying anything about him. Perhaps people were simply looking past him for friends located across the aisle, on the other side of the room. Maybe the murmurings were more along the lines of "Honey, did you remember to turn off the stove?" or "Let's make sure we give our tithe this week."

He hadn't actually seen anything so far to justify having negative feelings about these people. Nothing but friendly smiles had been flashed at him, many of them coupled with a heartfelt "good morning."

Easy, Delafield, he steadied himself, remembering that he'd already infiltrated one of Gruber's services—a cross burning, no less. *How bad could this be?*

Frank inched his way forward, eventually stopping at the center of the church. An usher waved frantically to him, pointing at a single chair situated in the middle of an otherwise-filled row. It sat between two longtime members: Barney Helms, an octogenarian whose tales about his life as a hobo during the Depression Era had been repeated many times during church picnics; and Martha Lipinski, a twenty-three-year-old Polish girl adopted in Krakow when she was only a toddler, then brought to America by her adoptive parents, who were still heading up Pastor Schmidt's missionary division.

Everyone slid back in their seats without complaining, more than happy to let Frank slip by on his way to the last empty chair. He could almost see a sign on the back of it that read, *Reserved for Late Arrivals—Unbelievers Only.* Fortunately, the journey took only a few seconds, and it was traversed with relative ease, at least until he banged his leg up against an attractive woman's bare knees. "Excuse me, I'm sorry," he blushed, feeling for a moment like he might never reach his destination. Finally, after a couple more steps and another second or two, his trek was over.

The music, by this time, was in full swing. It had started ten minutes earlier, at 8:00 a.m. sharp, led by Luke Schmidt, whose laid-back style of singing was perfectly complemented by a small band of young, exuberant musicians. Frank was particularly

impressed by the saxophonist, whose jazzy ad libs were strikingly reminiscent of the high-quality riffs one might hear during
a Bill Evans concert. It wasn't the kind of "church" music Frank
had expected—not at all like the funeral dirges still stuck in his
mind from when he was a boy growing up in church. He relaxed
a bit, and settled back in his seat.

The sermon Bill Schmidt delivered was an obvious response to
the week's events. He pointed to the Old Testament story about a
man named Job, a one-time influential businessman who lost his
health, his family, and his wealth. Yet he continued to worship
God. "Job was hurting. Job was frightened. Job was confused,"
Schmidt said. "But he never lost his faith, believing that there
must be some reason for his plight. And that God was with him
through it all."

Unlike so many televangelists that Frank had watched hawking
their miracle trinkets on TV and preaching a gospel of unlimited
prosperity, Schmidt taught that God was not in the business of
saving sinners for the sole purpose of making them happy.

"Remember that old Lynn Anderson song?" he asked his
congregation. " 'I Never Promised You a Rose Garden.' " He
started to sing it in a lighthearted way as his listeners smiled
and nodded, some chuckling slightly and looking at each other.
Schmidt went on to say that *God* never promised anyone a rose
garden either.

"Life," he explained, "has always been, and always will be, difficult. It's filled with tragedies. Not just for the unsaved, but also
for the saved. In Matthew 5:45, Jesus said that God causes the sun
to rise on those who are evil *as well as* those who are good, and
brings rain on the righteous *as well as* the unrighteous. So don't
expect to escape pain and loss. Our eyes shouldn't be focused on
this life, anyway. They should be looking to the next life. In John
16:33, Jesus taught, 'In this world you will have tribulation. But
take courage, be of good cheer. For I have overcome the world.' "
Schmidt stepped away from the pulpit behind which he had been

standing, speaking more intimately now, less like a teacher, more like a friend. "And do you recall when he said that?"

Frank surveyed the crowd, noticing a number of people gazing downward, deep in thought. A woman across the aisle, he saw, was tearing up.

"He said those words on the very night he was betrayed by Judas and taken into custody. He said that, knowing his hour of ultimate suffering had come. He knew that soon he'd be crucified for the sins of the world. For all of your sins, and for all of mine." Schmidt stopped talking, and after a lengthy pause, his voice hoarse, he continued, "And yes, he even died for the sins of those terrorists who hurt so many people this last week." An almost tangible shiver swept through the congregation.

"My friends, we *must* forgive them, and whoever else is behind these attacks, just as we ourselves have been forgiven. 'Forgive our trespasses, as we forgive those who trespass against us,' the Lord's Prayer says. You see, God doesn't want us to hold grudges against those who have wronged us. That's not his way, and as Christians, that can't be our way. Now, it doesn't matter if we've failed to forgive in the past, we need to keep striving to do better and to move on. We should leave no room for unforgiveness in our hearts. Allow no place for bitterness to lurk. Because, you see, not a single person, except Christ, has ever lived without committing some kind of a sin. Done something wrong. I know it's true for me. And I think you know it's true for you too. The book of Romans tells us that all of us have sinned and fall short of God's glory and holiness. What right do we have to not forgive others when we have been forgiven so much?"

Frank could see that Schmidt was now talking not only to his flock, but also to himself, about himself, his past, his hurts, his sins—about how to overcome the world with love and conquer evil with good. Finally he led a prayer: "God, I'm sorry for the things I've done wrong. I ask for your forgiveness, and accept by faith, Jesus' death on the cross and his resurrection from the dead, so that I can live eternally with you in heaven. Amen."

Frank appreciated the simplicity of the words and found them comforting for reasons that escaped him. It was nice to see others who had found something or some*one* they could turn to in times of need. A small part of him, in fact, wanted that kind of faith. But he was a confirmed agnostic—and quite sure he would always be one after being schooled in the ways of skepticism by his profession.

At the conclusion of the service, Schmidt made one final announcement, then handed the stage over to his grandson, Luke, whose band played a final song as everyone made their way out to the patio for doughnuts and coffee provided by the church. As the congregation exited the sanctuary, they sang an upbeat tune with great enthusiasm:

> *I'm so thankful, Lord, I praise your name,*
> *Since you found me, Lord, nothing is the same.*
> *Each day my spirit's dancing, I sing a song that's new,*
> *Everything I need I've found in you!*

Suddenly, it struck Frank like a fist in the stomach—the memory of the only time he and Blair had gone to church. It was the Easter before she died. They were vacationing at a romantic getaway and saw a brochure for a sunrise service and decided to attend. It was held in an open field, where the sun rose over a glen on the outskirts of Malibu, near the ocean. It was a wonderful experience for both of them. After they got back to L.A., they both wanted to go back to the resort for Christmas, maybe even see if the same church was holding another early-morning celebration. But Blair was killed. And he never went back to church again.

He wished she could've been with him to hear Schmidt and tell him her thoughts. He loved talking to her about such things, and without even trying lost himself in memories of their life together—until he was abruptly brought back to the present by Schmidt. "Mr. Delafield!" the pastor warmly greeted him. "What are you doing here?"

Frank swallowed hard and smiled reflexively, remembering just in time why he had come to Christ's Chapel. "Good morning, Bill. I was hoping I might get a chance to speak with you about a few more things. I had some additional questions."

"Not a problem. I'm actually going to have Luke preach the next message—let him get some experience under his belt in front of larger crowds. We can talk as soon as the nine-thirty service starts. Would you like something to eat in the meantime?"

"Uh…sure," replied Frank. "I'm not one to turn down free food."

"Good," the pastor said, patting his midsection. "I feel the same way."

Frank laughed and walked outside with Schmidt to the area where refreshments were being served.

Meanwhile, not far away but well out of sight, the Reichsmarschall watched the two men with great interest.

26

Enemy-occupied territory is what the world is.

C.S. LEWIS (1898–1963)

★ ★ ★

Bill Schmidt stared at the photographs of the three martyred terrorists. Frank had obtained the pictures from Stark, who after handing them over, suggested that perhaps someone in town might be able to help I.D. the killers.

"Where did you get those?" he asked, sitting attentively on the edge of his living room couch.

Frank squirmed in his chair next to the pastor, trying to find an answer that wouldn't be a complete lie. After all, this was a minister, a holy man of God, a pillar of the community—not to mention someone he genuinely liked. "Bill, I can't answer that. As a journalist I have to protect my sources. I can only say that they came from a very reliable contact. What I need to know is, can you identify these men? Maybe give me some background information on them?"

The first photograph—frame #21366 from the grainy, black and white video footage shot by surveillance camera B-17 at the Woodfield Mall in Illinois—showed a twenty-something man standing in front of the Rainforest Café.

"That's Johnathon Larkin," the pastor said matter-of-factly. "Sad story, that one. Like most of them."

Frank was a bit taken aback by how quickly and confidently the former racist leader had identified the terrorist. "Are you sure?"

"Oh, I'm sure alright. His father was a small-time thief and drug dealer. Did a few years in jail, nothing too drastic, though."

"Anything else?"

"Well, I'm not sure how important this might be, but Johnathon took the name Thor when he was a teenager growing up in Northern California."

"Thor?"

"Yes. Let me explain. You see, his mother was about as morally corrupt as they come. Every weekend she'd go out trolling the bars and without fail bring home some fella who'd spend the night. Usually the guy would hang around her home in the trailer park for at least a day or so, maybe a week. Just long enough to borrow a few bucks, drain the house of liquor, and smack Johnny around. The only time this boy ever had any peace was in the late afternoon when his mom and whoever she was shacking up with were gone. He must have been about eight or nine. That's when he'd watch reruns of *The Mighty Thor* on Nickelodeon. You know, that old cartoon from the 1960s based on the comic-books superhero Thor, the Norse God of Thunder?"

"I remember."

"Anyway, he always had this thing about Thor, so he took that nickname when he joined up with the Aryan Soldat Front. Ever hear of them?"

"Vaguely."

"It's a fairly radical group out of Oregon, somewhere around Salem, I think."

"How do you know this?" asked Frank incredulously.

Schmidt half grinned. "Now, Mr. Delafield," he began facetiously, "I can't answer that. As a pastor I have to protect my sources. I can only say that the information comes from a very reliable contact."

"Okay, you got me," Frank countered, then moved on without further comment.

The second picture was a screenshot from the Coral Ridge Mall attack. It had been taken with a cell phone belonging to Gary Michael Davidson, a thirty-nine-year-old asphalt and concrete layer who was just about to place a call as he started walking from the parking lot to the mall's entrance. But instead of seeing just a crowded entrance, he saw a man gunning people down.

After making a frantic plea for assistance from 9-1-1, Davidson had actually shadowed IronCross through the shopping center, recording the deadly rampage every step of the way. He captured four minutes of footage, including a five-second close-up of the shooter's face when IronCross unexpectedly turned around. The video abruptly stopped there in a hail of gunfire, marking the exact moment that Davidson died with eight bullets in his chest, two in his neck, and one in his head.

"How about this guy?" asked Frank, pointing to the second photo.

"Just a minute," Schmidt mumbled, thinking hard. "He's familiar. I believe he's also from the Aryan Soldat Front."

Frank, however, needed another name. "Take your time," he coaxed reassuringly. "No need to rush."

"I got it." The pastor exhaled loudly. "You're looking at George Nelson, one of the most hateful, dangerous followers of the movement I ever met."

"Did you know him well?"

Schmidt shrugged. "Not really. I talked to him a few times and was kept apprised of his activities through the grapevine. From what I recall, he played an active role in at least two murders, several beatings, and one firebombing of a black church in, uh, Tennessee, I believe."

"But he looks too young to have been so active when you were in the movement."

"Well, he's a lot older than he appears. And that used to drive him insane, because whenever he'd go to some big gathering of leaders, the ones who didn't know George always thought he was a new recruit, and treated him as such—a bit dismissively, if you know what I mean. A group of older Klansmen, in fact, always referred to him behind his back as Baby-Face Nelson, after that 1930s gangster. But George is actually well into his late forties by now."

"*Was* in his late forties," Frank corrected him as he slid the third and final picture across the table to the pastor.

"Oh yeah, good riddance, I say." Schmidt caught himself. "I'm sorry, Frank. That was uncalled for. Sometimes my old, angry self gets the better of me. I still have a lot of difficulty getting close to this stuff. These people. It brings back a lot of memories."

Frank placed his hand on Bill's shoulder. "I understand. And I hate to put you through this, but I really think you can help. Could you just take a look at this last shot?"

Photo three, the most disturbing one of all, was snapped by a color-enhancement camera mounted on a remote-controlled robot unit that was sent into the Mall of America by the government's Chemical–Biological Incident Response Force. It was of Terrorist101, his mouth frozen open in a horrifying rictus; exploded, dried blood caked over his eyes—the terrible results of the nerve agent he had released.

"Oh, Lord," Schmidt muttered. "No, I...I don't know this man. At least I don't think I know him. Maybe I do, but I can't tell from this picture."

Frank immediately slipped the photo back into the file from which he had taken it. "That's fine," he assured the pastor. "We don't need to look at these anymore."

For another hour or so Frank talked more with Schmidt about the two men he'd identified—their past activities, who they'd associated with most often, and how they might have gotten their hands on the weaponry used in the attacks. The grenades and machine guns, Frank learned, wouldn't have been hard for them to obtain, especially given the fact that about eight percent of the men and women in active military service were members of white-supremacist organizations. This wasn't common knowledge, although various incidents going back for decades told the story plainly enough.

In 1976, Schmidt told Frank, a KKK chapter of one hundred marines was uncovered at Camp Pendleton in Southern California. The group was exposed after a cross burning, and a brutal beating of two black marines. An investigation later revealed that commanding officers had for months allowed soldiers to regularly display their Klan regalia and had even allowed the distribution of literature throughout the camp.

During the 1970s it was also discovered that sailors on various navy ships were in the KKK. Some had actually donned Klan robes and confronted black shipmates. There was even a cross burning on one aircraft carrier while it was out at sea. And back on shore, toward the end of that same decade, a large KKK unit was uncovered at Fort Hood. Some of the soldiers in this group actually stood guard at a Texas Klan rally that featured David Duke and his hate-mongering buddy, Louis Beam.

Then, in 1985, law enforcement authorities found that the White Patriot Party in North Carolina had not only recruited soldiers with neo-Nazi sympathies but had succeeded in purchasing from them about $50,000 worth of Claymore mines, rockets, grenades, and small arms. They were caught only after an undercover agent heard about the weapons-for-cash exchange and set up an extensive sting operation.

Frank took in Schmidt's information, jotted down copious notes, and shared his own recollections about a 1995 scandal involving army personnel stationed at Fort Bragg in Fayetteville, North Carolina. The 82nd Airborne Division, as it turned out, had about a dozen skinheads in its ranks. Three of them, all in their early twenties, ended up murdering an African–American civilian couple, primarily so one of the men could earn a "spider tattoo"—awarded to a skinhead if he kills a black person.

"And don't forget about Timothy McVeigh, the Oklahoma City bomber, and his army buddies," Schmidt reminded Frank. He went on to explain how for years he'd seen not only basic recruits like McVeigh, but also officers, exhibit rampant, racist behavior. The pastor said he had even witnessed army, navy, and marine special forces personnel participating in the diversion of countless small arms, millions of rounds of ammo, and tons of explosives into the white-supremacist community in preparation for the Racial Holy War they believed to be on the horizon. "I told the feds about this when I left the movement," he complained. "But they did nothing. And it's still going on today."

"How could this be happening?" Frank asked.

"You'd be surprised at how little security exists around military weaponry. The government's inventory-control procedures wouldn't even fly in the warehouse of a neighborhood Home Depot. Military weapons disappear every year and are never found. To make matters worse, the government actually allows a huge supply of weapons to be bought on the open market. Did you know that just last year our Defense Department sold more than four *million* pounds of outdated explosives to private citizens and companies?"

Frank grew more uneasy about the nation's safety with each new revelation he received from Schmidt.

"Of course, Uncle Sam doesn't bother tracking where it goes after the money's made," Schmidt continued. "I can guarantee you, a lot of these supplies are going to white-supremacist groups like the Aryan Soldat Front. This doesn't even include the weapons we lose every year."

The shocked reporter stood and began pacing back and forth in the pastor's living room. "I don't think I want to know the answer to this, but I am going to ask you anyway: What do you mean, the weapons we *lose?*"

"Remember Iraq?" Schmidt began.

Frank nodded, but said nothing.

"Well, as of this year, three-hundred-eighty tons of high explosives are still missing from the al Qaqaa military installation that was supposedly being guarded by U.S. troops back in 2003. Some of it—a lot of it, in fact—came ashore in Florida, was split up and shipped in U-Haul trucks to hundreds of small towns across the country, then distributed to the leaders of nearby racist enclaves."

"Like Gruber's?"

"Like Gruber's," answered Schmidt.

Frank hesitated, but finally found his voice.

"Then I guess it's time for me to interview Gruber. See what he has to say."

Schmidt shook his head. "No way, Frank. Leave it alone. I don't want to see you get hurt."

"Bill, I'll be fine, I can handle—"

Just then, the lock on the front door clicked open, and in walked Luke, his Bible in one hand and the Sunday paper in the other. "Hello."

"Luke," Bill said, rising from the couch. "This is Frank Delafield. He was at the service this morning."

"Oh, sure. Nice to meet you, Frank."

"Same here. Your grandfather's told me a lot about you."

"Well, don't believe everything you hear these days, especially from preachers," he quipped nonchalantly as he flipped open the *Los Angeles Times.*

Its front-page headline silenced them all: "White Supremacists in Custody—Terrorism at an End."

27

★★★

Neither Frank, nor Bill, nor Luke knew what had been going on in the news until they read the shocking headline and the accompanying articles. A lot of people, in fact, were taken aback by the rapidly unfolding events, especially those unfortunate enough to be working in the main offices of the nation's largest newspapers, where frenzied night crews were forced to scramble so their front pages would reflect what had transpired in the wee hours of the morning.

The early edition of the *Los Angeles Times*, for example, was successfully revised only after a multitude of tasks were miraculously completed by a team of dazed reporters who were told around two a.m. about a series of postmidnight raids by federal authorities. The operation came close on the heels of an emergency FBI bulletin issued to all major news services late in the evening. It stated that a number of arrests would soon be made and that select government officials would be available for comment. Managing editors at newspapers in Boston, New York, Chicago, L.A., and every other large city responded by immediately rousing their most deadline-conscious reporters out of bed, ordering them to sculpt the government's dry-as-a-bone facts into riveting pieces of journalistic art.

According to the FBI, white supremacists—not Muslims—had been behind the terrorist attacks. This information, however, was not new. The same thing had already been unofficially reported the day after the assaults, thanks to an unnamed Iowa City police officer who'd leaked information about the recording found next to the body of IronCross. Experts in the field of racism in America almost immediately deciphered the cryptic "RaHoWa" as a reference to "Racial Holy War." It had also gotten out that this same message had been found in one form or another at the other two malls. Moreover, dozens of people who'd survived the deadly onslaughts repeatedly told authorities the attackers were white.

What was surprising was the recent news that twelve suspects had been apprehended—the alleged ringleaders of the terrorist network behind the attacks. They had been taken into custody at various locations throughout the country, some in close proximity to a racist enclave. One of the men was captured within ten miles of Yahweh City, an isolated white-supremacist compound outside of Denver. Another was caught living in a cabin near Justice Township, a whites-only community on the border between Michigan and Indiana. Each of the arrestees was associated with extremist organizations under the banner of the Ku Klux Klan, Christian Identity, or neo-Nazism, except for one man who could only be linked to a radical private citizen's militia.

"We're quite confident these men represent the upper echelon of a very sophisticated terrorist network," announced Duncan Phelps, Secretary of Homeland Security. "A lot of hard work went into finding them, and I for one, am proud of our joint task force of FBI, Secret Service, and Homeland Security agents. They operated smoothly and with extraordinary care to achieve the objective."

Finally, it was communicated that Phelps would be taking over leadership of the law-enforcement teams and divisions that were investigating the terrorist attacks. This fueled rumors that Secret Service Director Lance Vaughn had somehow muffed the investigation so badly that dismissing him was a necessary action—despite his previous service record and well-known friendship with President Beckett.

Frank, Bill, and Luke sat around the kitchen table, dividing up the newspaper's contents and examining each article. "This is ridiculous," Bill commented as he scanned the first few paragraphs of the story titled "Hierarchy of Hate."

"You must be reading the article I just finished," said Frank.

The pastor looked up from the table in disgust. "I know these guys. And every single one of them, except this militiaman who isn't even a white supremacist, are low- to mid-level soldiers in the movement. Their primary jobs are organizing rallies, relaying messages, and carrying out the grunt work. Some of them can certainly be tied to a few violent hate crimes. But leaders in a hierarchy? Absolutely not."

"The police might know more about these terrorists than you do," Luke suggested. "It's been a long time since you were involved."

Schmidt glanced at his grandson. "Maybe," he said. "But not likely."

"I think your grandfather's right, Luke. I've never been affiliated with any racist organization, and from my research even I can identify some of these characters as less-than-impressive representatives of the white-supremacist subculture." He gazed down at a sidebar labeled "The Dirty Dozen" and shook his head. "I mean, c'mon. Matthew Hawk? I talked about him in the last installment of my series. He isn't anything more than a gofer for the Aryan Patriots of America, ever since he messed up their grand scheme to get rich."

Schmidt rubbed the back of his neck. "You mean the computer hack into CitiBank?"

Frank nodded. "Right—for credit-card numbers. He spilled

the beans to some undercover agent. Four APA members were arrested, convicted, and sent to the state penitentiary. I'm actually surprised Hawk is even still alive. A few of the other groups that were supposed to get some of the cash from that job really hate his guts. Getting arrested probably saved his life."

Luke stood up from the table, then crossed over to the refrigerator, and pulled out a pitcher of lemonade. "Anyone want some?" he asked. But the two men declined, too engrossed to care much about food or drink. "I don't think we need to worry so much," he told both of them. "I can't believe the government would make such serious mistakes about who should and who shouldn't be arrested, especially given what's at stake."

Bill stopped reading. "I wish to God things were that simple, Luke. But I don't believe they are. I guess the best we can do now is just keep this whole thing in prayer."

"And help out where we can," Frank added.

The pastor gazed thoughtfully at the tired reporter. "Yes. I think you're right."

"Well," said Luke, placing the lemonade on the table, "I need to get up to my room and start studying for this Wednesday's message and also write a few letters to our missionaries in Rwanda. So, if you'll excuse me."

"Sure, no problem," his grandfather said. "But personally, I think you need to get out a little. Take a drive or hang out with some of your friends in the singles group."

Luke hesitated a moment. "Okay," he relented. "I'll call a few of the guys. Probably drive up to Bakersfield and go out for a late lunch."

Bill smiled, relieved that his grandson would not be working all day. "Great."

"Nice to finally spend some time with you," Frank said, as he stood up and shook the young man's hand.

"Same here," Luke replied before heading upstairs. "See ya later, Grandpa."

"Alright," he answered. "Have a good time."

Bill and Frank immediately went back to reading the articles and discussing what could be done. "Well, I'm *definitely* going to have to go talk to Gruber now," Frank affirmed. "Any advice?"

"You know I'm against this, right?"

"I know."

"But if you're going to do it anyway, you'll have to get by Gruber's right-hand man, Erich Strom. Don't know much about that fella. Showed up out of the blue a year or so ago, and now practically runs the place. He's an odd one, though. Can't figure him out." The pastor paused for a moment. "Listen," he started again, "when you get to the gate, ask for Strom right off the bat."

"Shouldn't I call first?" Frank said half-jokingly. "I'd hate to catch him in the middle of dinner or something."

Bill laughed. "They don't use landline phones out there. Computers—sure. DSL hookups—of course. Maybe a cell phone or two, okay. But even then, they usually have only the disposable kind around, 'cause they can't be traced."

"I guess your basic cordless on the desk is far too easy to monitor nowadays," observed Frank.

"And that's something Gruber and his kind don't want." Suddenly, Bill leaned in toward Frank. "One more thing," he said.

"What?"

"When you start walking toward the gate from the property line, make sure you have your hands up, and your jacket open, so they can see you don't have a weapon."

At first, Frank thought that Schmidt was pulling his leg. "Really? And what if I forget to do that?"

"Well, what'll happen is that their sentry guards will consider you a trespasser and shoot you where you stand for being a ZOG spy. You'll find yourself lying on the ground, if you're still conscious, just beyond the sign that says, TRESPASSERS WILL BE SHOT—YOU HAVE BEEN WARNED. The only time they take that sign down and relax security is during Gruber's famous weekend barbecues. Just about everyone is armed then, at least the soldiers are, especially the ones visiting from other compounds. They like to bring along a lot of guns to show them off."

At this point in the conversation, Schmidt noticed the look on Frank's face and asked him if he needed something to drink. The reporter wanted a double scotch on the rocks, but he settled for lemonade.

28

Woe unto them that call evil good, and good evil.

ISAIAH 5:20

★★★

Not long after Frank left Schmidt's home, the Reichsmarschall requested the presence of Der Neue Führer in the War Room. He was afraid that in his eagerness to vanquish the enemy, he'd jeopardized the movement's whole future. Had the mall attacks been a miscalculation? Was too much force used too soon? For the first time since being named Der Neue Führer's second in command, the Reichsmarschall was worried that the job he'd so diligently pursued might be beyond his leadership abilities, especially now that a significant threat had arrived on the scene, in the form of Frank Delafield.

The Reichsmarschall first spotted the pesky reporter during the town meeting, working the crowd, asking everyone questions. Then he'd shown up at the Traitor's house. And today, the nosey journalist had attended Christ's Chapel. The Reichsmarschall had watched him throughout the church service, studying his every move and response, hoping that perhaps his being there was just a coincidence. But then his worst fears were confirmed when Delafield met again with the one man who could ruin everything.

After a few minutes, the Reichsmarschall was distracted from his brooding by the sound of boots snapping heel-to-toe on the large concrete stones that lined the floor of the passageway leading from the outside world into the War Room. Der Neue Führer soon appeared in the entrance archway, stopping beneath the portrait of Adolf Hitler, which was hung in a place of prominence—between a banner that declared *"Ein Volk, Ein Reich, Ein Führer"* and the group's flag, which displayed a Nazi swastika, an iron cross, and the German eagle.

Der Neue Führer strutted into the room and proudly surveyed the isolated hideaway, which never failed to bring immense pleasure to his soul. It was not only a functional retreat, but also an homage to the grand purpose of the Nordic Brotherhood. The archway entrance symbolized heaven's gate, through which only the faithful entered. And the steel beams supporting the cavernous ceiling of uncut rock represented the strength of each soldier who was willing to bear the great weight of his or her destiny.

This place, he thought as he approached the Reichsmarschall, *is only the beginning of many glorious things to come.* He marveled at how quickly it had been constructed by his protégé, who now stood before him, dressed in his finest uniform, sporting a German Luger holstered on the hip. "Greetings, Herr Reichsmarschall."

"Heil Hitler," the young man replied stiffly, giving the *Sieg Heil* salute.

"What troubles you, my friend?"

"Delafield. He's gotten too close to us," the Reichsmarschall explained, his voice strained.

"That stupid reporter?"

"Yes. He's met with Wilhelm Schmidt twice already."

Der Neue Führer slapped the Reichsmarschall hard on the cheek. "Never mention that name again!" he shouted in anger. "You will *always* refer to him as the Traitor. Do you understand?"

"Yes, mein Führer," he replied reverentially, his head still cocked at a sharp angle to one side, frozen where it had come to rest after being struck. "Forgive me." With some hesitance, he slowly turned his face back toward Der Neue Führer. "What should be done?"

"What do you think should be done?"

"He must be eliminated."

The stern leader looked at his pupil. "And who will see to it that the job is successfully completed?"

"I have a few soldiers in mind—dedicated followers. Each one is willing to do whatever you tell them to do."

"What about you? Are you willing to carry out my orders without question as well?"

The Reichsmarschall instantly came to attention, smartly clicking the heels of his boots together. "Jawohl, mein Führer."

Der Neue Führer walked around to the side of the Reichsmarschall and eyed him closely. He leaned into his ear. "You volunteer, then?"

The Reichsmarschall didn't answer immediately. He'd never before been asked to actually commit such an act himself. He was a planner, coordinator, decision-maker. No blood had yet stained his hands directly. He considered himself a military commander, no closer to real battlefield action than the Washington politicians he'd seen giving orders to America's troops from half a world away, choosing who lives and who dies.

"Yes...yes, I volunteer," he stammered finally.

"Then take care of it," ordered Der Neue Führer, who by now had circled the Reichsmarschall and was staring at him face-to-face. "Any more questions or concerns?" he asked matter-of-factly.

The young man paused. "What about...the Traitor?"

Der Neue Führer nodded. "Yes, the Traitor," he repeated thoughtfully, as if seeing in his mind a wide assortment of final solutions to Schmidt. "He shall be taken care of in due time. At this point, however, I have other, more pressing matters that require my attention. I'm already late for a very important meeting."

"Of course," the Reichsmarschall said contritely.

"You're young," Der Neue Führer said in a somewhat gentler tone, "but you're capable. If I didn't have confidence in you, I would have abandoned you long ago like so many others have done. Yes?"

"Yes, mein Führer."

"No one else sees in you what I see in you. Rest in that knowledge. Live in that truth. Draw upon it for strength when you are weak."

"I will," he answered resolutely.

Der Neue Führer turned and left the bunker without saying another word. But instead of standing at ease, the Reichsmarschall remained rigid, hands at his sides, eyes locked in a forward stare until the distant sounds of Der Neue Führer's boots echoing in the corridor could be heard no more. Only then did he drop his shoulders and breathe more calmly. After a few more moments alone, the Reichsmarschall finally composed himself and began focusing his attention on the task he'd been given, pulling courage and resolve from the war paraphernalia decorating the walls as well as from the magnificent structure he himself had designed and constructed.

"Frank Delafield," he snarled through gritted teeth, "your days are numbered."

29

★ ★ ★

By Monday afternoon, December 29, the fear and anxiety that had been plaguing the nation for weeks had started to give way to a palpable sense of relief over the previous day's arrests. Duncan Phelps took credit for the country's positive mood swing, and rightly so, since it was his decision to round up the suspected terrorists. They were held without bail in a special terrorist-only detention center built three years earlier in an isolated area of South Florida.

The maximum security prison, known as the Southern Sector Detention Facility (SSDF), consisted of 175 cells arranged in a circular pattern that gave the prison's 115 guards a 360-degree view of the structure's complete internal layout. The $152 million it took to build the technological marvel also bought taxpayers seven-and-a-half miles of barbed razor wire; 128 remote-controlled cameras; 722 steel doors for corridors, entrances, and exits; 12 guard towers; 175 see-through polycarbonate cell doors, which provided not only security, but also an unobstructed view of the prisoners one hundred percent of the time; and in an apparent tribute to medieval Europe, a moat, forty feet deep and twenty feet wide. It surrounded the entire complex—a feature strikingly reminiscent of the trenches used to separate tourists from wild beasts at animal parks and zoos.

The newly arrested terrorists ranged in age from twenty-three to forty-seven and came from a wide cross section of America's extremist groups. Together they represented six states and ten separate organizations. And they had collectively served a total of fifty-eight years in jail for one-hundred-forty-two different misdemeanors and felonies. The most recent charges they were facing would put them all away for much longer: conspiracy to commit terrorism, conspiracy to possess and discharge firearms in the furtherance of violent crimes, conspiracy to maliciously damage and/or destroy public property using explosives, and conspiracy to levy war against the U.S. government via terrorism.

"The Dirty Dozen," as the press called them, were unquestionably enemies of the state. Each one hated the federal government, Washington politicians, and law-enforcement officials. Each one also had invested a significant amount of time and energy attacking the government in one way or another. Nevertheless, some distinctions existed among them. Several of the men, for instance, were extremely intelligent. Others, however, had little or no education and a below-average IQ. All but one were decidedly vicious and deserved to be confined for the rest of their lives.

The odd man out at SSDF was a skinny and obviously terrified computer geek unknown to the other white supremacists. This was not surprising since he was not a racist at all; a hater of the government, to be sure, but he didn't have a white-supremacist bone in his scrawny, one-hundred-twenty-eight-pound, five-foot-nine-inch body. His only crime was signing up with a Southern California militia that had been under surveillance by the FBI after a tip came into the office about the group's stockpiling of weapons. They put the beleaguered militiaman in cell #122, between Matt Hawk in #121 and Donny Blank in #123.

Hawk pressed his face up against the polycarbonate cell door, which although bulletproof, was not soundproof. "Hey, man," he said to the freshly arrived detainee after the guards had left. "Where'd they pick you up?"

No answer.

"Hey—122! I'm talking to you."

The trembling prisoner put his ear up to the clear door, then angled his head toward Matt's voice. "M…me?" he stammered.

"Yeah, dummy. Where'd they get you?"

"Umm…California, around the Nevada state line."

Matt Hawk smiled, recalling some pretty wild times he'd had in that area. "I used to do some work around there. Organized a bunch of rallies for the Imperial Klans of the Southwest. Helped them get marches going in Vegas, Riverside, and Bakersfield. What's your name?"

"S…Sammy. They call me SammyHack. Sometimes just SamHack, or SH."

Hawk scratched his head as he strained to look sideways into Sammy's cell. An impossible feat, but Hawk tried anyway. "Hack? Is that like with a computer, like hacking and stuff?"

"Uh-huh," he answered sheepishly, retreating from the door and sitting on the thin cot that had been placed against the side wall, its posts of steel driven deep into the concrete flooring.

"You with the Klan?" Hawk continued.

No answer.

"Hey! Are you deaf? I said, you with the Klan?"

Donny Blank, who had been listening in #123, spoke up. "That ain't no Klucker, Matt. He's too young."

"Well, he ain't with the Skins," argued Matt, stifling a snicker. "Too small."

Blank let out a loud guffaw as he banged his fists on the polycarbonate. "Kinda like a weasel, if you ask me."

Hawk roared with laughter at Blank's comeback, doubling up with his back against the door, until at last he had calmed down enough to speak again. "Hey, Hack, no offense, just kidding," he said through his last chuckles. "Seriously, who you with?"

Still no response from #122.

"Maybe he passed out, Matt. You know those feds kept me up for thirty-six hours; didn't even give me nothin' to eat or drink. Their Jew masters probably told them to starve us and make us go bonkers or something. He's probably half-dead, like I was."

"Sure…maybe," Hawk agreed.

"Leave him alone. We'll talk to him later—maybe he can help us find some way to break outta this concentration camp."

But Sammy hadn't passed out. He was lying on his back listening to everything being said, kicking himself for having gone against his instincts. He knew that he shouldn't have put a contact address down on his militia enlistment form; and he also knew he should've stayed totally off the grid, not gotten involved with people again, not in the real world. And now here he was. *Stupid.*

He had no idea that the Desert Militia had been stockpiling automatic weapons, nor did he suspect that its members would be so willing to blame their newest member for the cache of AK-47s when federal agents came knocking at the door. The government couldn't have been happier about finally catching up to the elusive SammyH. A nice coincidence. And being able to pin something on him as serious as terrorism was like icing on a cake. He'd be put away for the rest of his life if convicted. *How did I get myself into this?* he thought regretfully.

SamHack, born Morris Samuel Finster, had started on his journey away from society when he was only fifteen years old. By then he was already accustomed to life as a social outcast, having been ostracized as a nerd and abused in the hallways of his Southern California high school by cheerleaders and jocks. So instead of going to football games and dances, he sat for hours at his computer, enjoying one of the most popular Massively Multiplayer Online Role-Playing Games, Eve Online—a space adventure where he could pilot various kinds of extraordinary ships in a fantastic universe. And there he made his first real friends; many of whom were from distant parts of the globe.

It was in his early days of playing Eve that Sammy learned how to make a living by simply being more skilled than his competitors. He discovered that the supplies, ships, and valuable commodities he acquired in-game could actually be sold in the real world for hard cash to fellow players who wanted, but did not have the skills to obtain, what he was able to collect during his travels throughout the cosmos. So he'd play for hours at a time to secure a special missile launcher, rare skill book, or powerful spaceship, then tell other players about what he had. When an item was requested, he'd sell it to his customer, sometimes for hundreds of dollars.

Before long he was making quite a decent living, and realized that the more time he spent online, the more cash he could earn. Other games soon joined Eve in SamHack's money-making repertoire: Day of Doom, Good & Evil, Revolution VII, BattleQuest. The profits kept pouring in from countries as far away as England, Iceland, and Germany. He lacked nothing, except what most people might consider a normal life. But generally speaking, SH was pleased with how things had turned out, especially given his ability to earn a living tax-free. No government. No IRS. No bureaucratic regime breathing down his neck, watching over his shoulder, just waiting for him to mess up so he could be buried under red tape and greed.

That's what had killed his mother. First came the HMO insurance company runarounds after she was diagnosed with cancer. Then the IRS audits hit, thanks to a few minor errors on some of his mother's old tax returns. The IRS agents were relentless. They wanted those back taxes; they wanted them with interest.

Even Sammy's under-the-table earnings couldn't cover the enormous bills that kept landing in the mailbox almost daily. Mrs. Finster didn't have a chance—the stress, the bills, the lack of medical care. Her fight was over before it even began.

SammyHack would never forgive. Never forget. The corporate and political monstrosity that had killed his mother revealed to SH that America was in much worse shape than he'd ever imagined. So he made a vow to himself that at least one person was going to start telling the truth to anyone who would listen—and he'd do it pulling no punches.

He started out by registering with multiple online message boards where he'd post trivia about government and corporate lies he'd uncovered: "Big Brother Spies on Your Phone Calls"; "Government Gets the Oil & Consumers Get the Shaft"; "Pharmaceutical Companies Pay Off Politicians."

That was satisfying for a while, but Sammy eventually wanted to put an even more focused sting into his diatribes. So he created his own Web page dedicated to bringing down the guy who, to his mind, was one of the most corrupt politicians in recent times: President Peter Beckett. It amazed SH how Beckett was still the country's leader in light of the grievous lies that had been told not just by him, but by his staffers, from the vice president all the way down through his cabinet. Finally, in frustration, Sammy let loose with his harshest criticisms, using threatening language on an Internet blog he called "President Peter Piper's Pickled Peppers."

Maybe I screwed up there, he admitted to himself, lying on his bunk at SSDF, his eyes closed, head turned toward the wall. *But it wasn't like I actually was going to hurt anyone.*

After thinking long and hard about his decisions, his years on the road, and his mother, SamHack fell asleep. He was more tired than he thought possible. Like Matt Hawk, SH had indeed been awake an extraordinary length of time. About thirty hours, he thought. He slept undisturbed for the next eight hours, a pilot again, flying a Machariel battleship through pirate-infested regions of space in Eve Online.

He awoke in utter darkness, cold and disoriented. Then he remembered where he was, and realized it would probably be a very long time before he played again on the Internet. So he tried to fall back to sleep…tried to return to Eve. But as the back-and-forth chatter from #121 and #123 about ZOG and Hitler went on and on, not allowing him to rest. Sammy couldn't decide if he was more disgusted or frightened.

30

*You cannot do a kindness too soon, for you never know
how soon it will be too late.*

RALPH WALDO EMERSON (1803–1882)

★★★

Stark slammed down the receiver of the hotel phone so hard it cracked. The other agents briefly looked at him and each other without saying a word, then continued packing up the equipment. Only Carlyle stopped what she was doing and faced her partner.

"I'm guessing your conversation with Mr. Phelps went exactly the way we thought it would," she said.

"What a grade-A-son-of-a…"

"That's what I thought." She lifted her shoulders in resignation. "At least you tried."

Stark let out a long, exasperated sigh. "He's making a big mistake if he thinks I'm going to end this investigation just so he can look good."

"Well, I hate to be the bearer of bad news, but there's really not much you can do." Carlyle handed her fuming mentor a cup of freshly made hazelnut-vanilla coffee—medium-hot, no cream, four tablespoons of sugar. "Here," she said. "This'll make you feel better."

Stark thanked her and took a few sips, hoping to calm himself. He'd been talking to the Secretary of Homeland Security for over an hour, trying to convince him that closing down the operation would be terribly unwise, not only because the agency was, in his opinion, zeroing in on the real terrorists, but also because one of his agents was still working deep undercover at Gruber's camp and wasn't ready to leave.

"First of all," argued Phelps, "we *do* have the *real* terrorists. And unless you can show me some evidence to the contrary, please do everyone a favor by keeping your irresponsible opinions to yourself. As for your undercover agent, whoever he is, you tell him to pack up his walkie-talkie and secret decoder ring and get out of there pronto. He has seventy-two hours. I won't have this operation stretching into the new year. It's already cost the administration millions of dollars. A total waste of funds, in my opinion. So I want your boy back in L.A. by Thursday afternoon, January 1, at the latest, and at HQ for debriefing next Monday. Do I make myself clear?"

"*Very* clear," Stark answered rigidly. Three days, of course, left him and Carlyle almost no time to follow up on the leads they'd received over the weekend. But there was nothing else to be done. The mission would end once Coletti was extracted, so they had to somehow come up with proof that Gruber, or someone in his camp, was tied to the terrorist network responsible for the recent attacks against America.

Stark was convinced that a link did indeed exist.

According to local residents, unfamiliar individuals were seen in the town of Rosamond shortly before the mall strikes. And their descriptions matched those of Johnathon Larkin and George Nelson, named by Schmidt, as well as the third man Schmidt didn't know, but whose fingerprints had finally identified him as Chester Pate, a self-styled racist with no particular affiliation.

The trio had arrived separately, on three consecutive days, and checked into different hotels under aliases according to the registration books Carlyle had obtained from the Motel 6, Rosamond Inn, and Desert Cactus—the town's cheapest lodgings.

They eventually showed up together at Norma's Pub, where they drank and shot some pool on the Monday night before the attacks; Karl's Hardware & Rental Center, where on Tuesday afternoon they were seen loitering in the "Guns & Ammo" section of the store; and at My Place Bar & Grill, a popular watering hole, where they played some darts and had lunch on Wednesday. After that, they weren't seen again, except for Nelson, who was captured on a security-cam video at a gas station on the edge of town. He filled up a 1986 LeBaron with fake Nevada license plates, then headed north on CA-14.

Stark theorized the three terrorists had come to Rosamond to either meet a contact or pick up weapons. Then afterward, they'd separated and traveled by car to Iowa City, Bloomington, and Schaumburg. But he needed something more substantial than a theory to raid Gruber's compound—preferably some proof that the men had gone to his enclave or received assistance from at least one of his followers. Money given to them would qualify as aiding and abetting a terrorist. Even if the men had merely stopped by to meet Gruber for a few moments or gotten directions from a camp member while in town, that would be enough to secure a search warrant.

Stark and Carlyle decided they weren't going to let the next seventy-two hours go wasted. The problem was, they were on their own. The other agents were busy shutting things down and seeing to it that the agency's equipment was made ready for transport back to Los Angeles. So they split their investigation up. Stark would contact Coletti again, this time face-to-face, give him his exit orders, and tell him that if he was going to find the War Room, then he'd better do it immediately. He'd also show him the photos of the terrorists to find out whether they'd ever visited the compound. For the operative's safety, this would happen far from town. Meanwhile, Carlyle would continue looking for witnesses who might have seen any of the men heading toward Gruber's camp.

"What about Delafield?" Carlyle asked, pulling on her jacket.

"He's supposed to be going by Gruber's place today. So let's see what our star reporter can find out for us. You never know what might happen."

Carlyle raised one eyeborw. "Stark, do you think we should be letting him go through with this interview?" She paused. "I mean, he could get seriously hurt."

Stark knew that this was his partner's way of voicing strong disapproval. She'd always put it in the form of a question: "Don't you think that...?" "Doesn't it seem like...?" "Wouldn't it be better if...?" He appreciated her tact, and once in a while she actually got him to change his mind. But this was not one of those times.

"I don't like this any more than you do, Chris," he admitted. "But I'm willing to do whatever it takes to bring the real terrorists to justice. I don't want to see Delafield get hurt. He's an okay guy. I know that. But I also know that if we don't figure out what's going on around here, a lot more innocent people are going to be wiped out. Besides, he knows what he's doing. He's chosen to stay here of his own free will and snoop around. That's what guys like him live for."

Carlyle shrugged. "Yeah, well, I just want to make sure he goes on *living.*"

"Okay, then, let's get out there and do our jobs. And I'll tell you what. If you want, you can sort of keep an eye on him while I'm out of town meeting with Coletti. Deal?"

"Deal," she said, relieved that someone would be watching out for Frank.

31

*Heroism is not only in the man,
but in the occasion.*

CALVIN COOLIDGE (1872–1933)

★★★

The first bullet would've killed Frank instantly had it struck him in the heart, which is where the Reichsmarschall was aiming. An inch or two up or down, or to either side, would've made no difference because of the high-velocity round. He very likely wouldn't have even made it to the hospital, dying instead at the scene from shock or massive blood loss before the paramedics arrived.

But the .308 hollow-point slug missed its mark by a good foot-and-a-half. The Reichsmarschall, one hundred yards away, hadn't taken into account the powerful Santa Ana winds when he squeezed the trigger of his Springfield M1A rifle. A twenty-five-mile-per-hour gust of cold desert air was all it took to alter the projectile's trajectory.

Had the unsuspecting journalist been standing motionless, he would've gotten hit in the shoulder or arm. But he was moving sideways, and that was enough to save his life. He'd noticed that the woman behind him was in a hurry. So he'd pivoted when exiting the Short Stop Mini Mart and held the door open for her and her little boy. Frank had smiled politely at Mindy Laughlin as she walked by him, holding her son's hand. *Cute kid*, he thought.

She had smiled back, just as a silent splatter of red landed across Frank's light-blue shirt. At that same instant, Mindy felt a sharp pain in her upper back. She and Frank stood there for a second or two, simply staring at each other, neither realizing what had just happened. Mindy didn't do anything except look Frank directly in the eyes, a grimace on her face. Then she began quivering and looked down at her chest, where the blood was soaking her lemon-yellow sweater.

"I'm hurt," was all she could say before collapsing in front of her son, Cameron, who started screaming.

Frank quickly knelt over Mindy, who'd fallen outside the store, using his light jacket to stop the bleeding. His efforts were futile. Blood was everywhere, some pooling beneath her, some running down the tilted curb into the gutter. She was unconscious, mercifully unaware of what was going on.

The second bullet struck the mini-mart's front window, which exploded into thousands of glistening shards that flew in every direction. Another bullet followed quickly, hitting the wall next to Frank, who now understood someone was shooting at him. Amid the screams and panic, he pulled the boy and mother into the store, hoping to find some cover.

"Call the police!" he shouted. But before the cashier could respond, bullet #4 struck the man in the forearm and he went down. "Call 9-1-1!" Frank hollered again as he moved further inside, dragging Mindy and Cameron with him, away from the doors and windows.

He crouched as low as possible, keeping a tight grip on the hysterical boy with one hand while trying to put pressure on Mindy's wound, desperately hoping to stop the blood that was gushing freely. He hadn't yet realized the twenty-eight-year-old mom was already dead.

The call for help was finally made by a kid at the back of the store. "Someone's shooting at everyone," the frightened teenager shouted to the 9-1-1 operator. "I'm at the Short Stop Mini Mart, and someone's shooting."

At least a dozen sheriff's and highway-patrol units arrived

within ten minutes. By then, however, the Reichsmarschall was long gone.

★★★

Agent Carlyle got to the scene about an hour after the incident. Dozens of spectators were milling around, gawking and speculating. Although Mindy Laughlin's body had been removed, the coroner was still wrapping up his investigation.

Frank sat alone on the curb near the entrance, gazing off into the distance, transfixed by the desolate landscape that stretched for miles beyond the small town. Carlyle approached him, and knelt down only a few feet to his right.

"Frank?" she said gently.

The distraught journalist slowly turned. She could see that his shirt was still damp with blood, which had also soaked into the legs of his jeans.

"Oh," he responded in a daze. "It's you."

Carlyle sat down next to him. "You okay?"

He thought for a moment. "No, Agent Carlyle. I don't think I am."

Carlyle said nothing.

"She died right there in front of me. I couldn't do a thing to help her."

"I know. But at least her son is going to be all right. You saved his life."

Frank wrung his hands, noticing the blood still on them. "If I would've just gone up to Gruber's camp without stopping for a stupid soda, she'd be alive right now."

Carlyle placed her hand lightly on his arm. "You can't second-guess these things. It'll make you crazy."

The reporter looked into Carlyle's eyes and saw genuine compassion. She truly cared. Actually felt bad about what had happened to him, and what had happened to Mindy. *Beneath that tough exterior,* he thought to himself, *there's a real person.*

"It wasn't your fault, Frank."

"I know," he said, scanning the desert. After a long pause, he continued. "You ever see someone get shot?"

Carlyle nodded. "Yes."

"It's not like in the movies. They don't get blasted backward. They just…drop to the ground. Straight to the ground where they're standing, like a bag of bricks."

"A lot of things are different in real life than they are in the movies."

Frank looked away from her, back out toward the scenery, wishing he could do nothing else but sit there for a few hours and watch the sun go down.

Carlyle dusted off the tops of her legs, unsure of what to say next. "I guess this means you won't be going to see Gruber."

Frank snapped his head around. "You're kidding, right? Of course I am."

Carlyle stood, and fixed the reporter with a firm stare. "You can't. It's too dangerous."

He looked up at the agent, ready to make his case. "Well, regardless of how you feel about it, I've *got* to find out what's going on. I want whoever did this to be punished. Not for my sake, but for that woman I saw them haul away in a body bag."

Carlyle put her hands on her hips and looked down, frustrated. "Don't you get it?" she argued. "It could be *you* next time."

"Oh, I get it," he explained as he started toward his car. "But what *you* don't seem to get is that I don't care. All I care about is making sure that these murderers are caught. My interview with Gruber is *on*, and no one's going to stop me."

"C'mon, Frank," she tried one last time, even though she knew that he was set on his course of action.

"No," he yelled out as he crossed the parking lot. "Tomorrow morning I'm gonna talk to that sicko. I'll stop by the hotel suite afterward to let you know what happened—if I'm still alive, that is."

Carlyle could only watch as the stubborn journalist got into his car and drove away.

32

★★★

It was almost one o'clock in the morning, but Frank couldn't sleep. He couldn't stop thinking about Mindy, her family, how Cameron, her little boy, was doing. He could still hear the sound of the window exploding, Mindy's last words to him, and Cameron screaming. *I hope the kid's going to be okay,* Frank thought as he lay in bed, staring at the ceiling of his hotel room.

The bar downstairs was still open, of course, waiting patiently for anyone needing a little stress relief. And the exhausted reporter knew that a couple of martinis backed by a shot or two of tequila would certainly be enough to knock him out. Instead, he climbed out of bed, walked over to his laptop, and began typing.

Random, disorganized thoughts trickled slowly out of his brain and onto the screen as he mindlessly tapped the keyboard, a word or two at first, disjointed and meaningless: "Death comes… dying…evil…shadows…dark…alone…" A smattering of short sentences followed after several minutes, until at last he found his thoughts flowing, writing paragraph after paragraph. A cathartic rush of emotions, observations, and questions poured forth.

With our first breath we unknowingly beckon to our side
a companion who, for the rest of our earthly days, will

166

remain closer than any friend, yet more feared than any enemy. This invisible observer shadows our every move as deftly as a predator stalking its prey, watching us as we make our way through life, day after day, night after night, never truly alone.

Only when every cell of our being is saturated with the mad rush of the world around us do we forget for a few moments that our ghostly companion is there. But this respite never lasts. We invariably recall our accursed acquaintance—after a nightmare; while being prepared for surgery; just before the dawn, when we fret about what tomorrow will bring.

We are most vulnerable to the Grim Reaper while tender infants, when our unformed psyches are blissfully unaware of the silent attendant who cradles us on the edge of this world and the next. But our ignorance of mortality diminishes as we mature—we plummet from the dizzying heights of a tree house; we choke on the contents of a bottle beneath the sink. In response to this new and terrible knowledge, we do the most unnatural things: climb more carefully; swallow only what Mom gives us.

The lifelong game of hide-and-seek has begun. Though it is a game that we will never win, we play with all our strength. But year after year, as friends and loved ones are spirited away after their battle with Death has concluded, an odd sensation of fear mixed with wonder invades the souls of those left behind, still playing the game, as we ask a chilling question: <u>Is that the end of it all?</u>

At 2:28 a.m., Frank hit the SAVE button one last time. He went back to bed—sat for a while in the dark, his mind a restful blank. "I hope tomorrow goes well," he muttered. Then he set the alarm, lay back, and closed his bloodshot eyes, letting his body drift off as the hum of the heating unit lulled him into a sleep without dreams.

33

*Those who can make you believe absurdities
can make you commit atrocities.*

VOLTAIRE (1694-1778)

★★★

It wasn't my fault, the Reichsmarschall kept telling himself.
*She got in the way…she just got in the way. Things like this happen.
Civilians get killed. It wasn't my fault.* He paced back and forth,
confused, arguing with an invisible prosecutor standing beside him
who was charging him again and again with murder. *No, no, no,* he
answered his accuser, hoping each denial would bring a measure
of reassurance. *I didn't mean to kill her. It was an accident.*

He replayed the incident in his mind, trying in vain to dis-
cover where he'd made a mistake. *It was a perfect shot…a perfect
shot.* He'd lined up his target from a hundred yards away using a
top-of-the-line sniper scope. Frank was well within range, moving
slowly toward an unobstructed spot, but then he'd stopped—just
stood stock-still. A bull's-eye practically painted in his chest.
The Reichsmarschall remembered inhaling slightly, holding his
breath, and then—as he had done so many times before during
his training exercises—gently squeezing the trigger.

But suddenly the woman had been in the crosshairs, not
Delafield. "NO," the Reichsmarschall had yelled in the moment
he saw his bullet strike her. Her expression of shock and pain
would forever be frozen in his mind.

But there was no time to mourn. He had to take down the

journalist—had to complete his mission. *Where is he? Where is he?* the Reichsmarschall panicked, scanning the area through the eyepiece. *There!* He pulled the trigger again, this time firing too early, shooting wide as he moved his rifle toward Frank. Then a third round, followed by a fourth. But it was too late. The opportunity was gone.

Now, hours later, in the War Room, the Reichsmarschall knew his willingness to do whatever it took to obtain victory was wavering. He was doubting himself, doubting his tactics and abilities. He overturned a table, still fuming over the debacle, then kicked a chair. Suddenly, he realized what he had to do—look to the man whose words had inspired millions. He turned to the back of the room and flipped on a recording of Adolf Hitler's 1933 Proclamation to Germany. It boomed throughout the War Room at full volume. It was one of the Reichsmarschall's favorites—a speech filled with promises and truths to encourage the soul and embolden the heart in the direst of circumstances.

"The inheritance which has fallen to us is a terrible one," the Nazi leader declared. "But we are all filled with unbounded confidence for we believe in our people and their imperishable virtues. Every class and every individual must help us to found the new Reich."

Each word reverberated in the Reichsmarschall's ears. *Yes, yes,* he agreed, straining to find absolution for the death of the young woman. He walked back over to the console that listed more recordings: Hitler's Munich orations, 1922 to 1924; the Stuttgart, Nuremberg, and Weimar speeches of 1933, 1936, 1938; and his wartime speeches in Berlin. From the last collection, the Reichsmarschall chose the Reichstag discourse of May 4, 1941.

He closed his eyes imagining what it might have been like to be present as the chancellor railed against the enemies of Deutschland: England, France, America, and all the "Jew-ridden democracies" that were committed to destroying the Fatherland. He let Der Führer's potent voice penetrate and heal his soul.

To the families of those who had paid the ultimate price, Hitler expressed his deepest sympathies, but then went on to say, "Taking the measures as a whole, however, the losses suffered are so small that they constitute supreme justification: first, for the planning and timing of this campaign; second for the conduct of operations; third, for the manner in which they were carried through."

The losses suffered are so small that they constitute supreme justification, the Reichsmarschall repeated in his mind, then whispered quietly. "I had no choice. Nothing must stand in the way of victory." He stopped the recording. After a few more minutes of basking in the afterglow of Hitler's words, he left his hideout and returned to the small, airless room where he lived in town.

"It's Delafield's fault. That's why she's dead," the Reichsmarschall concluded at last, finding peace within himself, understanding he was guilty of nothing. He was not responsible. It was not his fault. "That Jewish lapdog is probably being paid by the government to cause all this trouble," he muttered, hanging up his coat. "The Traitor too. They're in this together. I'll take care of them both next time. Punish them for their transgressions. And Der Neue Führer will be pleased with me. He'll see that I can do this. When it's all over, everything will be as it should be."

The Reichsmarschall sat down at his worn, wooden desk and opened his journal, which Der Neue Führer said would someday be a valuable document. In it, he'd been keeping a record of the war since it had started, and before that, he had chronicled his rise through the ranks, the day he became second in command, and the initial plans he and his leader had made so many years ago. He gripped his pen firmly and began another entry:

> I killed a noncombatant today. A woman, an Aryan sister, the mother of a small child. God will forgive me, however—of this I am sure, for he knows I was only trying to do what had to be done. As in all wars, many people, not just soldiers, must die. Sacrifices lifted up to God the Father, just as his Son the Christ was lifted up as a sacrifice for many.

The blood I shed would not have even been spilled had it not been for the Jews' desire to destroy Yahweh's holy people. The Zion monsters and their hirelings, like Frank Delafield and the Traitor, seek to ruin God's kingdom. They work to slander the good reputation and integrity of the white race, God's righteous nation. They devise plans to dilute the royal white bloodline through miscegenation: blacks and whites creating mongrelized, cursed offspring, befouling the holy acts of sex and procreation. And, of course, they spread the satanic plot of multiculturalism.

They started this war. Guilt for the woman's death, therefore, ultimately rests on their heads. I am absolved. God will judge them. As for me, I shall continue to fight, although surrounded on all sides by enemy soldiers, Jew slaves, spies, and betrayers. The country lies in ruins, with ZOG in control of the nation's liberal media, the banks, the health-care system, the food industry—and most certainly Hollywood, a cesspool of sexual degenerates and Jews, with movies and TV shows flaunting countless scenes of negroes kissing white women. I am sickened, but my disgust only drives me on, makes me long even more for the day when the Fourth Reich will rise from the burning ashes of what was once <u>called</u> America, but was in reality the accursed kingdom of ZOG.

That day will be glorious.

For now, however, I must endure the daily sufferings of my own isolation and bear the anguish of watching my people live in slavery, bound by the chains of the Zionist totalitarian regime in Washington. Until our liberation, my primary goals will be to simply promote and support the revolution for as long as I am able, dreaming of the era when God's natural order of a white American republic will be established on this continent, forever and ever, amen.

There will be more dark days ahead, I am sure. But I know that my God, Yahweh the King, and my commander, Der Neue Führer, will see this conflict through to its end. Many heroes have gone before me in the struggle: Richard Butler,

> William Pierce, George Lincoln Rockwell, Bob Matthews,
> William Potter Gale, Timothy McVeigh, to name but a
> few. I can only hope that someday my name will be added
> to this list of brave warriors—soldiers whose labor and
> blood over the years helped establish the rise of the Fourth
> Reich. <u>Heil Hitler. White Pride. Hail Victory!</u>

The Reichsmarschall closed his journal. Perhaps he would publish these writings after the war was over, use them as a teaching tool in a redesigned school system in which white children would be safe, no longer afraid of the blacks with their guns and knives and sickening rap music. For a brief moment, he even envisioned the journal as a kind of nonfiction version of *The Turner Diaries*, his favorite novel. He had read the story by William Pierce numerous times, relishing its vivid description of the very struggle in which he now found himself. It perfectly reflected the movement's goals as well as the hopes and dreams of every Aryan warrior.

The Reichsmarschall was finally ready to relax, exhausted by his trying time on the battlefield. "Tomorrow will be a better day," he promised himself, staring fixedly at the moon shining through the window. *White Power, Hail Victory*, he whispered as he dozed off, the crowds in his mind chanting their responses. He envisioned himself and Der Neue Führer standing before the adulation of the masses. *Glorious*, he thought, smiling, his eyes closed. *Glorious.*

34

War is hell.

WILLIAM TECUMSEH SHERMAN (1820–1891)

★★★

At 5:30 a.m. on January 21, 1968, the first barrage of 122mm rockets and 82mm mortars slammed into the U.S. marine base at Khe Sanh, Vietnam, just south of the DMZ. Soon afterward, small-arms and automatic-weapons fire, sustained and focused, erupted from the dense jungle that surrounded the base's perimeter, making the fierce onslaught even more intense and terrifying.

Not long after the attack began, a rocket found its mark, landing a direct hit on the primary ammunition dump. It sent an enormous plume of flame and searing smoke high into the pre-dawn sky, a billowing ball of orange-white heat visible for miles. When the assault ended, forty marines had been wounded, and eighteen more lay dead.

Thus began the seventy-seven-day siege of the base at Khe Sanh and the marine camps in nearby hills. The offensive came as no surprise, at least not to President Johnson or General William Westmoreland, commander of U.S. forces in Vietnam. Up until 1968, the North Vietnamese Army had remained a mysterious force, unpredictable and wily, seemingly able to appear and disappear at will. So Westmoreland decided to flush them out—force them into a head-on clash. He set his trap by allowing Khe Sanh and its hill outposts to be encircled by North Vietnamese forces, using as bait 6000 U.S. soldiers—mostly marines under the age of twenty-one—with limited resources and no possibility of evacuation.

Eighteen-year-old Eddie Stark, Private First Class, USMC, witnessed that first assault on the main base from his position on Hill 861, a few miles northwest of Khe Sanh proper. Earlier that same morning, his unit had endured its own bombardment, followed by a ground assault by two-hundred-fifty North Vietnamese soldiers, who blasted pathways through the protective wire around the outpost.

Shouting, gunfire, and explosions enveloped him as he battled for what seemed like forever, all the while tripping over bodies, firing his weapon, and lobbing grenades. He was bleeding from somewhere, but felt no pain—too much adrenaline.

Stark wanted to run away and never look back—or hide in a foxhole, play dead until it was over. But through the haze of smoke, he would catch a glimpse of fellow soldiers trying to stay alive, and that alone gave him the courage to go on. He eventually found himself in hand-to-hand fights that night. And when it was all over, he'd killed five men in close combat, choking the last one to death with his bare hands.

Thanks to the heroic efforts of PFC Eddie Stark and the rest of his battalion, the Hill 861 attack was eventually repelled and the NVA troops routed, but not before the deaths of four young marines. About a dozen others were wounded, including Eddie, who took a handful of shrapnel in his left side and suffered a deep gash in his thigh. But he wasn't sent home. The medic just stitched up the gaping wound without anesthetic, then removed the shrapnel and taped the holes shut after filling them with Merthiolate.

But others who survived the initial engagements were not so easily repaired. Lance Corporal Mitch Perkins lost his left arm three inches above the elbow. Second Lieutenant Joe Campbell caught a bullet that sliced through his spinal cord near the fifth vertebra, leaving him a paraplegic. Private First Class Dan Barnes lost his sight to grenade fragments. They all got out on the same chopper. Perkins babbling incoherently on morphine. Campbell staring silently off into the distance. And Barnes repeating, "I can't see! I can't see!"

As for Eddie Stark, he went on to see more combat, more limbs blown off by land mines, more lives ruined physically, psychologically, emotionally, spiritually. He knew even as it was happening that he'd never forget the bloody images that filled his days and nights: the stench of death hanging everywhere, search-and-destroy patrols into hostile territory, ambushes, rats almost as big as dogs feeding off decaying bodies, women and children tortured and killed by the Vietcong for aiding Americans. None of it would ever be forgotten.

The insanity at Khe Sanh ended in mid-April when the U.S. high command decided to reassign the area's units to other parts of Vietnam and abandon the base and hill camps that so many men had fought and died to hold. By July of 1968, not a single marine was left in the area.

"What a waste," Stark grumbled as he touched the thick shrapnel scars through his shirt. They still hurt him whenever it got cold or damp, reminding him of those awful months in combat. He continued along Route 14 on his way to see Coletti, unable to stop thinking about the war. This usually happened during lengthy drives, especially at night when the tedium of the road took him back in time. *Politicians were playing their games then, and they're still doing it now.*

And Duncan Phelps, Stark thought, was the worst kind of politician, just like the ones in the 1960s who'd gotten so many kids killed so far from home. *All he wants to do is make himself look good and get more power,* the agent fumed, still amazed at the decision to shut down the Rosamond operation. Gruber was clearly behind the whole thing somehow. Of this, Stark was sure.

"We have the *real* terrorists," he said aloud, mocking Phelps.

He turned off Sierra Highway, taking Crown Valley Road toward downtown Acton, a sleepy hamlet less than an hour south of Rosamond. As he passed by a late-night café, he wished he could grab a cup of coffee. But he was running behind schedule. Coletti was probably already waiting. So he drove on, thinking again about Khe Sanh, where he often had to go for weeks without a hot meal. And even when C-rations were available, he sometimes had to settle for one ration every twenty-four hours, and survive without water for several days.

The road narrowed a bit and veered to the right, then to the left. No one was around, and the streets were lit only by a few lamps spaced far apart. He was heading for the Acton Community Center, the hub of local activities for the community of less than 10,000.

He stopped as far away from the building as possible, in a darkened corner of the parking lot, having shut off his headlights even before driving up the entranceway. *Where's Coletti?* he wondered as he opened the door and stepped out of his car. He heard nothing, took three steps, then froze when he recognized the unmistakable sound of a bullet being chambered into a 9mm Beretta.

"Put your hands up and turn around slowly," the voice behind him ordered.

Stark didn't put his hands up, but he did turn around. "Coletti, you have a sick sense of humor."

The undercover agent smirked, concealed somewhere in the shadows. "You're slipping, old man."

"You wish," Stark retorted. "C'mon, get in the car. I've got some bad news."

35

*The past is not a package that
one can simply put away.*

EMILY DICKINSON (1830–1886)

★★★

For the next hour, Stark and Coletti discussed their options in light of the operation's shutdown. One course of action was for Coletti to go back to L.A. straight from his meeting with Stark. He'd left nothing of value at Gruber's compound and could just walk across the parking lot to his Harley, climb on board, and ride home. It would've been an understandable choice. There was probably little more he could accomplish in the seventy-two hours Phelps had given him to wrap up any loose ends. On the other hand, if Coletti stayed at the camp, there was a slim chance he might uncover something the feds could use to secure a search warrant.

Coletti, of course, wanted to hold tight and push it to the deadline. The stakes were high. People's lives were on the line. And on a more personal level, he had a reputation to uphold. He always got his man, so to speak, from his days as a vice cop in Brooklyn to his most recent international undercover job, one that other agents in the department had referred to as "Mission Impossible." But if he didn't find the War Room, or at least link Gruber's camp to the attacks, then it would mean his first failure.

And he hated the thought of that. His hard-driving, authoritarian father, Angelo Coletti, had instilled in him at a very young age the need to succeed.

177

Though Coletti had abandoned most of what he'd been taught growing up, that value had stuck with him. *Be perfect. Never fail.* And now in Rosamond, he was facing his worst fear.

"So that's it?" Coletti asked angrily. "'Sorry, we can't let you stick around long enough to do your job. Time to go home.' What kind of an operation is that?"

"Hey, I feel the same way," Stark replied. "You know that if it was up to me, I'd let you stay for as long as necessary. But I'm not calling the shots."

The undercover agent slammed his fist down hard on the car's dashboard. "Unbelievable. I've spent almost a year inside that loony bin, and now Phelps is going to flush all of my hard work down the toilet." Coletti turned and stared out the car window in frustration. "Well, he can forget it. I'm not going back to L.A. Not until I find what I've been looking for."

Stark sighed. "Don't do this to me. You can't ignore orders—though I realize you have a nasty habit of doing just that. If you're unwilling to quit tonight, fine, hang out for three more days. But I'm asking you as a friend to get yourself out of there within the mandated time frame. And for the record, any more stunts like the one you pulled in Singapore and you'll be canned so fast you'll be standing in the unemployment line before the ink on your pink slip dries."

"But—"

"I'm not going to argue with you about this, Mike. I'm trying to tell you that if you go rogue again, even if you apprehend the Nazi mastermind himself, it won't be tolerated. We can't have agents disobeying direct orders. I mean it."

"Alright, alright," Coletti said, giving up. "But I'll leave the camp my way. I don't want any desk agents showing up with fake warrants so they can haul me away in a black sedan. That would be totally lame."

"Understood."

Stark pulled out the pictures of the three terrorist suspects.

"Ever see these guys?" he asked as he passed them to Coletti.

"Sure. About three weeks ago. They came into the compound, walked around a bit, visited with some of the guys, then took off."

"Did they talk to Gruber?"

"No. Why?"

"Because those are the mall terrorists."

Coletti looked up in disbelief. "Are you thinking what I'm thinking, Ed?"

"Yep."

"All I need to do is verify that the guys I saw talking to these terrorists are still in the camp and we can raid the enclave."

"Looks like it."

"You should have brought these out first," Coletti said, tossing the photos back to Stark. "It would have saved a lot of time."

Stark took the pictures and put them back in an envelope. "I needed to get it straight with you that this operation is over by Thursday, whether you'd seen the terrorists or not."

"Fair enough. I'll head back tonight and look for the guys they talked with. They might even be able to give me more information about why the terrorists came to the compound."

Stark nodded. "Sounds good. And if you get a chance, take another sweep of the whole place. See if you can find that War Room. It's important."

"You got it." Coletti paused. "Hey, by the way, not to change the subject, but how's that partner of yours doing?"

"Carlyle's fine. She's checking out a few more leads in Rosamond while trying to keep tabs on Delafield. Wants to make sure he doesn't get himself killed—or worse."

"He still nosing around?"

"Yeah. Guess he's gonna go up to the compound tomorrow and try to get an interview with Gruber."

"That should be interesting."

"Keep an eye out for him. Make sure none of those gun-happy goons take a shot at him."

Coletti laughed. "Sure. I'll see what I can do."

The two agents shook hands and bid each other farewell. Stark watched Coletti exit the car and disappear into the darkness. He was glad, in a way, that his friend would soon be concluding his assignment. The white supremacists following Gruber were a violent group, and it was impossible to know what might happen if Coletti was discovered. He'd seen too many agents lose their cover just hours before a mission was over. And the outcome was almost always fatal.

36

★★★

Tuesday came too soon for Frank. His head hurt and his body ached. He'd gotten barely four hours of sleep and was still shaken from the attempt on his life. The last thing he wanted to hear was the hotel phone. But that's exactly how his day started. He rolled over and answered it, having totally forgotten where he was.

"Hello…hello?"

A computer responded. "G-o-o-d m-o-r-n-i-n-g. T-h-a-n-k y-o-u f-o-r s-t-a-y-i-n-g a-t t-h-e H-i-l-t-o-n. T-h-i-s i-s y-o-u-r w-a-k-e u-p c-a-l-l. T-h-e t-i-m-e i-s s-i-x t-h-i-r-t-y. F-e-e-l f-r-e-e t-o e-n-j-o-y o-u-r c-o-m-p-l-i-m-e-n-t-a-r-y b-r-e-a-k-f-a-s-t o-n t-h-e s-e-c-o-n-d f-l-o-o-r. H-a-v-e a n-i-c-e d-a-y."

"Thank you," he said unthinkingly, then put the receiver down and slowly pulled himself up. Moaning as he threw the covers back, unable to go any farther than the edge of the bed, he sat there for a few more moments with his eyes shut, trying to recalibrate his senses. *What are you doing, Delafield?* he thought groggily, already second-guessing his decision to waltz into Gruber's stronghold in broad daylight on the off chance of getting a private interview with the head hatemonger himself. Even if he got past the entrance gate, Erich Strom would be waiting. What would Gruber's right-hand man do?

"Good job, boys," he imagined Strom saying to a cadre of salivating camp guards. "You've caught yourselves a Jew trespassing on our property. Now drag that child of Satan down into the canyon and dispatch him to the throne room of Yahweh for eternal judgment."

Frank shook his arms to get the blood flowing, cocked his neck back and forth, then rolled his head around a few times before lightly slapping his right cheek. "Wake up," he ordered himself. "Time for a free breakfast." He stumbled out of bed and flung open the faded curtains. *Well, at least it's not raining.*

On his way to the bathroom, he apprehensively flipped on the TV, exhaling a sigh of relief after seeing there were no early morning emergency news reports.

That's a nice change.

After channel-surfing awhile, he finally settled on a talk show featuring a collector of PEZ dispensers. He cranked up the volume, then headed for the shower. A glimpse of himself in the mirror told him that he also needed a shave. *Delafield, you look like a bum.*

An hour later, Frank was downstairs working his way through pancakes, scrambled eggs, bacon, corned-beef hash, and a heaping plate of French pastries, washed down with a gallon of black coffee.

He breezed through the *L.A. Times, Wall Street Journal,* and *USA Today*—they were still running stories about The Dirty Dozen, bringing out details of their arrests and giving in-depth profiles of each man in custody, complete with family reactions, law-enforcement observations, and shocked comments by old high-school acquaintances. "Truly exhilarating stuff," Frank grunted.

One thing, however, did pique his interest. There was precious little information released about the odd man out: Morris Samuel Finster, a.k.a. SammyHack. "Hmm," he mumbled as he chomped down on another strip of greasy bacon. *There's a story here. I think I might have to pay Morris a visit.*

Something was very fishy about Sammy's arrest, but Frank had far too much to do at the moment to allow his mind to wander. He glanced at his watch and decided he'd better head off to meet his fate. He wanted to arrive at the compound by nine. That would give him plenty of time to get through the gate, find Strom, and interview Gruber before noon.

Notepad: check.

Digital recorder: check.

Cell phone: check.

List of questions: check.

For a brief moment, the journalist wished his inventory included a .38 revolver. He recalled the sleek sidearm he'd seen on Stark and wondered how it'd feel to wear one. In his mind's eye, he saw himself looking pretty tough with one of those strapped to his ribs. *Too bad you've never fired a gun. You'd probably just blow your foot off.*

"Anything else I can get you, hon?" the waitress asked, interrupting Frank's musings.

"Oh, uh…no. I'm good." He took one last bite of pastry and washed it down with a final swallow of coffee.

Wallet: check.

Press ID: check.

Frank stood quickly, strode out of the hotel, and crossed the parking lot to his car, still unable to formulate a precise plan for what he was going to do when he got to the camp's gate. But that wasn't unusual. He tended to perform better on the spur of the moment anyway, like so many of his colleagues (although on this particular occasion he would have been more than happy to be the kind of reporter who approached things less spontaneously).

It'll be fine, he tried to convince himself as he started up his rented Honda.

If the day went without a hitch, he figured he might be able to squeeze at least two hours of rock-solid information out of Gruber. If things didn't go smoothly...that was something Frank tried not to dwell on. Yet the possibility of a serious mishap couldn't be discounted. So he decided to stop for some gas first and strike up a conversation with the attendant, just to let someone know where he was going. It probably wouldn't make any difference, but for some reason the idea of it steadied his nerves a bit.

At the nearest Exxon, he topped off the Accord's tank and stepped up to the cashier's booth. "Nice day," he began.

"Sure is," said the platinum blonde working behind a window of protective glass. "Nothing like December in California. Wish I didn't have to stay inside all day."

Frank nodded, taking notice of her chipped nail polish and ragged cuticles. "Yeah, that's too bad. I'll be driving around most of the afternoon, so I'll be able to enjoy the weather. But first I have to take a trip over to Yahweh's Holy Temple."

Dolly stopped counting his change. "Why you goin' up there?" she asked.

Frank saw a tiny spasm flick along her sagging jawline. "I write for a magazine, and I'm gonna to try to get an interview with the camp's leader, Karl Gruber. Ever heard of him?"

Dolly deposited $8.34 into the window's change drawer and slid it out in a single hurried motion. "Who hasn't?" she replied. "Good luck."

"Thanks," he said, picking up the money. "See ya."

"Goodbye," she said, then lit up an unfiltered cigarette.

Frank didn't like the sound of that. *Goodbye? Why didn't she say "See ya around," or "Okay, have a nice day"?*

After getting in his car, he seriously contemplated what he was about to do. Was it worth it?

Yeah, it's worth it, he answered himself. One last thing, though. He pulled out his wallet and dug through several credit cards, two coupons for Quizno's, and a crumpled assortment of receipts, until he finally found what he was looking for. *Ah, there it is.* He let out a long breath.

Organ-donor card: check.

37

★ ★ ★

Bill Schmidt climbed out of bed Tuesday morning after a fitful
night of sleep interrupted by one nightmare after another—the
result of a phone call he'd received Monday evening from Stephen
Alexander, a fellow pastor who lived across town. A member of
Stephen's church, Mindy Laughlin, had been murdered earlier
that afternoon, brutally gunned down in front of her young son,
who was now an orphan.

The congregation was heartbroken.

As far as anyone knew, she didn't have an enemy in the world
and was dearly loved by everyone among Alexander's parishion-
ers. She'd served in the children's ministry and directed the Little
Lambs kids choir.

Pastor Alexander requested prayer from Bill for himself as
well as for his church, and asked if perhaps Luke might be able
to sing a few special hymns for the funeral, which was scheduled
for Sunday.

"Oh, Stephen, I'm sure he would've had no problem doing
that for you," Schmidt told his grief-stricken friend, "but unfortunately he's out of town until next week. He decided to leave just

last night for a youth retreat up at Big Bear. I'm afraid he won't be back till next Monday."

The pastor understood. "That's alright, Bill. Give my best to him when he gets home."

"I will," Schmidt promised. "And if there's anything else I can do for you, just let me know."

"Thanks. I only hope they catch whoever did this."

"I do too."

Bill hung up the phone, emotionally off balance, pangs of guilt shooting through his soul. The feeling reminded him of those dark and confusing days immediately following his son's death. For a second time in his life, he wished he had done something *before* a tragedy occurred. *I should have helped Agent Stark when he first came to me,* the pastor chastised himself, *just like I should have left the Aryan movement long before my son's mind was polluted by hate and prejudice.*

But now it was too late—again.

Another life was tragically cut short, due in part to his unwillingness to do the right thing at the right time. He'd heard the sirens blaring down the street on Tuesday afternoon. *Some idiot ran that light at Fourth and Prospect again,* he'd assumed. But then local TV bulletins had interrupted regularly scheduled programming. None of the stations released the identity of the victim, but their coverage did mention the name of the man who was with the woman at the time of the shooting.

"Los Angeles journalist Frank Delafield," the newscasters repeatedly announced, excited and seemingly proud that a reporter had been in the thick of the action.

Schmidt immediately realized what had happened: a botched assassination. It was the only plausible conclusion. There were no random, drive-by killings in Rosamond. And Mindy was well-liked, had no criminal background, and lived a quiet life. No one had heard any gunshots near the scene of the crime. That indicated to Schmidt that in all probability a hunter's rifle had been used. He owned one himself and knew it could hit a moving target as far away as two hundred yards.

Bill considered giving Frank a call, but decided not to. The guy undoubtedly already had his hands full. Besides, the sharp-minded journalist didn't need to be told by an aging ex-Klansman that someone had tried to kill him. That was painfully obvious. Schmidt did pray for Frank, however. Spent a lot of time asking the Lord to protect him, keep him vigilant during his travels, particularly to Gruber's compound, and show him the direction he should go.

Guide his every step, Lord. He's a good man. Let him know you're with him.

He was praying for himself as well, asking God for strength to do what he knew needed to be done. There was no longer any doubt in his mind. He had to open up old wounds, step back into the past. A Bible passage he had read during his morning time with God was clearly a message meant for him: "Do not participate in the unfruitful deeds of darkness, but instead expose them."

Although Bill hadn't been active in the racist community for many years, he had remained connected to the complex network of white-supremacist groups and Christian Identity churches. He kept himself apprised of those who were still involved, those who'd left, and those who were straddling the fence. He even had a few contacts sprinkled throughout the KKK—men and woman disillusioned with the movement but unwilling to leave, either out of fear of reprisals or an inability to alienate themselves from the only people with whom they'd ever formed any meaningful relationships; the only place they felt they'd ever belonged.

They updated him about what was happening throughout the racist underground and supplied him with important pieces of data he might one day find a use for—like current names, addresses, and telephone numbers. In return, he encouraged them to get out of the movement. Offered them another way of life through the redemptive power of the Jesus of the Bible, rather than the perverse and hate-filled false Jesus exalted during white-power rallies.

Schmidt realized for the first time that perhaps he was the only one who could find out where, or even if, the elusive War Room existed. Maybe he could even uncover whether or not Gruber was directly linked to the terrorist attacks. But to accomplish all of this, he would have to meet with some dangerous people, ask a few pointed questions, immerse himself back in the culture of hate, if only for a single night. So he made a call he didn't want to make, a call he never thought he'd have to make again—to a former associate with whom he was not on the best of terms. Fortunately, Schmidt would not have to identity himself. Just having the number to call was sufficient.

The phone rang eight times before being answered. "Hello."

Schmidt paused for a moment before uttering the phrases he still had buried deep in his memory. "Greetings, brother."

"Greetings," said the man at the other end of the line. It sent a chill up and down Schmidt's spine. Macon Hatfield's voice sounded exactly the same. Upbeat and youthful, with a slight Southern twang, the remnants of a syrupy drawl he had worked hard to soften after moving to California from rural Mississippi, where he had served in the Klan as a Kleagle—a recruiter.

"I was wondering if you have any white sheets for sale?" Schmidt continued, trying to disguise his voice.

"I believe so, brother. I believe so."

Bill began perspiring and swallowed hard, almost stuttering his next line, but he somehow managed to keep his nerves in check. "Are you open tonight?"

"As a matter of fact we are. Several of our outlets are having a sale this evening. Would a Bakersfield location be convenient?"

"Yes, that would be fine."

"Good. Are you coming from the north or south?"

"South."

"Then just take your first exit, head east for about six miles, turn left at Alameda Junction, then straight ahead to our desert location."

Schmidt repeated the directions in his mind. "I appreciate the help, brother."

"And make sure you check out the Coyote Lounge while you're here in town," Hatfield suggested. "They have a great Happy Hour that starts at 9:00 p.m. sharp."

"I will," the pastor said, then he heard a click.

Schmidt put the receiver down and moved into his study to get a piece of scratch paper. Picking up a pen, he wrote: *exit 1, east, six miles, left at Alameda J, straight. PASSWORD: Coyote.* Attendees of the Klan meeting would be decked out in full regalia. An anonymous sea of white. *Thank God.* His identity would be concealed.

Schmidt tucked away the directions and headed out to the storage shed, a 10 x 10 structure he'd built with Luke when the boy was fourteen. It was one of the last projects the two of them had worked on together. Years of memories had been unceremoniously stashed there: Luke's rusty tricycle, clothes donated to the church, extra cans of paint, and assorted bins filled with junk that ranged from wire hangers to electronic equipment that needed repairing. He pushed through the mess to the large, battered, cardboard carton sitting against the far wall, the only one unmarked, and braced himself.

He slit the tape with his thumbnail and slowly opened the flaps. The box smelled of mothballs and dust. The clear plastic bag inside was still closed, taped shut, just as he'd left it so many years ago. He broke it open and reached inside. The fabric was smooth and chillingly familiar. "God forgive me," he uttered under his breath, then pulled out the robe and hood he'd worn too many times to count when he was young.

Sewn securely over the heart he saw the infamous red, black, and white crosswheel emblem of the KKK. And beneath that, his old moniker: "White Knight."

38

★★★

Karl Gruber's desert retreat—as he liked to call it—rested on ten acres of prime Southern California real estate located on the sunrise side of Highway 14, just a stone's throw north of Rosamond's city limits. The area had originally been settled by the Newberry family around 1850, but by the 1990s only one parcel was still family-owned, and it was finally snatched up for a cool million by Sid Greeley, a Las Vegas promoter and producer.

The property, however, unexpectedly came up for sale again when Greeley disappeared one night after driving out to his newly acquired property to have a look around. No one ever saw him again. He had wanted to check out the sunset from what was supposed to have been the site of his new hotel—an upscale, Wild-West stopoff for vacationers on their way to L.A., and gamblers making the trek to Sin City.

But instead, Sid had ended up dead. Or at least, that's what the authorities assumed. They concluded he never would've simply walked away from such a potentially lucrative source of income. And since neither his body, nor his car, were ever located, the police and FBI decided to blame the mob—a reasonable culprit given some of Sid's less-than-savory connections in Nevada.

But local residents cast their suspicions primarily on Karl Gruber, who had coincidentally put in a bid for the land only twenty-four hours after an anonymous tip told authorities that Greeley was missing. The newspapers had not even broken the story about Greeley, and yet there was Gruber, making a petition for the property in the county assessor's office. When the case was closed, Gruber was first in line to buy. He got what he wanted for $850,000.

No one knew how he came up with that much cash, but rumor had it that the money was stolen during several bank robberies committed by white supremacists during the 1980s. Somehow it had landed in his pocket. He sat on it, then eventually pulled out the loot to make his purchase—the site of his new compound.

Its eastern flank was skirted by a bubbling creek that ran a few inches deep every spring, thanks to melting snow that trickled down from nearby mountains. The camp's south side, in contrast, was lined by enormous boulders, their surface a colorful wash of reddish-brown and orange. They rose from soft, beige sand, making for a perfect postcard or snapshot photo opportunity. To the west sat Highway 14 while to the north lay miles of picturesque flatland punctuated every few feet by wild cactus and purple sage. All in all, a very nice place to call home.

Frank arrived at the turnoff to Gruber's compound around a quarter past nine and pulled onto the dirt road leading up to the front gate. It snaked along for about a mile before straightening out near the camp's entrance: a barred metal gate, ten feet high. The gate was linked on either side to a glinting barbed-wire fence like the kind that usually surrounds prisons—a twelve-foot-high deterrent to all who might consider approaching it, complete with spools of curled razor wire on top to prevent anyone from even thinking about climbing over.

Frank stomped on the brake and stared out the windshield.

The road had narrowed to little more than a walking trail for perhaps a few horses and several people, but it was not nearly wide enough to accommodate a car. So the last three hundred feet would have to be traversed on foot, which was not what the journalist wanted to do. The enclave looked different during the daytime—far more intimidating. In fact, he had barely noticed the metal gate that first night of the cross burning: it had been thrown invitingly open, with a welcome sign hung on it that read *Bar-B-Q 2NITE*. Everyone had simply walked through on their way to good times and good food.

But today things were different. Frank could see several men in the distance patrolling back and forth just on the other side of the fence, like Nazi soldiers watching over a concentration camp. "Oh, great," blurted the perspiring reporter as he saw one of them unshoulder a gun and point it in his direction. A second soldier quickly ran up to his fellow guard, looked toward Frank, then leveled his rifle just as eagerly.

Frank popped open his car door at the same moment that the camp gate swung open. The men inside began running down the trail. He could hear them shouting, but then their voices were drowned out by a siren that began to howl from deep inside the complex. His mouth went dry.

The journalist remembered Schmidt's advice and raised his hands high over his head. *Very* high. It could clearly be seen he did not have a weapon. But would that be enough to keep them from gunning him down on the spot?

"Get your hands up. Get your hands up *now!*" shouted one of the men from about thirty yards away.

The others, five of them, soon joined in, yelling commands.

"Turn around!"

"Keep your hands up!"

"Get on the ground! *On the ground!*"

Well, make up your minds, the journalist thought frantically, beginning to wonder if the last thing he'd see in life would be a bunch of skinhead punks ranting and raving. He thought for a split second about which command to follow first—keep his hands up, turn around, or get down on the ground—then wisely decided to do all three of them at once.

39

*The less reasonable a cult is,
the more men seek to establish it by force.*

JEAN-JACQUES ROUSSEAU (1712–1778)

★ ★ ★

"Stay down!" shouted the first compound guard to reach the reporter. The hulking skinhead looked eerily similar to his fellow soldiers, who arrived only seconds after him. They each wore a kind of makeshift uniform (black jeans, dark T-shirt, and heavy leather boots), and proudly sported tattoos on their shaved heads, necks, and arms: *SS, 88* (a coded reference to Heil Hitler), swastikas, Nordic runes, and other blatant racist messages.

"I'm down! *I'm down,*" the journalist yelled.

"Don't move!" ordered the gun-toting man as his crew surrounded them. It sounded to Frank like a herd of wild stallions. All of the men were young, in their late teens to early twenties. Fit as boxers spoiling for a fight and hyped on adrenaline.

"Who are you?" one of them barked loudly, still panting.

"What's your name?" asked another, prodding Frank in the side of the neck with the business end of his rifle.

"Who sent you?"

"Anyone else in the car?"

The rapid-fire questions came in no particular order.

"Take it easy, guys!" Frank bristled as a pair of muscular hands grabbed him roughly by the shoulders where he lay on the ground. A knee came down between his shoulder blades, followed quickly by a hand on the back of his head that pushed his face firmly into the dirt, rendering him helpless. Someone he couldn't see frisked him up and down.

"I don't have any weapons!" he yelled, inhaling a mouth full of trail dust.

"Shut up!"

"I need to talk to Erich Strom," Frank continued, still pinned down like a defeated wrestler.

"What for?"

"My name's Frank Delafield…I'm a journalist from L.A." He struggled to catch his breath. "I just want ask him if I can get an interview with Karl Gruber."

"You're a *spy*," spat a young man who looked barely old enough to shave.

"Yeah," another agreed, "I say let's teach him a lesson."

Frank tried to see who was speaking, but his head remained smashed into the dirt. "No! No!" he said with a rising sense of panic. His time for making small talk and explanations was running out. "I'm *not* a spy. I was told to contact Erich Strom."

"By who?"

Can't answer that one, Frank realized. *Think fast, Delafield.* "Everyone in town knows that Gruber's in charge of this compound."

The silence that followed made the already nervous reporter even more uneasy. He registered nothing more than the wind rustling through the leaves and branches of nearby trees. *What now?* he thought. *This can't be good.*

Finally, the man who seemed to be the leader took control of the situation: "Compound?"

Uh-oh, Frank thought. *Shouldn't have said that.*

"Stand him up."

The reporter was jerked to his feet and spun around. "Compound?" the big man said again, taking a few steps closer. "This

ain't no compound. This is our home. It's our church. It's our sanctuary of light in the midst of Satan's Kingdom of Darkness."

Frank nodded deferentially. "You're right. I...I didn't mean
any disrespect. I'm sorry."

The group leader grinned expansively—another bad sign.
"Well, if you're not sorry, you're sure gonna be." He raised the
butt of his gun and readied himself to pulverize the journalist's
face.

Oh, geez, here it comes. Frank cringed, and tried to lean his head
away from the coming blow—a difficult move since he was being
held in place by a couple of six-foot ogres.

"Willy!" came a sharp command, putting an immediate stop
to the action. *"Put that gun down right now!"*

Frank peeled open his eyes and beheld a powerfully built man
with white-blond hair and piercing blue eyes approaching. The
guy looked like some sort of twenty-first-century Leif Erickson,
a Viking if there ever was one. He marched toward them with a
stride that said to everyone watching, *I'm the one in charge here.*
He made the other men look like boys in comparison.

"Willy, what's wrong with you?"

To Frank's amazement, the formidable lead guard was instantly
transformed. "We...we found a spy," he stammered.

"Well, how are we going to interrogate him if you bash his
teeth in? You must learn to think before you act!" The man then
turned to the others. "The last thing we need is to get local law
enforcement coming out here. I've told you that before—and I'm
not going to tell you again. Do you get me?"

"Yes, sir!" they answered in unison.

"Do any of you want to lose the privilege of guard duty?"

"No, sir!"

"Then, I suggest you start paying more attention to what I
tell you and stop acting like a bunch of twelve-year-olds. Am I
making myself clear?"

"Yes, sir!"

"And put your rifles down," he added in a calmer tone. "This intruder's not going anywhere." Guns were slowly lowered as the commander walked up to the captive. "So. You a spy?"

"No. Absolutely not. Like I told them, my name's Frank Delafield. I'm a journalist. And I need to speak to Erich Strom."

The man shot a glance at the guards still holding Frank by the arms. "Let him go."

Frank shrugged away as they released him and gave them each a dirty look, his halfhearted attempt at salvaging some dignity.

"I work for a magazine in Los Angeles, and I was hoping to get an interview with Pastor Gruber. I wanted to get permission from Erich Strom."

"Well, all you had to do was ask," said the blond Viking, smiling coldly as he held out his hand. "Erich Strom—pleased to meet you."

Frank looked down and cautiously took his hand, not knowing if it was a genuine gesture or just a ruse to get him into some kind of Nazi death grip. "Good to meet you too," he finally answered.

"Welcome to Yahweh's Holy Temple," Strom proclaimed, gesturing grandly with his arm outstretched toward the property, then added apologetically, "Excuse me for a second." He turned once again to the guards. "Would anyone like to tell me who's patrolling the gate?"

The six skinheads looked back at their deserted posts. The camp was completely exposed to attack. Not only was no one patrolling, but the gate was flung open so wide that forty head of cattle could've been driven through.

"Get back to your stations!" Strom hollered. "And close that gate!" The men actually jumped sideways. Then they took off even faster than when they'd made a beeline for Frank. "Sorry about those boys," Strom said, nailing the reporter with his steely blue eyes. "They can get somewhat excited at times."

"Yes," Frank agreed. "I noticed."

"Do you have a press card and some identification?"

The reporter pulled out his wallet and produced his ID. "Here."

Strom examined it carefully. "And you write for who?" he asked, lightly scratching his chiseled jaw.

"A magazine in L.A. called *BTI*. Very well respected, and with a fairly large circulation."

"Is that so?" Strom asked as he handed back Frank's credentials. "Well, I suppose a little accurate reporting about who we are and what we believe could possibly help the movement."

Frank tried to work up a smile. "You know what they say: 'All press is good press.'"

Strom stared at him, his expression as dead as a tomb. "Is that what they say?"

"Yeah, it's...just a...you know—" Frank stammered, not knowing if Strom was serious, making a joke, or just being weird.

"So you want to talk to Karl?" Strom interrupted.

Frank breathed in relief. "If possible."

"Well, anything's possible," Gruber's second-in-command replied enigmatically. "Why don't you come in with me. We'll see whether or not the pastor is interested."

Frank began brushing himself off, slapping the dirt and mud out of his shirt and pants. "Thanks," he said. "I'd appreciate it."

"And Mr. Delafield..." Strom said as they began walking forward.

"Yes?"

"A word of advice—I wouldn't go wandering around the camp unescorted if I were you. You might be mistaken for a spy, and that would be—*unfortunate*, if you catch my drift."

Frank nodded. "I gotcha."

40

★ ★ ★

Willy pushed open the gate just barely enough to allow Strom and his unexpected guest to slip inside. The wrought-iron barricade looked even more impressive up close than from a distance. It was a single piece of metal formed without seams, complete with short, sharp spikes that studded its outer surface. Frank could almost feel those javelin-like points piercing his skin. Also noticeable was the angle at which the gate leaned forward, making it impossible to climb even if one could somehow avoid being skewered.

This thing must've cost them a bundle, Frank calculated to himself.

"Okay, lock it up," said Strom. The guards responded with a quick series of well-ordered movements. *Clang. Crash.* The deadbolt was shoved decisively into place, sealing off the only route of escape for anyone wanting to make a speedy exit.

Well, here I am, the reporter thought with a mixture of wonder and trepidation. He followed Strom, fascinated by his surroundings, excited about finally being given the opportunity to tour the enclave. But no matter what happened or what was said, no matter how seemingly cordial Strom was being, Frank never let

himself forget this was a perilous place to be. He couldn't get so
wrapped up in the experience that he stopped thinking about what
he might have to do if things started going south.

Had Gruber by chance read some of what he'd already written
about racists? What if Strom suddenly decided to start behaving
less pleasantly toward him? He still couldn't resist taking one last
peek over his shoulder toward the comparative safety and sanity
of the outside world. *So far, so good,* he reassured himself.

Strom zigzagged between several buildings that Frank hadn't
seen the night of the cross burning. Their route was taking them
deep into the heart of Gruber's stronghold—past the main worship
sanctuary, church office, fitness center, barracks #1 for single men,
barracks #2 for single women, and row after row of modest cabins
built for married couples and their families.

There was a surprising number and variety of people wandering
around the enclosure: toddlers, teens, young adults, even a few
senior citizens who were probably old enough to have been alive
and kicking when their über-hero, Adolf Hitler, was ordering the
extermination of every Jew in the Warsaw ghetto. In this alternate
version of normal life, things went on pretty much like they did
anywhere else, but with a white-supremacist twist, a racist slant
that made the adoration of specific bloodlines and the hatred of
darker skin tones the standard by which everything—absolutely
everything—was to be measured.

Most of the adults, truth be told, seemed outwardly no different
from Rosamond's other residents. They didn't act like wild-eyed
freaks, dress in bizarre outfits, or use cultic lingo understandable
only to the initiated. They were being friendly, even neighborly,
as the two men strolled through the camp's central courtyard.

"How you doing, Erich?" one man shouted from his cabin
porch.

"Morning, Erich," a middle-aged lady called out cheerfully,
smiling and waving as she passed them.

And yet something, *something,* was amiss everywhere. Frank

could feel it, but he couldn't put a name to it. Things were normal, but not normal. Then again, maybe *too* normal. Was that it? He wasn't sure.

"So, Mr. Delafield," Strom began, not breaking his athletic stride, "tell me, what's your background?"

"Well, I'm from California. Grew up in Orange County. I always wanted to be a writer, but didn't really start to—"

Strom interrupted him with a dry laugh. "No, no—I mean your ethnic background."

Frank paused. He couldn't remember the last time someone had asked him that. "Oh," he said, stalling, trying to actually work up something beyond *American*. "I guess you might say I'm kind of an English-Welsh-French blend. My mother was French. And my father was English and Welsh."

"That's alright. As long as you don't have anything else mixed up in there," Strom said with a grin, then gave him a stinging slap on the back.

"Yeah," Frank winced. "I mean, no. No…just those."

Strom rounded another corner and continued making small talk. "How long have you been writing?"

"Professionally? Since the year I graduated from UCLA."

"Hmm. Good school."

"Freelancing mostly, until I started working full-time for *BTI* a few years ago."

The two men traded more information as they skirted several long warehouses used to store extra food, water, clothing and, Frank imagined, various kinds of weapons and ammunition. The seasoned journalist knew it would be uncharacteristic for such an extremist organization to not have those kinds of things in its possession.

Strom and Delafield finally reached the last building that could be seen in the immediate area. Last perhaps, but certainly not least. And it was by no means at the end of the property, which extended out quite a bit further. Obviously, more than enough room for serious expansion. *PASTOR'S OFFICE*, the sign read in faded green letters. Beneath those words were two verses written in the kind of curling, fancy script that often appears on wedding invitations:

> *By defending myself against the Jew,*
> *I am fighting for the work of the Lord.*
>
> —ADOLF HITLER, "MEIN KAMPF"

> *You shall know the truth,*
> *and the truth shall set you free.*
>
> —JESUS CHRIST, JOHN 8:32

Two heavily armed guards stood ramrod straight on either side of the door. They looked different than those patrolling the front gate. Neither of them were skinheads jockeying for a position or bent on getting into random violent mischief. These were mature men, serious and intense, probably ex-military. They wore dark uniforms reminiscent of Hitler's SS and had close-cropped hair, and they stood as grim and motionless as gargoyles bulked up by layers of sinew and muscle.

"Wait here," Strom said, then turned and ascended the stairs into the office.

Frank watched the heavy door slam behind Erich and waited, trying not to stare at the guards' loaded assault rifles. *M-16s? AK-47s?* "So," he indicated with a casual wave of his hand, "what kind of guns you got there?"

They ignored him utterly, putting to death his first and last attempt at being sociable.

A few minutes later, Strom's gleaming blond head appeared around the edge of the office door. "Mr. Delafield," he intoned dispassionately, "Pastor Gruber will see you now."

41

★★★

The Reichsmarschall desperately needed something to eat after the six-hour drive north to Yountville, so he pulled into the first inviting place he saw: Los Amigos Bar & Grill.

He liked spicy Mexican food, as well as Chinese takeout and peppery East Indian cuisine, despite their decidedly non-Aryan origins. It was a glitch in his paradigm, to be sure, but one that he tolerated. *Food is just food,* he told himself. He wrote it off as a weakness of the flesh—something amiss in his character, but nothing so serious that God wouldn't overlook it, especially given his otherwise obedient lifestyle.

Yountville, a rural community of about 3000 residents, sat comfortably nestled in the rolling hills of Napa Valley. The four-hundred-mile drive from Rosamond was a lot of effort, but it would be well worth the trouble—eventually. On this day, however, the Reichsmarschall would have to be content with ironing out some details related to the final operation that he and Der Neue Führer believed would topple ZOG once and for all.

"I'll have two carnitas tacos, a basket of tortilla chips with extra guacamole, and a large Coke."

"Jou wan salsa wit dat?" asked the counterman, tossing a handful of greasy black hair away from his shining forehead.

The Reichsmarschall suppressed a twinge of disgust. "Yes."

"Mild or hod?"

He thought for a moment, then snapped, "*Hot*," sharply enunciating the *t*.

"Anyting else, senõr?" The server's accent was so thick the Reichsmarschall could barely understand him.

"No," he answered with thinly veiled annoyance. "That's all."

It was only a little past noon, which left the Reichsmarschall a good while to wait before his three o'clock meeting. Perhaps he would go to a local winery after lunch. He had always wanted to go on a tour, partially because of an interest in wine-making, and partially because of the free samples in the tasting rooms.

The tour might calm him down. Besides, the whole area would soon belong to the new Reich. So why not experience the pleasures it had to offer? He pulled out a map and looked up the vineyards in his immediate area as his food was being placed on the table.

As he bit into his first pork taco, the Reichsmarschall was starting to feel a lot better, and not just because of the delicious meal. He was glad to have gotten out of Rosamond for a while. The death of the innocent woman at his hands had unnerved him. But he was back on track now—he was sure of it—and thankful that his blunder had not jeopardized the main objective of the movement—to install Der Neue Führer as president of the United States.

The great man himself, surprisingly, had not been particularly put out by the Reichsmarschall's failure. In fact, he'd almost seemed to expect it, and even voiced deep approval of the Reichsmarschall's dedication, zeal, and willingness to do whatever it took to ensure the success of the movement. "You are a faithful soldier," he had reassured him. "And your loyalty will take you far in my administration when I assume the presidency."

"But what about Delafield?" the Reichsmarschall had asked, still concerned about the reporter's snooping.

"Delafield will find nothing. He is a heathen whom God will curse. And the Traitor, though he might be able to hurt our plans, will never get involved. He is weak and frightened. His *Jew*deo-Christianity is a false faith. An impotent substitute for the true faith of God once and for all delivered to the saints. It is a lie from the pit of hell, spawned by Satan, spread via Jew-invented myths, and swallowed by gullible children who are afraid to wage war. Our faith is the faith of Yahweh. Our faith is the faith of the white race. Our faith is the faith that Scripture tells us will one day triumph. No man, including Delafield, and least of all the Traitor, will ever be able to stop it."

Gourmand's Delight Farm, the Reichsmarschall's three-o'clock destination, specialized in the organic cultivation of only the finest mushrooms—the kind usually featured in cooking contests and used by America's award-winning chefs in their posh restaurants. He was impressed by what he saw. Thirty aluminum sheds greeted him, each one covering about 1800 square feet and designed with hi-tech operational and environmental control systems. The Reichsmarschall emerged from his car, walked through the office's front door, and was greeted by the receptionist. "May I help you?" she asked politely.

He nodded. "Yes. I'm here to see Mr. Gunther Smythe."

"And your name?"

A pause. "Just tell him his three-o'clock appointment is here."

After about fifteen minutes, Smythe walked into the reception area and greeted his visitor warmly. "Well, there you are," he said with a look of elation on his aged face. "So glad you could make it." The botanical scientist proudly shook the Reichsmarschall's hand. "Please, follow me."

The two men strolled over to the labs, where Mr. Smythe did the majority of his work as the company's head researcher. Smythe unlocked the door to Lab 7C, which was housed in the farthest building from the main offices. "Please," he motioned with one hand, "after you."

The warm room was musty, humid, and smelled richly of fresh soil. Countless racks of mushrooms were stacked twelve feet high lining the enclosure from end to end. "Where are they?" the Reichsmarschall asked.

"This way." Smythe led the Reichsmarschall toward the rear of the laboratory. He finally stopped at a small table covered with thick white muslin cloth. "Behold," he said with a flourish as he flicked back the cover.

"They look delicious," the Reichsmarschall joked.

"Oh, they are, they are," said the scientist. His mouth lifted crookedly. "And also very deadly."

"How did you do it?"

"I was able to cross the highly toxic death-cap mushroom with a variant strain of shiitake to produce this marvel." He gazed affectionately down at the table. "A fungus that is twenty times more potent than the destroying angel mushroom and ten times deadlier than the death cap."

The Reichsmarschall lightly touched the new strain, designed for the victorious culmination of the grand scheme. "They're beautiful. You followed my orders precisely." He carefully lowered his face to within a few inches of the deadly caps. "And what is the mortality rate?"

Smythe grinned from ear to ear. "Ninety-nine percent."

"How much is needed to do the job?"

"One ounce."

The Reichsmarschall stood up and looked at his brother in arms. "Perfect," he whispered, a tiny catch in his throat. "Perfect."

42

★ ★ ★

Frank walked past the two guards, relieved to no longer be pinned under their soulless eyes.

"Come on in," Strom said evenly as he opened the door.

The waiting area didn't look particularly religious, nor did it have a markedly military feel. Its furnishings were sparse: a mahogany sofa on which wagon-trail scenes had been embroidered, a hefty coffee table that was actually a large tree stump, and several rough-hewn chairs sat on a plank floor. All very rustic—decidedly a *Little House on the Prairie* atmosphere. On the walls were a variety of black-and-white historical photographs, and adding a crowning touch was a huge bearskin rug.

Strom led Frank to a door at the far end. It was grooved and sturdy. The word *PASTOR* was branded into it. Strom gently pushed it open to reveal Gruber's office, a medium-sized room decorated frontier-style.

"Pastor Gruber?" Strom said, quietly addressing the old man behind the huge desk at the opposite wall. "This is Frank Delafield."

Gruber looked up from his papers, smiled broadly, and stood.

"Mr. Delafield, it's so good to have you here at Yahweh's Holy Temple."

The reporter put on his best it's-great-to-see-you-too face and extended his hand. "Glad to be here," he gushed. "I really appreciate you taking time out from your busy schedule to see me."

"No trouble at all," the pastor responded, momentarily placing his hand on his chest, then extending it forward. "My pleasure."

His grip was surprisingly firm for a man in his seventies, and it took the journalist by surprise, as did Gruber's physique. He was tall and straight, and carried himself like a man who at one time had been as formidable as any of the skinhead guards. His face, however, gave away his true age. Deep crow's feet fanned out like scars from the corners of his eyes, his forehead was marred with heavy horizontal lines, and grayish liver spots mottled his sagging cheeks.

"Have a seat." He gestured toward an overstuffed leather chair.

"Thank you."

Gruber sat down and looked at Strom, who had remained by the door. "Erich, I think we'll be fine here for a while. I'll let you know if we need anything."

Strom nodded. "I'll be over at the warehouse." He turned crisply and left.

"So," the pastor began, steepling his fingers in front of his chin, "you'd like to do an interview with me. Is that right?"

Unknown to Gruber, however, the interview had begun the moment Frank walked into his office. He had instantly started taking note of everything around him.

The floor-to-ceiling bookshelves that lined the walls held such works as Eustace Mullins's *The Curse of Canaan*, Gary Smith's *Land of ZOG*, James Combs's *Who's Who in the World Zionist Conspiracy*, and Richard Harwood's *Did Six Million Really Die?*

Hanging on the wall behind Gruber's desk, a large painting

of Adolf Hitler enjoyed pride of place, set elegantly in a gold frame and flanked on either side by two flagstaffs—one with the Third Reich battle flag, the other with two flags: the famous 1777 Revolutionary War flag with thirteen stars in a circle, and the Confederate Stars and Bars.

And on Gruber's desk lay a copy of the *Protocols of the Learned Elders of Zion,* along with some publications that had been distributed around Rosamond throughout the preceding year: PR pamphlets and tracts; grotesque caricatures of Jews with hooked noses and African-Americans with outrageously protruding lips; and lying next to an open Bible, a flyer featuring a photo of a white woman and a black man smiling in each other's arms with a caption reading, *The Ultimate Abomination: Kill on Sight.*

Frank scooted forward and pulled out a notepad and pen. "What I'd like to get is your take on the recent events in this country, especially in light of the fact that the terrorist attacks during this past month have been linked to individuals allegedly involved in the Christian Identity movement."

Gruber leaned back in his chair and rested his hands together. "*Terrorist* attacks?" he asked. "I suppose that's all a matter of perspective, isn't it?"

Frank tried to keep his face calm. *Steady, Delafield. He's just testing you.* "Yes, I suppose it is. And that is exactly what I'm here for—to get *your* perspective. The perspective of Christian Identity, which is, I gather, very different from the one currently being expressed throughout the nation."

"True," Gruber agreed. "But why are you so interested in my unpopular perspective when you obviously don't share my faith?"

Tread carefully, Frank cautioned himself. "Well, I'm a journalist. And journalists make a living by writing articles they know people will want to read. I'm convinced that what you have to say will be interesting to people." He tapped his pen on his notepad three times. "So, I get a good story, the subscriber gets a good read (whether they agree with your faith or not), and you get a platform for your views. It's win-win-win."

Gruber thought for a moment. "Where will this be printed?"

Frank knew then he had him on the line. *"BTI,"* he said confidently. "A magazine that has a national circulation of 500,000."

The preacher looked doubtful. "Hmm, I've never heard of it."

"Well, it has a highly specific readership: people interested in pop culture, religion, social issues, politics. Those sorts of topics."

"I see." Gruber stared intently at the reporter. Then he seemed to reach a decision. "Alright, I'll do it. But on one condition."

"Name it."

"You print precisely what I say. Verbatim. No editorializing."

Frank tried not to show his excitement. He felt like a used-car salesman whose customer had just offered to pay top dollar for a clunker. He feigned a few moments of hesitation. "I suppose I could arrange that"—*pause, pause, pause*—"Yes...I think I might be able to convince my editor to go with a straight transcript format. It's highly unusual. But so are the circumstances."

"That's my condition, Mr. Delafield, take it or leave it."

"Well, in that case, I guess I have no choice." Frank pocketed his pen and put down his notepad. "I'm going to have to record the interview, if that's acceptable to you. That way I'll be able to play it back and get everything exact."

Gruber threw his hands up. "I have nothing to hide."

"Super," replied Frank, relaxing for the first time since his arrival.

"Oh, and one more thing, Mr. Delafield. Now listen closely, because this is extremely important."

"Sure."

Gruber leaned forward. "Please be absolutely accurate," he said, "because if you aren't, I'll be very displeased with you. And if I were ever to become displeased with you, then my flock of faithful soldiers would become displeased with you, which in turn might result in unpleasant consequences. I'm sure you wouldn't want that."

"No," Frank said, fully comprehending. "I wouldn't want that at all." Exhaling slowly, he plunked down a mini digital recorder on the desk. "Shall we begin?"

43

Our mission is to conquer the earth and have dominion over it.
ARYAN NATIONS FOUNDER RICHARD BUTLER (1918–2004)

★★★

Delafield: I'm now beginning my interview with Karl Gruber, December 30, at Yahweh's Holy Temple. Pastor Gruber, would you please state your name and confirm for me that I have your permission to record this conversation?

Gruber: Of course. My name is Karl Gruber. I'm the founder and pastor of Yahweh's Holy Temple, which is located in beautiful Rosamond, California. And it's perfectly fine for Mr. Delafield to record this interview.

Delafield: Okay, then. Let's start with a few basic questions.

Gruber: Fire away.

Delafield: Sir, in a nutshell, what are your religious beliefs— the ones you consider most essential to your Christian Identity faith?

Gruber: That's easy. Like all Christians, I believe in the Triune God—Father, Son, and Holy Ghost—and that the Son came to this earth as Jesus Christ. He was one-hundred-percent God and one-hundred-percent man, lived a sinless life, died on the cross for our sins—including yours, Mr. Delafield—then rose again on the third day. And he will come again to judge the living and the dead, after which time a new heaven and a new earth will be established forever. I also believe, of course, that the Bible is God's infallible Word and that it has final authority over our conduct and faith.

Delafield: But Identity advances more views than just these widely held tenets of Christianity. It's my understanding that you, unlike other Christians, claim that Jesus wasn't a Jew. Doesn't this mean you actually believe in an altogether different Christ than the one commonly presented by, say, mainline Protestants?

Gruber: Correct. Jesus was not a Jew, contrary to popular belief. He was a white man, a Caucasian. We do indeed, therefore, embrace as our Savior and Lord an utterly different Christ than the one held out by the *Judeo*-Christian faith, which, truth be told, is not the Christian faith at all. It is a subverted faith. A false Christianity. A diabolical lie concocted over the centuries by enemies of God seeking to mislead the world.

Delafield: Subverted by whom? By the Jews?

Gruber: Correct again. Look, I know this may sound…repulsive to you. Truth is sometimes difficult to accept when for many years a person has been brainwashed into thinking a particular way. But those with an open mind, who are willing to look at the evidence, will see that historical documentation establishes beyond a shadow of doubt that whites are God's true "chosen people." Now, bear in mind the fact that Jews have been saying this same thing about themselves for centuries—that they are God's chosen ones. Are they called racists? No. Not a single person would dare level that charge against the Jews. *We,* however, are thus vilified. Does that make any sense to you?

Delafield: But don't you think there's a difference between how you claim to be God's people—indeed, a racially superior people—and how the Jews, as well as those who hold to Judeo-Christianity, say the people of Israel are God's people? I mean, they only use that expression in reference to their belief that God, for whatever reasons, chose to interact with humanity through Israel. There is no inference of racial superiority.

Gruber: You see, there's where you're dead wrong. Nothing personal, but I think you've been getting most of your information from Jew propaganda. Firstly, the Jews *do* consider themselves racially superior. Secondly, the Israelites of the Old Testament were white men and women, Caucasians, just like Abraham, Isaac, and Jacob—all the way back to Adam and Eve. This whole idea that the Old Testament Israelites were Jews is part of a great and terrible lie.

Delafield: And that's why you believe Jesus was also a white man? Because he was of the house of Israel, which was actually a Caucasian nation?

Gruber: That's right.

Delafield: Interesting. But I have to say…and mind you, I'm no biblical scholar…that I don't see what you're talking about.

Gruber: The problem is that you haven't been exposed to the truth. What you have to do is turn to the first chapter of Genesis where it speaks of Adam. The Hebrew word for "Adam" literally means "to show blood in the face, to have a ruddy complexion, or to turn rosy." Obviously, only a white person can blush. So, I think it's quite clear that Adam and Eve were white.

Delafield: So the Old Testament Israelites were white people?

Gruber: There is no doubt about it.

Delafield: What about the Jews? Where did they come from?

Gruber: They are descended, so the Bible tells us, from the unholy spawn that came forth after Satan seduced Eve into having sexual relations with him. The devil took on a physical body in order to impregnate her, hoping that his vile crime against God would hinder the Lord's plan to create a pure race who would serve, honor, and glorify him. That was Eve's sin in the garden, by the way, copulating with Satan. Genesis 3:15 talks about the "Seed of Satan." That foul act produced Cain, an abomination from the beginning, just like his descendants.

Delafield: The Jews?

Gruber: Yes. They are quite literally children of the devil.

Delafield: With whom did Cain have these Satanic progeny?

Gruber: Pre-Adamic races that God created as experiments—first attempts, you might say, at creating beings who would reflect his image.

Delafield: You call them "mud people."

Gruber: Yes. Also "beasts of the field," according to Genesis 1:25. Cain intermarried with them, had offspring, and from then on it has been one long war, a battle between the children of darkness and the children of light. Need I remind you that the Jews murdered Jesus Christ? How obvious must the truth be for people to acknowledge it?

Delafield: I guess it's safe to assume, then, that you don't like Jews very much.

Gruber: Do policemen like thieves? Do parents like child molesters? Do free societies like dictators? This is what we're talking about, Mr. Delafield. Satan's children, walking the earth seeking whom they may enslave—while at the same time trying to utterly obliterate God's holy race of righteous believers.

Delafield: So *every* Jew is evil?

Gruber: Oh, there might be a few who aren't actively engaged in hostile activity. But in general, yes, collectively, I believe they are evil. And I don't think it would be an overstatement to say that by nature, they are totally corrupt and conniving, although some of them may not act out their instincts with as much fervor as others. The bottom line, however, is that a Jew can no more deny his or her own satanic nature than a fish can decide not to breathe underwater or a bird can choose not to fly.

Delafield: To be honest with you, I've known many Jewish people, and they didn't seem that bad to me.

Gruber: [laughs] Don't be so naive. Satan is not going to come up to you, shake your hand, and say, "Hello, I'm evil incarnate, nice to meet you." No, no, no. The devil is far wiser than that, as are his spawn. But if you observe history and examine current events with a spiritual eye, you will see that Jews have been behind every social evil and cultural dilemma. Poverty, abortion, war, inflation, the so-called civil rights movement. The filth that's pouring out of Hollywood, polluting the minds of our young people under the guise of entertainment. And of course, miscegenation. It's the greatest assault being made against white people, and is simply a Jewish attempt to dilute the Aryan bloodline by convincing everyone that whites should interbreed with other races. They want the natural barriers that separate races to be dismantled. Charles Weisman from Minnesota, who wrote *America: Free, White, and Christian*—I'll give you a copy of that before you leave—he astutely observed that this is why we repeatedly see Jews running to the aid of the nig…Negro and colored races. Jews want to elevate them while lowering the status of the white man. That's what intermarriage is about, you see. But that's something God never intended. In fact, he commanded us to do the very opposite.

Delafield: Where exactly does it say that in the Bible?

Gruber: Genesis 1:24. God said, "Let the earth bring forth every living creature after his kind." *His kind.* It couldn't be any plainer. He didn't say after some *other* kind. This is why in Deuteronomy 7:3-4, God reminds his people, "You shall not intermarry with them," speaking of other nations. "You shall not give your daughters to their sons, nor shall you take their daughters for your sons."

Delafield: What if your daughter fell in love with someone of another race and married him?

Gruber: That would never happen.

Delafield: But what if it did?

Gruber: [short pause] She would no longer be welcome in my home. I would immediately disown her outright as my offspring—consider her a traitor to our race and a hell-bound heathen. She would, in effect, become my enemy.

Delafield: That's awfully harsh, don't you think?

Gruber: No harsher than befits the sin committed.

Delafield: But I see Jesus in the New Testament as someone who is far more—excuse me for saying this, I mean no offense—loving and forgiving toward others.

Gruber: [long silence] She'd be lucky if I didn't shoot her.

Delafield: But Jesus didn't advocate violence.

Gruber: Really? Jesus said in Luke 22:36 that he who has no sword, "must sell his cloak and buy one." He also called the Pharisees a brood of vipers, sepulchers filled with dead men's bones, and blind guides—that's how he described the Jews who eventually crucified him. God's enemies are my enemies. They should be your enemies too.

Delafield: And others in the movement—others whom society might label as racists—would they—

Gruber: Excuse me. We are not *racists*. The correct term is *racialists,* please.

Delafield: I'm sorry…racialists. Would other racialists share your views on this issue?

Gruber: Several great men in the movement have made our beliefs plain over the years. Louis Beam, for instance, noted that racial treason "is the greatest crime a member of our race can commit." And David Tate of the Aryan Nations declared many years ago, and rightly so, that God "hates a race traitor." So, in answer to your question, yes, I would say that white racialists are united in considering race traitors to be our greatest enemies.

Delafield: Even greater than Jews?

Gruber: Yes. Because race traitors are not only guilty of aiding and abetting the devil's schemes, but through their actions they are literally killing off our holy bloodline.

Delafield: Why is it so important to keep the white race, or for that matter any race, pure?

Gruber: Well, as I have said. This is God's will. That's the way he set it up. It's part of Yahweh's divine plan for the white man and woman. We were meant to have dominion over the earth. We are in a war, a spiritual battle of cosmic proportions that will have eternal consequences. And it won't end until God's will is accomplished.

Delafield: Speaking of war, I'd like to discuss the recent attacks. Before we started this interview, you seemed to indicate to me you felt these...*events*...were not necessarily "terrorist" attacks. Can you explain that?

Gruber: Yes, but before I do, I want to make it crystal clear that we at Yahweh's Holy Temple grieve at the loss of innocent lives. Also, it is vital for people to understand that innocent lives are sometimes lost during a war, which is what is going on at present in our country.

Delafield: A "Racial Holy War." *RaHoWa,* I believe you call it. Is that right?

Gruber: [nods] America is the Promised Land that God said would be given to his people—the New Jerusalem. Right now, it's in the hands of the enemy—ZOG, or the Zionist Occupational Government. According to prophecy, the United States is supposed to be our home, so it must be taken back. Once this is accomplished, God's heavenly kingdom will be established, as prophesied in the book of Daniel, chapters 2 and 7.

Delafield: Then you think it's acceptable to bomb, shoot, and gas innocent people?

Gruber: I never said that.

Delafield: So what *are* you saying?

Gruber: I'm merely trying to point out that within the movement there may be some zealous, faithful soldiers who feel that we're past the point of peaceful negotiations—that the time has come for more extreme measures. Whoever they are, you must understand that…from their perspective, this is a war. And whatever they do they view as acts of war.

Delafield: What about your perspective?

Gruber: I don't necessarily feel that we should be confronting the enemy so directly or forcefully at this time. There have been other members of the movement, however, godly and honorable men, who for years have been searching patiently for another solution to our predicament. And they feel differently. But let me be clear. We are not the aggressors here. Let me read you a statement made in 1986 by Thom Robb, a pastor like me, a God-fearing and trustworthy servant of Yahweh. [looks for newspaper article]

Ah, here it is. Robb said, and I quote, "There is a war in America today and there are two camps. One camp is in Washington, D.C., the federal government controlled by the anti-Christ Jews. Their goal is the destruction of our race, our faith, and our people." Clearly, it's the Jews who are on the attack. We are on the defensive. And in the end, there will only be two classes of people left—citizens and slaves. Which one would you rather be?

Delafield: It sounds to me like you're making a case for terrorism.

Gruber: And to me, it sounds like you're not listening. Whoever carried out those attacks were not terrorists. Try to understand that. Were they misguided? Perhaps. Unwise? Maybe. But were they criminals? Hardly. They were warriors. Aryan warriors of the highest rank.

Delafield: As I said, I'm no biblical scholar, but I would imagine that true Christianity would have an emphasis on love, instead of hate.

Gruber: Indeed. And what we do, what we believe, what we teach, is all based on love. People see us as hateful thanks to stories they've been force-fed by the jewspapers, and thanks to those so-called special reports on white supremacists they've seen on the Cable Jews Network. But believe me, it's not hate that causes the white man to be filled with disgust when he sees a Negro defiling a white sister, making mongrel babies with her. It's not hate that boils up in a housewife when she hears about another pedophile who's been let loose by our Jew-built court and parole system. It's not hate that makes a hardworking white man shake his fist in impotent rage when he sees another truckload of mud creatures illegally crossing our borders so they can take jobs away from us. It's not hate that causes anger to swell in the heart of a white Christian farmer when he watches billions of dollars in aid being given away to worthless Africans or to some backward Asian nation while he can't get a break from the government to save his farm! No, Mr. Delafield, it's love that motivates us. Love for our people. Love for our country.

Delafield: You have to realize this seems extraordinarily harsh to me. It's a lot to take in. It's so contrary to what I've been taught for years.

Gruber: Of course.

Delafield: [brief silence] Now, I must ask these next few questions simply because they are so obvious, and also because we have been discussing the violent actions taken against what you perceive to be enemies of your race.

Gruber: *Our* race, Mr. Delafield. You're one of us.

Delafield: Okay—so here are my last questions. Do you know who set off the explosives at the various places in mid-December?

Gruber: I do not.

Delafield: Or who launched the attacks against the three malls?

Gruber: No.

Delafield: What about the men arrested—do you know any of them?

Gruber: Not personally, no.

Delafield: Is there anything else you'd like to say?

Gruber: Yes. People need to open their eyes. And I hope this interview will help them do that. The fact is that the white race has been dispossessed. Our land, our heritage, our right to exist as a pure people is being taken away from us. Anything that is done against our enemies is done only in self-defense. Armageddon is coming. And people need to start choosing the side they are going to be on.

Delafield: Well, that should do it.

Gruber: Good. It's been my pleasure.

44

Satan himself masquerades as an angel of light.
It is not surprising, then, if his servants masquerade
as servants of righteousness.

2 CORINTHIANS 11:14-15

"Thank you, Pastor Gruber. I'm sure you've given me plenty of material for the article. Hopefully, I'll finish it up next month, which means it should be in print no later than February or March."

"Good. I'm looking forward to reading it."

Gruber stood and crossed to the window as Frank began packing up his things.

Pen: check.

Notepad: check.

"Isn't the view spectacular?" asked the leader of Yahweh's Holy Temple as he proudly surveyed his property.

Frank rose from his chair. "Yes, it is."

"You know, Mr. Delafield," began Gruber, still gazing out at the arid terrain, "if you'd like to spend a couple of nights here, you're more than welcome. We have a comfortable cabin at the center of our 'Families Only' area that I keep reserved for special visitors. It might do you some good to spend a night or two with your own kind."

My own kind? Frank thought, a chill going up his spine. "Uh... I..."

Gruber turned and looked pointedly at Frank, whom he had pegged sometime during the course of the interview as a potential convert. "In our main dining hall tonight, we're going to be serving an excellent pot roast and homemade apple pie. You can sit at my table, along with Erich and some of the other staff members."

The journalist rocked his head from side to side, seemingly indecisive. "I'd like to, I really would. But I have to get back to the hotel and start putting this whole thing together." He faked a smile and hoped he had sounded as inoffensive as possible.

"Alright, no pressure," Gruber responded, casually waving his hands in the air as he walked toward him, "although to be honest with you, I think you need some time off. You strike me as the kind of man who works too hard."

"Do I?"

"That's a fact. Just call it my pastor's intuition. But if you feel you must keep your nose to the grindstone, perhaps you might consider remaining here as a sort of working vacation. Think about it. You could dine with us, visit with more of our members. Even interview them if you want to. Then tomorrow night, I'd be honored to have you attend our special New Year's Eve celebration as my personal guest."

Interesting offer, Frank mused, snapping off the recorder he'd forgotten about until that moment. "No, really. Thanks, but I just can't."

Gruber pursed his lips. "Oh, I understand. I understand. But listen, how about a short tour of the camp before you leave us? I'll have one of the boys take you around. Go wherever you want— except for restricted areas."

The reporter hesitated. *Why not? No harm in taking a look around.* "That would be great."

Gruber picked up a walkie-talkie on his desk. "Erich?" he said, pushing down the button. "Come in."

Pop...zzzz...click. "Yessir."

"Erich?"

Zzzz…click. "Go ahead, sir. This is Erich."

"Mr. Delafield and I have completed our interview. Can you come by to pick him up?"

"Affirmative. I'll be there in two minutes."

"And Erich?"

"Go ahead."

"Bring one of the Rank Five security boys with you. I'd like to have him accompany Mr. Delafield on a tour of the grounds."

"No problem. Will T.R. do?"

"T.R. will be fine. Thank you, Erich."

"We'll be right there."

Gruber tossed the walkie-talkie onto a nearby chair. "Awfully convenient to have these little gadgets around. Technology is a wonderful thing, don't you think?"

Frank agreed, and for several minutes the two men conversed about some of the electronic innovations in the modern world.

Finally, there was a knock at the door. "Come in," Gruber said.

Erich briskly entered the room. "Sorry I took so long. I was briefly held up."

"Don't worry about it. Mr. Delafield and I were having a splendid time together."

Gruber draped his arm around Frank as he walked him to the door. "I look forward to seeing that article as soon as it comes out. And you'll remember my friendly word of caution, won't you?"

"Yes…I'll get it right," he answered. "I'll send you a copy of the article as soon as it's published."

They shook hands and, an instant later, Frank found himself again outside with the two guards and Erich Strom. With them was a young man about seventeen years old, eighteen at most, far smaller than any of the other guards. His head was shaved, but that only made him appear oddly vulnerable, like an orphaned baby bird. He was holding a gun, but didn't give the impression he actually knew how to use it. Frank almost felt sorry for him.

Erich cleared his throat. "This is one of our latest recruits—T.R."

"Nice to meet you, T.R.," Frank said, still studying the scrawny sentry.

The boy nodded, trying to act tough. "Hey."

"T.R., I want you to take Mr. Delafield on a tour of the camp. Show him whatever he wants to see—except, of course, High-Security Zones 1B and 3X."

T.R.'s head wobbled confidently in response. But Frank could tell he was thinking hard to recall where these zones were located. "Uh-huh—yes, sir," he answered, then carefully repeated, "Zones...1B and 3...X."

"Well done," Erich said, punctuating his praise with a slap on the boy's back. He quickly refocused his attention back to the reporter. "It was good to meet you. Maybe we'll see each other again. T.R. will serve as your guide until you're ready to leave, then he'll show you to the gate."

"That'll be fine."

Strom grinned and crushed Frank's hand in an iron grip, then disappeared around the side of a building.

"Where to first?" asked Frank, eager to begin his tour.

T.R. shuffled a bit and looked nervously toward the two men still standing at attention on either side of the door to Gruber's office. "I...I don't know...umm, where d'ya wanna go?" he finally managed to say.

No help here. "Well...how about we start with the chapel?" the journalist suggested.

"Okay."

"By the way, my name's Frank Delafield. What's yours?"

"T.R."

"No, I mean your full name."

He looked somewhat puzzled by the question for a few seconds, then shrugged and shifted his rifle to the other arm. "Todd... Todd Ryan."

45

★ ★ ★

"Will these little wonders of yours still be viable twelve weeks from now?" the Reichsmarschall asked, studying the smooth, deadly fungi growing plump under the warm, red pulse of the overhanging heat lamps. The mushrooms appeared rich and dense, almost fleshy, especially the creamy white flaps surrounding the base of each stalk.

Dr. Smythe enthusiastically bobbed his head up and down. "Yes, yes. Remarkable, isn't it? In fact, the levels of phallotoxins and amatoxins in them will be even greater by that time." He chuckled. "The smallest morsel in the mouth will put a person into a coma from which they will never awaken, or into anaphylactic shock, which in turn will result in subdural hematomas leading to irreversible brain damage. The poisons, you see, start to be absorbed into the bloodstream even before swallowing, through the mucous membranes of the oral cavity. Fully ingesting them will most assuredly result in death."

"But won't the other guests be alerted if they see our main target choking and writhing in front of them?"

Smythe poked a bony finger at the Reichsmarschall. "I'm glad you asked. The true marvel of these beauties is, there's a delay of at least six hours before symptoms begin to manifest themselves. By then, however, it will be much too late for medical intervention. Shortly thereafter, every attendee of the breakfast will be dead—or close to it."

The Reichsmarschall carefully replaced the cloth over the mushrooms. "Any chance of these dying, or their potency waning in a less ideal environment?" He motioned around the stifling hothouse with one arm. "I mean, is all of this *really* necessary?"

"No," answered the good doctor. "This new variety is much heartier than its less deadly counterparts. They are fragile only during the first few weeks of life. The mature ones you see here can survive virtually anywhere, as long as they are kept in a dark place with a basic heat lamp about a foot away."

"Excellent, my friend," the Reichsmarschall beamed approvingly as he placed his left hand on Smythe's shoulder and stepped closer to him. "You have served the movement faithfully and will be remembered for many years to come."

The elderly horticulturalist closed his eyes, and nodded in humility. "I am touched," he replied—just as all seven inches of a double-edged blade ripped upward into his abdomen. Nothing but a wet, gurgling sound escaped Smythe's throat. His eyes bulged, and his lips gaped, releasing a thick trickle of blood.

The Reichsmarschall whispered softly, "Go to your reward. Your work is over. May Yahweh smile upon you as you enter his kingdom." With the benediction complete, the Reichsmarschall jerked the knife to the side and released his old friend. Smythe fell backward, knocking over a table of chanterelles and porcinis. Within a second or two his blue eyes rolled back in his head.

"I'm sorry," said the Reichsmarschall, trembling slightly as he wiped off the blade and pushed it back up his sleeve into its sheath. "I couldn't risk you identifying me. We're too close to let anything go awry. But rest assured, I will tell Der Neue Führer of your honorable sacrifice for the cause."

Silence—except for the droning hum of a generator next door.

The Reichsmarschall turned away and picked up the two racks of mushrooms and one of the heat lamps. He stepped over the body and headed for the door, swiveling around for one last look. "I *do* wish there could have been another way," he said, wondering how he'd come to this.

He was a murderer now.

46

★ ★ ★

Frank and T.R. made their way back through the compound in the direction of the chapel, walking along the edge of a field used to grow fruits and vegetables. Soil had been trucked in to create a farming area that was irrigated from the camp's main water tower.

"Impressive," Frank observed as he glanced across the garden.

Todd shrugged, but said nothing.

Next, they headed in the direction of a grouping of small cabins—the "Families Only" area. Kids were everywhere, playing games and laughing.

"Hello, T.R.," a small girl squeaked shyly, pausing from her attempts to master the art of jumping rope.

T.R.'s mouth twitched upward in greeting.

"Hey, Todd," called a skinny little boy with dirty knees who, once he'd gotten T.R.'s attention, stood at attention and gave the Nazi salute.

Behind the children sat rows of tiny but sturdy-looking log cabins. Some appeared to have two or more bedrooms, while others seemed to have just one room with a loft for sleeping.

"Ever stay in one of those?"

T.R. shook his head.

Two storage warehouses then came into view. One had a *Verboten* sign out in front. The other, however, was wide open and bustled with people going in and out. Frank saw piles of clothes, food, and furniture laid out neatly on tables. All donations to Yahweh's Holy Temple.

He paced down the long aisles until Todd unexpectedly broke the silence. "I donated that to the church when I first came here," he mumbled, gesturing at a six-string guitar resting on a shelf next to a half-dozen other dusty instruments.

"You play the guitar?"

"I used to."

"Any good?"

There was a momentary pause as Todd weighed the question with some care. "Uh-huh."

Frank found himself starting to warm up to the guy. "So why'd you give it away?"

"I didn't *give* it away. I can still play it whenever I want, but this way others can play it too."

"That was nice of you," Frank said, wondering how in the world T.R. had gotten caught up with someone like Gruber in the first place.

"Whatever. Pastor Gruber says we need to share what we have. Take care of each other."

Frank ran a hand through his hair and glanced at his watch. "Maybe we should start heading to the chapel."

"Okay," Todd answered agreeably.

They sidestepped around the line of people waiting to sign out supplies, and soon were on their way up the path. Todd coughed quietly. "The Jews…they're trying to kill us all off, you know."

Is that what T.R. really believes? Frank wondered. "So I've heard. D'you think that's true?"

"I *know* it's true," the boy continued as they left the warehouse area and proceeded toward the chapel. "Pastor Gruber says so, and I totally trust him. He's smart."

"Why do you trust him?" Frank asked lightly.

Todd didn't reply immediately, but kept walking for a bit. "Um," he finally began, "I guess…'cause he's always been good to me."

"What do you mean?"

"Well, he takes care of me. You know, he gave me a good home and such. Talks to me when I want to ask him something. Even threw me a birthday party." His eyes flickered toward Frank. "That's a lot more than anyone else has ever done for me."

"Don't you have any family?"

"No. My mom's dead and I never knew my father. He left when I was about two months old." T.R. kicked a rock on the path and faced the reporter. "I can tell you one thing—if Pastor Gruber would've been my father, he never would've left. I…I know it. And I can say for sure, seriously, he's my father now…He's a father to all of us. Every single one of us."

They reached the compound's chapel. Inside, it was peaceful, much like any other church, but with a few shocking additions: a large crucifix with a Nazi flag draped across the shoulders of Christ; a bronze sculpture of a German eagle suspended from the ceiling; and a podium marked with a large, red swastika.

"You like attending services here?" Frank tried to suppress his incredulity.

T.R. gave a half-hearted shrug. "I guess. It's okay. I mean, I believe in God and everything."

"So you think it's okay with God for you to hate people?"

Todd lowered his brows, vaguely confused. "I don't hate anyone."

"How about blacks? Jews?"

"Oh, well, they hate us! We're just trying to survive."

Frank leaned against the doorway of the chapel and folded his arms in front of his chest. "Can I ask you something?"

"Sure."

"You ever meet a Jew?"

T.R. dropped his head, working hard to recall the names and faces of the people he'd come into contact with during his life. "Um...I...I don't think so."

"Then how do you know they're evil? Couldn't Pastor Gruber be wrong?"

"No...I don't think he's wrong."

Frank watched several camp members casually strolling around. "But nobody's perfect," he added.

Todd began fidgeting with his gun strap, uncertain as to what he should say next. "So why are you here anyway?" he finally asked.

Frank realized he had reached the bottom of the well, so to speak, and decided to try a whole new tactic. "I, uh...just came to interview your pastor for a news article I'm writing. And also to see if I could find anybody who might know a few guys that probably came through here a couple of weeks ago."

"Yeah?"

"I have their pictures." Frank pulled out the photos of Johnny Larkin and George Nelson, holding back for obvious reasons the picture of Chester Pate's contorted face.

"That's Thor," said T.R. quickly. "And that's George."

Frank stepped in closer. "You know these men?"

"Uh-huh. They were here with another guy named Charlie... um, I think a few weeks ago. Came down from California City." He handed back the pictures. "Stayed a few days. Then, I guess they went back."

Frank tucked the photos back into his pocket, his heart hammering in his ears. "So, d'you happen to know where they were staying in California City?"

Todd scrunched up his face once more, tipped his head back, and shut his eyes, "Lemme see...454 Sienna Drive." His eyes popped open. "I was there when Pastor Gruber wrote down the address for them. It was my job to walk them out to the gate."

"Did Erich Strom know about them meeting with Gruber?"

"I don't think so, 'cause they came into the camp when he was gone and met with the pastor right away. By the time Erich got back from town, they'd already left. Later that afternoon they came back, but didn't talk to Pastor Gruber again. Just hung out for a few days, then took off."

"Interesting," Frank said, now eager on to be on his way. "Well, I think I'm about ready to go."

"Okay."

As T.R. walked Frank toward the gate, just one thing ran through the journalist's brain—*Next stop, California City.*

47

We march and fight, to death or on to victory.

AMERICAN NAZI PARTY FOUNDER
GEORGE LINCOLN ROCKWELL (1918–1967)

★ ★ ★

Walking at a fast clip down the White House hallway, the four men simultaneously checked to see whose cell phone was beeping. The owner of the offending device snapped open his PDA and stepped off to the side, allowing the Secretary of Defense, FBI director, and Chairman of the Joint Chiefs of Staff to pass by. When the other three noticed that one of their group had halted, they stopped and turned.

With a quick wave of his hand, he motioned them on.

They nodded and resumed their course, until at last they disappeared around the corner.

"Yes?" Der Neue Führer whispered into his BlackBerry.

There was a momentary silence. Then a familiar voice crackled excitedly over the poor connection. "Sir, I have excellent news."

"I told you never to contact me on this line." The Nazi commander eyed the corridor for anyone who might be watching.

The Reichsmarschall was driving south on Interstate 5 toward Rosamond. Once he set up a place for the mushrooms to mature, he would wait for the time to send them to Washington. Though he had dialed Der Neue Führer's private number against explicit instructions, he was confident his revered leader would want to be apprised of the day's important events.

"Yes, sir, I know. But I have a disposable cell phone. So it can't be traced."

Der Neue Führer noticed two federal agents approaching. He grinned and spoke loudly. "Fine. But make it fast."

"I have them!" the Reichsmarschall responded exultantly. "The mushrooms—they're going to work perfectly."

"And Smythe?"

The Reichmarschall recalled the scientist's contorted face again. But he had reconciled himself to the sacrifice. "You have nothing to worry about. Our secret has gone with the good doctor into eternity."

"Well done," Der Neue Führer said, pushing his glasses up higher on his nose. "Where are you now?"

"En route to Rosamond. I'm going to stop off in Santa Barbara overnight, then complete the rest of the drive on Wednesday. I should arrive at home base by early afternoon."

For the first time, Der Neue Führer felt as if the master plan, which had taken decades to put into place, was about to succeed. He wished his beloved father and grandfather were still alive so they could witness the historic transference of power in America—from ZOG back into the rightful hands of white, Christian leaders.

No one else had come close—not The Order, not Yahweh's Defense Force, not the Army of God. They had possessed the zeal and dedication, but not the necessary connections to make it happen. Der Neue Führer, on the other hand, had all the connections he needed. He was strategically positioned to assume command of the country as soon as the right circumstances arose. And those circumstances would soon arise, he had no doubt, thanks to the events he himself would soon initiate.

"Guard the cargo with your life," Der Neue Führer charged his protégé.

"You can count on me, sir. I won't let you down."

Der Neue Führer nodded at several cabinet members walking past him. "Wonderful," he bawled, flashing a toothy grin in their direction. "In that case, I look forward to speaking with you again." He flipped the phone closed and dropped it into his suit pocket.

"Good morning, sir," CIA Director Mark Hellingsford said in greeting.

Der Neue Führer picked up his briefcase. "Hello, Mark."

Hellingsford glanced at his watch. "I guess we'd better get a move on," he said. "We're already late as it is."

Der Neue Führer took an exaggerated look down at his own timepiece, then fell into step beside the CIA director, striding with him toward the meeting that was about to begin in the office of their friend and commander in chief, President Peter Beckett.

48

*America will never be destroyed from the outside.
If we falter and lose our freedoms,
it will be because we destroyed ourselves.*

ABRAHAM LINCOLN (1809–1865)

★ ★ ★

"Glad you could make it, everyone. Have a seat," said President Beckett as the latecomers trickled into the conference room. Several key cabinet members were in attendance, including the vice president, Secretary of State, Attorney General, and Secretary of Homeland Security, along with top-level representatives from the FBI, CIA, and Secret Service. It was time to lay out a definite strategy for the months ahead, take advantage of the positive political climate.

The nation's voters were once more behind the president, whose approval rating, according to the latest polls, had reached fifty percent. That came as no surprise to political analysts and social commentators who'd watched Beckett's popularity steadily rise after the apprehension of The Dirty Dozen. Pro-Beckett messages from the corporate media hadn't hurt either.

The majority of citizens now seemed to be willing to allow the government to take whatever steps deemed necessary to keep the country from further harm. Secretary of Homeland Security Duncan Phelps immediately recognized the opportunity and contacted the president in hopes of arranging a conference to address much-needed measures for internal security.

First on his agenda was a renewal of the controversial Protection Act, which allowed for suspected terrorists, including U.S. citizens, to be detained for thirty days without legal representation at any undisclosed location considered appropriate by Homeland Security.

Second on the secretary's list was a domestic spying policy change. Terrorist suspects marked for surveillance, he argued, should be selected at the sole discretion of the president and a special board of appointed advisors. This would alleviate the workload of other law-enforcement leaders, thus freeing them up to concentrate more on actual investigations and operations.

Finally, Phelps wanted to promote new legislation that would require all individuals to register their names in a special database to track travel between states, as well as into other countries. The government would be able to see at a glance the movements of citizens throughout airports, bus terminals, and train stations. The "National Travel Pass" would also be used at checkpoints built along state lines.

The secretary received responses that ranged from tentative approval to vehement objection. After several hours, however, his detractors were unable to counter his many arguments, especially in light of the president's support. Beckett repeatedly mentioned how it was the secretary, after all, who had succeeded in averting any further disasters.

"We must work hard to keep this great land moving forward," Beckett declared. "Things aren't the same now as they were before the December attacks. It's our job to consider the future, and implement changes that will last well beyond this administration. The plans we're making here will promote not only our safety, but also the security of our children and grandchildren."

Five hours later, the meeting disbanded. The officials filed out, many still doubting the wisdom of their decision to approve the measures. But the political atmosphere left them no viable alternative. The president, the vice president, the Secretary of Homeland

Security, the CIA director, and the new Director of the Secret Service, Craig Malone, were all united behind the initiatives. That was more than enough clout to win the debate.

Only Lance Vaughn, former head of the Secret Service, would have been able to raise enough doubts to pull the president in another direction. He'd gone toe-to-toe with Phelps before on such issues and successfully convinced him and federal law-enforcement officials to respond to the threat of terrorism with moderation.

But that safeguard was no longer in place, a fact that pleased Duncan Phelps to no end.

49

Courage is doing what you're afraid to do.
EDDIE RICKENBACKER (1890–1973)

★ ★ ★

Frank didn't arrive in California City, a small town half an hour north of Rosamond, until around eight o'clock Tuesday night. Although he'd left Yahweh's Holy Temple around noon, he didn't immediately follow up on the lead that T.R. had given him. First of all, he needed to head back to the hotel and go over his interview with Gruber. Second, he wanted to wait for darkness to fall before wandering around in search of suspected terrorists.

Better safe than sorry, Frank figured, though when he actually took a few moments to think, he wondered how "safe" it was for him to be hunting down violent racists to begin with. The answer didn't thrill him, but he believed it was an important enough story to justify the risks. So he pressed on. He *had* to go to California City—period.

Sienna Drive was narrow, lined with palm trees and lit by antique-style street lamps. The houses were expansive and modern, with impeccably groomed lawns. It was not what Frank had expected. *Maybe T.R.'s memory wasn't so great after all,* he thought wearily, eyeing the miniature mansions.

After several more minutes he reached #454, a palatial ranch-style home at the south end of a handsomely landscaped cul-de-sac.

The corner lot offered not only additional privacy, but a spectacular view of downtown California City.

He parked three doors down, behind a dense row of Japanese boxwood. He purposely pointed his Honda downhill, away from the house, and left it unlocked. He'd seen too many movies where the hero missed an easy escape because he had to execute a tricky turnaround, or couldn't get "Key A" into "Lock B." Frank also reminded himself to check the rear seat when he got back in—nothing worse than being garroted from behind by some maniac in a ski mask and leather gloves.

The house was empty, lights off, door locked. It appeared as if the residence had been deserted for weeks. He crept around to the side, scaled a fence, and inched his way closer to the house, then started checking the windows.

Guest room—*nope.*

Downstairs den—*strike two.*

Living room—*bingo.*

He slid the glass open an inch, then braced himself for an alarm. Silence. Nothing except for the eerie whistling of a cold wind out of the southeast. He'd forgotten how chilly it could get at night in the California desert in wintertime. He quickly slipped inside, where the air wasn't much warmer. Frank could barely feel his fingers enough to flip the switch on his penlight.

Finally, an intense stream of light shot around the living room. The brilliant beam reminded him of Yoda's miniature light saber. "A fool in danger, you are," he rumbled in his best imitation of the Jedi master.

Surprisingly, there were only a few pieces of furniture: a loveseat shoved into a corner, a couple of torn futons, a card table with three fold-up chairs next to it. No TV. No stereo. No signs of life whatsoever. *This doesn't make sense. Why decorate a beautiful home like a crack house?* He moved on quickly.

Den—*empty.*

Downstairs bedroom and bathroom, the garage—*empty, empty, empty.*

He ascended the carpeted stairs slowly.

Master bedroom—*nope.*

Storage closets—*nothing.*

Finally, one last room, toward the side of the house farthest from the street—*Jackpot.*

It was a complete home office: desk, two chairs, printer, fax machine, LCD monitor, computer system. Not just any computer system, either—a top-of-the-line PC tower. From what Frank could tell, it probably had a couple of high-end graphics cards and an ultrafast CPU.

Racist tracts and pamphlets were tossed everywhere, along with sheets of loose paper scrawled with telephone numbers, addresses, and odd names: ReichMan, VampireKiller, Soldier488, H31LH1T73R, IZAN. Some had been crossed out, a few so heavily marked over they were unreadable. Of the names he could still make out, the only one Frank recognized sent a chill up his spine: *THOR.* And next to it was a date—December 26—the day of the mall attacks.

The journalist quickly jammed as many of the papers as he could into his pockets, then weighed his options. Leave now or look for more? Being caught might prove fatal. He knew that now. But he chose to dig around a bit more.

At first he didn't find much, just a few dirty paper plates, a crumpled Carl's Jr. wrapper, and a jar of pencils. But then he spotted a CD case. It was empty. Its label, however, showed it was for a videogame titled Rise of the Fourth Reich. *I've never heard of this one,* he thought, flipping to the back cover. *Deutschland Games, PO Box 672381, L.A., California.* No rating, no content description—which meant it wasn't being sold on the mainstream market. *Must be underground stuff.*

Frank tucked the case into his jacket and was about to boot up the PC when he heard a noise downstairs. He froze. All he could imagine was some Nazi gorilla stomping upstairs with a Luger in his hand. He crossed to the room's window. Fortunately, it opened onto a side-porch roof that sloped gradually downward. He slid on his stomach along the Italian tiles until he reached the rain gutter. He grabbed it and swung himself over the edge, got his balance, then dropped about four feet to the grass below.

The journalist ran as fast as he could back to his car, immediately noticing a black sedan parked on the opposite side of the street. It hadn't been there when he'd arrived. Had he been followed? In thirty seconds he'd reached his car, jumped inside, and took off. *Made it,* he thought, until he looked in his mirror and saw a dark figure emerge from the house and sprint to the black sedan. A flash of headlights and the squeal of tires told him he'd been seen. He swore and punched the gas pedal to the floor.

The two cars fishtailed around one turn after another down Sienna Drive. Frank pushed his skills to the max, braking and accelerating like a demolition driver on a figure-eight track. If he could just make it to the freeway, he might be able to shake the sedan. But whoever was following him was a pro. The guy wasn't having any trouble negotiating the turns and was closing fast.

Finally, Frank saw the main cross street that led to the freeway. But he hit the left turn too fast. His rented Honda spun in a three-sixty, then slammed into the bottom of a ditch, airbag deployed, engine dead.

I gotta get outta here, was all he could think as he stumbled out of the wreckage, dazed, and began to climb out of the gully in which the vehicle had come to rest.

The black sedan had already reached the site, and its driver was out of the car. Waiting for him.

50

★★★

The reporter finally wrapped a hand around the guardrail his Honda had just smashed through. Suddenly, he felt someone grab his arm and yank him hard up to the roadway. Frank rolled onto the pavement, tensing his muscles to receive a kick or a punch. Instead, he saw the one person he least expected.

"What are you doing here?" he gasped, adrenaline still shooting through his veins.

"I was just about to ask you the same thing," Carlyle snapped. "That is, until you bolted out of that house like it was on fire."

"Seemed like the right thing to do at the time." Frank propped himself up on his elbows, his head pounding and his ego in shreds. "Where'd you learn to drive like that anyway?"

The Secret Service agent reached down and pulled him to his feet with disconcerting ease. "Same place I learned to shoot," she answered with a slight grin.

"Some secret spy academy?"

"No," she answered. "My dad."

"Nice of him," said the journalist, unsteadily brushing the dirt and gravel from his pants.

"Yeah, I always thought so."

Using his coat sleeve, Frank wiped a rivulet of blood off his upper lip, then moved his shoulder back and forth, testing for more injuries. "So again, I ask—what are you doing here?"

"I'm making sure you stay alive."

Frank glanced over at his car in the ditch. "Well, Special Agent Carlyle, I'm no expert, but it looks like you're not doing a very good job."

"It would've made things a lot easier if you'd decided to talk to me earlier today after your meeting with Gruber. He obviously gave you the address. What I'd like to know is, why?"

Frank limped over to the black sedan and collapsed on the bumper. "Actually, I got the address from a guy named T.R."

The agent narrowed her eyes. "Okay, I'll play along. Who's T.R.? And what did you find in that house?"

"Whoa, there. Slow down. I'll tell you everything you want to know. Maybe even share some interesting things I retrieved from the house. But first I gotta get something to eat—and drink." Frank winced at the blood spattered on his jacket. "Oh, yes—I could *definitely* use a drink right now."

A bruise forming on Frank's forehead caught Carlyle's attention. "Do you think you need a doctor?"

The journalist shook his head. "No. I'm fine. Really. I just have to put something hot, and preferably unhealthy, in my stomach. I haven't eaten anything since this afternoon."

Carlyle moved to the passenger door of her vehicle and swung it open for him. "Fair enough," she said. "Let's go."

Frank climbed inside. He found himself watching her closely as she crossed in front of the car—captivated by her poise, her strength, her looks. She had a subtle natural beauty he couldn't ignore—or resist.

Sitting there, feeling about as appealing as a smelly old goat, Frank suddenly realized that Christine Carlyle was the first woman to catch his attention since Blair's death. *Wonderful. After all this time, I end up falling for a cross between Wonder Woman and Columbo.*

The agent slid behind the wheel, started up the engine, and pulled out her cell phone. "This is Carlyle. I want Cooper and Jones positioned outside 454 Sienna Drive." *Pause.* "Well, I don't care how late it is. Just get 'em there. But under no circumstances are they to enter the premises. I repeat—do not enter. Until a warrant comes through, I just want some eyes on that place. Keep me informed. And update Agent Stark on the situation. Let him know I'll be back in Rosamond tomorrow."

Out of the corner of her eye, Carlyle noticed the reporter studying her. "What?" she asked, concerned that his head injury was more severe than it looked.

"Nothing," he replied, averting his gaze. "I, uh…I was just wondering where you were taking me. That's all."

"Don't worry." The corner of her mouth twitched in a smile. "I know a good place. You'll feel better soon."

51

★ ★ ★

Schmidt arrived at the Klan meeting fifteen minutes before it was scheduled to start. At any other time, the abandoned ranch outside of Bakersfield would have been the perfect place from which to admire the stars overhead, their heavenly brilliance undiminished by the glow of city lights.

The pastor eased his car into a tight space between a new Jeep Wrangler and a classic flatbed Ford, then grabbed his satchel. It was black with a red-stitched cross and a flap embroidered with a triangle symbolizing the Holy Trinity. An asterisk representing the letter *K* at each point of the triangle marked it as dating from the 1920s, when the Invisible Empire boasted a membership of three million. Bill knew the sack would attract someone's attention and mark him as a die-hard Klucker.

He forced himself to breathe normally as he neared the entrance to the meeting place—a huge equestrian center with a bare, unfinished wood exterior, a dark green roof, and yellow lantern lights winking out of small windows on the ground floor. He knew the hooded, shotgun-wielding security guard—a Nighthawk—might question him. He'd already donned his robe and hood a few miles down the darkened road. But that was no guarantee he'd get in, especially since the guards had been told to be wary of lone Klansmen.

Bill let two other men pass him and tried to follow only a few feet behind them. Hopefully, the Nighthawk would think he was with them. But no such luck. He was halted abruptly by the barrel of the guard's shotgun coming down in front of him like the gate at a toll booth. The pastor took a silent breath and looked through the eyeholes of his hood at the Nighthawk. "What's the problem, brother?"

"Where's your escort?" the guard asked coldly.

Bill threw up his hands. "He got the flu. Can you believe it? I *told* him to get a shot, but he said he didn't need one. Poor fool still thinks he's the man he was forty years ago. Oh, well—whaddaya gonna do?"

Bill tried to move on, but the man wasn't convinced. "AYAK?" The guard barked the coded term meaning "Are you a Klansman?" and prodded the pastor in the chest with his gun.

Bill swallowed hard, but managed to hold his nerves in check. "AKIA," he answered—meaning, "A Klansman I am."

The guard nodded and lifted his weapon. "Greetings, brother. Sorry about that. Just doing my job."

Bill placed his hand on the man's arm. "Forget about it. Can't be too careful these days." He gave the Nighthawk a couple of friendly pats on the back. "I'd rather see you doing your job than not."

Schmidt walked on, and couldn't believe his eyes when he entered the barn. There were at least sixty Klansmen milling about, congregating beneath a huge loft on which had been erected an altar, three ornate thrones, and a pair of flags: America's stars and stripes and the KKK's banner, which featured the same insignia on everyone's robes.

Seated upon the thrones were three high-ranking Kluckers. The first, in a red robe and hood, was the Titan—the district leader. The second, in a purple robe with many stripes on the

sleeves, was the director of that area's Klavern, or local chapter—
the Exalted Cyclops. The third, dressed in a golden robe that bore
many stripes and also two patches on the chest, was the Kludd—
the authority over the whole surrounding territory.

As the Exalted Cyclops paced to the front of the loft, silence
fell on the gathering, which had swelled to nearly one hundred.
"Brothers," he began in a throaty baritone, "I welcome you: fellow
Klansmen, honored guests, and all of you fine men who are about
to join our ranks." He gestured with pride toward a row of young
men in civilian clothes.

After the shouts and applause subsided, the Exalted Cyclops
continued. "Allow me, if I may, to quote a fellow believer, a friend
of mine, whose words rang true when spoken years ago and still
ring true today." He spread his arms wide.

"We are the Ku Klux Klan. We hate n——rs. We hate Jews.
We hate homosexuals. And we hate foreigners. We don't have to
have a reason to hate 'em. Just because they breathe, we hate 'em.
You need to wake up. This is America. The n——rs are taking
over along with the Jew. And I hate Jews! I hate 'em because they
exist. I hate 'em because they breed. I hate 'em because they're the
scum of the earth. WHITE POWER!"

"WHITE POWER!" the assembly roared in unison, a fitting
climax to the yells of support they'd voiced during their illustrious
leader's speech.

"Tonight is an important night, brothers," the Exalted Cyclops
went on. "Please give a warm reception to our esteemed visitor."
He motioned toward the Kludd, who stood up for the hearty
round of applause, then approached the front of the loft.

"Thank you," the Kludd intoned, bowing slightly from the
waist. He turned toward his now-silent audience. "You know, a lot
of people say the youth of America aren't worth much anymore.
They're rebellious. They're obsessed with sex. They're hooked on
drugs. They're disrespectful to their elders and disobedient to

authority. And unfortunately, that's a pretty fair assessment of what's going on.

"But I have to stop and ask myself, Why? Why has this happened to the generation holding the future in their hands? Well, I'll tell you why. It's because we got a bunch of Jews up in Washington controlling our country, telling us how to raise our kids and who we need to send them to school with. Telling us that we have NO RIGHTS anymore when it comes to who we eat with in restaurants or who we sit next to on the bus." He paused for a moment, as if enduring a sharp internal pain.

"Furthermore, we have Hollywood, crawling with even more stinkin' Jews, doing their best to shove the filth they call entertainment down our throats. Showing it's okay for black men to ravish our daughters, and pumping out documentaries full of lies about that satanic civil-rights movement, saying the n——r is my equal and that we should all just get along as equals."

The Kludd lifted a clenched fist into the air and shook it at his audience. "NO, SIR. I say the n——r is NOT my equal! AND HE AIN'T YOUR EQUAL EITHER!"

Wild shouts of agreement swelled from the crowd.

"HE AIN'T YOUR EQUAL. And don't you ever forget it. There ain't NO n——r that's your equal. There ain't no n——r equal to ANY white person. Yet they want our children to procreate with the n——r to defile our race, because once you lie down with a n——r, you ARE a dirty, filthy n——r. Once you go black, there ain't nooo coming back.

"But, thank God Almighty, there is a righteous and holy Invisible Empire that does not recognize the usurpers of authority in Washington. And we're here tonight to initiate more faithful believers into that empire. Those who haven't swallowed the demonic poisons the Jew has been force-feeding them their whole lives. Honest, God-fearing, white men committed to our cause. LOOK OUT, N——R, THE KLAN IS GETTING BIGGER!"

More cheers erupted from the hooded Klansmen. Bill Schmidt was quaking inside, grieved beyond words. *How could I have been like this?* he asked himself as the whoops and howls swirled around him.

The Kludd motioned for quiet.

"What we're doing here tonight, my brothers, is reuniting these young men with their heritage. Giving them something to be proud of. You know, Adolf Hitler—who wasn't the monster today's Jew-run media would like you to believe—said that someday his spirit would rise from the grave. That he would die for his people, but then one day would rise from the dead so the world would believe his message. Well, I see that great leader rising from the dead every time we take into our fold more dedicated followers like the ones you see standing here before you. HAIL THE YOUTH!"

"*HAIL THE YOUTH!*" the crowd chorused, splitting the cold night air.

"HAIL THE FUTURE!"

"*HAIL THE FUTURE!*"

"WHITE POWER!"

"*WHITE POWER!*"

The Exalted Cyclops rose briskly from his chair, as did the Titan. They moved to either side of the Kludd, who turned to the red-robed Titan. "Will you do the honors, brother?"

"I will," responded the Titan, who then summoned the row of young men. "Come forward."

The new inductees, two dozen or so, took three steps toward the loft.

"Men of honor, you are here tonight to take a solemn vow. Answer in the affirmative after each question, knowing that you are speaking your words not only before men, but also before God Almighty. Please kneel."

Each man knelt down.

"Are you a white, non-Jewish American citizen?"

"I AM," responded the group.

"Are you in favor of a white man's government in this country?"

"I AM."

"Do you believe in racial separation?"

"I DO."

"Then, by the authority invested in me, I now declare and proclaim you a citizen of the Invisible Empire, a Knight of the Ku Klux Klan, and bestow upon you the name *Klansman,* the most honorable title among white men."

The attendees remained at the initiation ceremony for several hours, congratulating the new members, recalling old times, and trading stories.

"The '60s were the worst," said one Klucker. "Nothing was ever the same after Johnson sent in the National Guard to protect those marchers from Selma to Montgomery,"

"You're right," another agreed.

"If you ask me, that was the beginning of the end. All the n——rs started voting after that. What a mess. Look what their votes have done to this country."

Schmidt stood off to one side, listening closely. "I remember it like it was yesterday," he chimed in.

"Were you there?" asked the first man.

"Sure was. Followed them all the way in my truck with a buddy of mine."

"No kidding?" asked the second Klucker.

"That's a fact," Bill replied, hating what he was about to say. "I was standing right there when our boys in badges whipped the tar outta them n——rs on the Edmund Pettus Bridge. Sent 'em running back across to Selma—yellin' and screamin' and cryin.' Whoo-ee, it was a sight! Me and my buddy were laughin' our heads off. "

Schmidt wasn't lying. He had indeed been there. And his buddy had been none other than Karl Gruber. Then, two weeks after Bloody Sunday, when the demonstrators once again staged their march, Gruber and Schmidt had gone right along with them, cursing them and chucking empty beer cans at them when the National Guard troops weren't looking.

The Klansmen were visibly impressed. "Never met anyone who was actually there—you must be an old-timer."

"I am for sure," Schmidt replied as the memories ate at his soul. He held up his satchel to the small group now clustering around him. "This was my father's. He had it made in 1919. Gave it to me and said, 'Son, don't you ever let this bag go to anyone else. Don't sell it. Don't lose it. Don't give it away. It's part of your family's heritage. It represents you, me, and our race.'"

For the next hour, Schmidt regaled the men with one story after another, raking the government over the coals. He was a natural leader, and in the past, fellow Klansmen had always enjoyed being around him. Little had changed. He went on until he felt a tap on the arm.

"Brother, can I have a word with you?"

Bill knew this man was different from the others. Something in his voice. "Certainly," the pastor replied, following him cautiously outside to the back of the barn.

"You seem to harbor some strong feelings against the government," said the heavy-set man.

"I do," Schmidt answered quickly. "One day, those Washington politicians working for ZOG are gonna fall to their knees and beg for mercy. But all we're gonna say is, 'Get in line for the gallows, or we'll take care of you right here on the spot.' And we won't use a bullet either, we'll just bash their heads in to save ammunition. Then they'll know that the thirty pieces of silver they took to betray this nation won't buy them salvation or mercy."

The man nodded his head. "Ever heard of the Nordic Brotherhood?"

"No."

"Good answer," said the husky Klansman. "You'd be dead right now if you'd said anything else. How about Karl Gruber?"

"Yes," Bill said thoughtfully. "He was the man who got arrested some years ago. Has a church around these parts. Who hasn't heard of him?"

"Another good answer."

Sweating profusely, the pastor felt like he was having a heart attack. *What next? What does this guy want with me?*

The hooded man laid a granite hand on Schmidt's shoulder and squeezed. "Listen, brother, I think I have some information you might find extremely useful."

52

"Getting to Know You"
OSCAR HAMMERSTEIN (1895–1960)

★ ★ ★

For a dozen years, Le Petit Bistro had been California City's best-kept secret, a real favorite among locals. It was nearly impossible to get seated without reservations, particularly during peak hours. But luckily for Frank and Christine, it was late.

"Two for dinner," Carlyle announced confidently as she approached the maitre d'.

The host instantly registered Frank's disheveled attire. "Oh... well, we're almost closed, *mademoiselle*. I'm so sorry."

Carlyle pulled out her Secret Service ID and flashed it in his impassive face. "But you *are* still open, right, until ten o'clock?"

"Um...of course...certainly, right this way." He hastily lifted two menus and led them to one of the best tables in the house.

Christine glanced back over her shoulder at Frank. "I love doing that," she whispered with a wink.

After being seated, Frank perused the softly lit room. *Very intimate*, he thought, pleased by the decor and the classical music playing in the background. With great anticipation, he opened his artistically decorated menu: *Mesclun de Marius, Coq au Vin, Tarte Fine aux Pommes...*

He frowned and looked up at Christine. "You speak French, I take it?"

"Yep."

"Well, Agent Carlyle, care to help me out?"

She raised her eyes from the menu, amusement dancing across her lips. "Okay. Or you could just flip to the next page."

The reporter turned over the gilt-edged paper, which felt as thick as canvas between his fingers. *Mixed field greens with vinaigrette, chicken braised in wine, apple tart...*

He cringed with embarrassment. "So much for me being a top-notch *investigative* journalist, huh?"

Christine let her head drop to the side. "You got a pretty nasty bump on your head. Don't be surprised if you're not quite yourself for a while."

"Do you speak any other languages?" he inquired.

She thought for a second, tugging on her earlobe, as if she were compiling a list in her head. "Let's see, besides French...Arabic, German, Russian, Spanish, Portuguese, Dutch, Latvian—"

"Latvian?"

"Don't ask. Long story."

"Wow," Frank said, temporarily forgetting his hunger pangs. "I'm impressed."

Christine waved her hand. "Don't be. It's just a facility. You write professionally, which means you probably have a ridiculously large vocabulary. I just happen to have a knack for languages."

"Maybe. But it's a pretty awesome talent, if you ask me. Sure would come in handy on a European vacation."

"Yeah...well, perhaps someday. But right now I think I like catching bad guys."

The waiter arrived to take their orders, carrying with him a woven basket of hot bread that he delivered with a flourish.

"Nice place," Frank observed, biting into a slice of sourdough slathered with butter.

"Yeah, I like it. It reminds me of a café I used to go to every Friday night when I lived in Paris."

"How long were you there?" asked the reporter, his curiosity growing.

"About a year, right after graduating from college. I wanted to see a little bit of the world before pursuing a career."

Frank took another slice of bread, then set the basket within Christine's reach.

"Where'd you get your degree?"

"University of Maryland," she answered, selecting a flaky roll. "How about you?"

"UCLA."

"Go Bruins!"

Frank laughed. "You know, I went to Europe after graduating, too. But my buddies and I decided to just backpack through a bunch of different countries for a few months. Germany, Austria, Belgium—had the time of our lives."

Christine grinned. "Sounds like fun."

"It was. But you know, the best time I ever had on vacation was when I hiked through Yosemite National Park during my senior year with my best friend."

"Ooh, Yosemite's great," she agreed. "I was there a couple of years ago with my mom and dad. I love the outdoors."

They continued to converse amiably throughout dinner, segueing with ease from one topic to the next. Frank was captivated by Christine's eyes—deep-set and penetrating, full of vibrant energy and passion. And Christine found Frank attractive and charming. But what really tugged at her heartstrings was how honest and vulnerable he could be.

By the time dessert was served, the two of them felt like they'd known each other for years.

"That looks yummy," Frank said, pointing to the diminutive plate that the waiter had placed in front of his companion.

"*Tian au Rhum*. Rum custard. You want a taste?"

"Do you really have to ask?" As he watched her scoop out a small portion, he held out a spoonful of his warm raspberry tartlet smothered in ice cream. "Here, try some of this," he said.

"Mmm…*Tarte aux Frambois.*"

"Yes, ma'am," he nodded, then piped in his best Inspector Clouseau imitation, "*Tartay oh framboyz.*"

Christine covered her mouth and laughed. "Do me a favor, Frank. Stick to writing."

Just then, the reporter's cell phone rang. He looked at the caller ID. "Do you mind if I take this?"

She answered by digging into her custard.

He flipped open his phone. "Hello?"

"Frank, this is Bill Schmidt. Where are you?"

"I'm in California City."

"Why are you…? Never mind. Look, you have to get over here as soon as possible. I just got back from a Klan meeting."

Frank straightened up in his chair. "A *what?*"

"A Klan meeting. I got dressed up in my old hood and robe to see if I could gather some information. And you're not going to believe what I found out. But I want this to stay between you and me. No feds."

Christine caught the odd look on Frank's face. "Everything okay?"

"Just my editor," he whispered to her, his hand covering the receiver.

Schmidt cut in. "Hello? Are you there?"

"Yeah, I'm here. Okay, uh…I don't have a car. But I think I can get a ride back to my hotel by…" He held his hand out toward Christine, hoping for an answer.

"Eleven-thirty," she replied, checking her watch.

"…eleven-thirty."

"Great," Schmidt exhaled, his relief obvious. "I'll pick you up tomorrow morning, then. Seven o'clock sharp. We need to make plans. I have an idea."

"Sounds good to me."

"What was that all about?" Christine asked as he pocketed his phone.

"Oh, my editor wants me to stay in tomorrow and put the finishing touches on an upcoming article. So I guess I won't be going anywhere for a while."

Carlyle dropped her napkin neatly onto her empty plate. "Too bad. But I have to admit my job's going to be a lot easier with you in one location. I have to get with Stark and go through that house. By the way, didn't you say you were going to tell me about this T.R. character? And also show me something you found in the house?"

"Did I?" Frank teased. He casually pulled out the scraps of paper and slid them across the table. "Take a look."

Christine's eyes widened. "You realize what these are?" she asked.

He leaned back, hands locked behind his head, knowing he had just scored some major points.

The agent folded up the notes and put them in her pocket. "C'mon, Frankie boy. Finish up your coffee. Time to go catch some bad guys."

53

We become just by doing just acts...
and brave by doing brave acts.

ARISTOTLE (384–322 B.C.)

★★★

Schmidt reached Frank's hotel at 6:55 a.m. Wednesday morning. After parking his car near the rear entrance, he called the journalist from a house phone at the far end of the building. "I'm here," the pastor said, "by that coin-op laundry room they have on the first floor."

Frank picked up his laptop. "Good. I'm gonna have to sneak down to the hallway that leads to where you are. I have a particularly efficient agent following me around, so I gotta make sure she doesn't see me."

"The brunette?"

"Yeah."

Schmidt changed the receiver to his other hand. "Well, there are worse things that could be tailing you."

"No doubt," Frank agreed, grinning a bit. "Be right down." He hung up and headed out the door.

A few minutes later, he was pulling out of the hotel parking lot with Bill, who was eager to get the ball rolling.

"I think we should go to my place to talk," he suggested. "I know it's still early, so I'll put on some coffee and cook you up one of my special omelets."

"Okay by me. Just as long as I get to hear about that Klan meeting last night." Frank glanced over at the pastor. "Have you lost your mind?"

Schmidt let out a hearty laugh as he turned a corner. "Oh, I lost that a long time ago."

The ten minutes it took to reach Bill's house was more than long enough for him to explain his reasons for attending the Klan meeting. It all made sense—go where there was a chance of finding information, and send someone who wouldn't be easily detected. And if anyone knew how to blend in with Kluckers, it was Schmidt. The reporter, however, still didn't know what his friend had actually found out. Bill waited to relay that bit of news until after he'd served up a couple plates of bacon, hash browns, and Southwestern omelets.

As Frank tucked away his meal, Bill explained how he'd stood around talking to the Kluckers just like he was one of them. "Then," he continued, "from out of nowhere, this huge guy— must've been at least six-four—raps me on the shoulder and asks to have a word outside. So we go, and after talking a little— you know, him sort of checking me out to see if I was the real deal—he says, 'I think I have some information you might find extremely useful.'"

The Klansman identified himself as Arty Jones, a member of the Nordic Brotherhood. The Brotherhood was stepping up its preparations for the impending Racial Holy War by getting everyone armed and ready for battle. And not just with regular items like shotguns, rifles, and handguns.

"None of that mainstream stuff," Arty scoffed when Bill asked. "I'm talking about serious firepower here: military-grade plastic explosives, automatic machine guns, hand grenades, shoulder-mounted rocket launchers—the works."

"Are you getting it from overseas?" Bill had asked coolly. "From Muslim countries?"

"No way. We don't want to have anything to do with those towel-head sand monkeys."

"Then who's your supplier? Shoulder-held rocket launchers aren't exactly standard issue."

Arty nodded. "True, unless you have access to government storage facilities. We've worked for years to get our guys into the right positions. And now we're finally seeing the fruits of our labor. Those weapons are coming right out of ZOG's own warehouses to sites where our members can go and pick them up. Then they're transported to where we need 'em. When we take down this totalitarian regime, we're gonna do it with ZOG's own hardware. How great will that be? And we've already been taking the war to the enemy."

Frank listened to the pastor, surprised but not truly shocked. The Brotherhood's strategy perfectly fit within the Christian Identity paradigm, and the decision to arm its members to the teeth seemed to be the logical next step toward Armageddon. But were these actions linked to the recent terrorist attacks, as Arty Jones had seemed to indicate? If so, how? And who was involved?

"That's not even the worst part," Bill added, leaning over the table and dropping his voice. "Guess where a major weapons cache is located around here."

"Yahweh's Holy Temple?"

Bill slapped his left thigh. "Yahweh's Holy Temple."

Frank paused. "Why don't the feds know?"

"The weapons are hidden underground at the far eastern corner of the property. Apparently, the only people who know about it are members of the Nordic Brotherhood. That guy I met last night was probably the only Brotherhood member at the meeting. So it's not surprising that very few at Gruber's camp would know about the weapons. And how would the feds find out?"

"And Gruber? Does he know?" Frank asked, spooning up a mouthful of eggs.

"Oh, he knows alright. In fact, that's why Arty wanted to talk to me. He said if I was interested in joining the Brotherhood, I'd first have to accept a mission to prove my worth. He instructed me to contact Gruber and ask for a final consignment of weapons. Gruber is supposed to provide everything nice and neat, complete with a fueled-up truck and directions to the drop-off point. I think somewhere out toward Denver. Apparently, this will be the last shipment from Yahweh's Holy Temple for a while."

"So you think Gruber was involved in the planning and execution of the terrorist attacks?"

Bill appeared uncertain. "To tell you the truth, I don't know. He might be directly linked. Or he might simply be a weapons supplier who is keeping himself ignorant of what happens to the weapons after they leave his hands. Whatever he's done, it's enough to put him away for a good long stretch."

"Okay then, we need to let Stark and Carlyle know as soon as possible so they can get a warrant and go in there."

The pastor sat back, dismayed. "You gotta be kidding me," he responded sharply. "What I told you is nothing but hearsay. And no judge worth his salt is going to issue a warrant on just that. What we need is cold, hard proof. And I have an idea—"

"Why am I suddenly so nervous?" Frank interrupted.

Just then, Luke walked in the front door. "I'm back!" he shouted, throwing his duffel bag on the couch.

Bill got up and walked into the living room. "What are you doing here? I thought the trip was supposed to last till Monday."

Luke collapsed into the nearest armchair. "It was," he answered with irritation. "But that stupid blizzard moved in, and we all had to get out of there before it dumped four feet of snow on us."

Schmidt patted his grandson on the shoulder. "Oh, well. At least you're safe."

"Yeah, I know." Luke scraped something sticky off the sole of his worn-out Nike, then suddenly perked up. "Hey, you wanna go out for dinner tonight? It's New Year's Eve, after all."

The pastor looked back toward the kitchen. "Actually, I...I'm probably going to be busy tonight—and I'll be out pretty late."

Luke looked momentarily confused. "Uh, late? When will you be coming home?"

The pastor pressed his hands together and fought to appear calm. "I really don't know."

54

★★★

Bill and Frank reached Gruber's camp just in time for the traditional New Year's Eve marshmallow roast—a favorite activity of church members, especially the kids. The bonfire at the center of the festivities blazed, sending flames high in the air and giving off more than enough heat for everyone to be comfortable. There was plenty of cocoa and hot dogs, a raffle every hour, and a band, which was playing on a stage a ways off.

"Well, we made it," Frank commented as he and Schmidt strolled unchallenged through the front gate.

"Did you ever have any doubts about us getting in?" the pastor asked.

"Getting in? No." He looked over his shoulder, then to his left and right. "Getting out is what worries me."

"Relax, Frank. God is in control. I live under divine protection."

"Yeah—well, good for you," the journalist retorted nervously. "I just hope some of that divine protection rubs off on me."

The two men followed the route Frank had taken the day he interviewed Gruber. After several minutes, they were beyond the last building and venturing out toward the eastern corner of the property, where the underground weapons cache was supposed to be.

"You got that nifty penlight of yours?" asked Schmidt, no longer able to see in front of him.

"Yep," Frank answered, pulling it out. He flicked it on. Even illuminated, the way was long and slow, leading across some open sand, then down a shallow gully and, at one point, over some rocks and boulders. Eventually, however, they reached a grassy knoll near the base of a hill that rose up steeply. Frank hurried on toward the hillside, hoping to spot a clue.

Suddenly, the pastor heard a thud, followed by a sharp groan and the sight of Frank's flashlight flying into the air. It landed on a small mound of earth, lighting up where the journalist had fallen—on his back, with one foot cocked unnaturally, in a dip that had been concealed by a mountain of pine needles.

"Are you okay?" Bill asked, rushing over.

"Actually...I don't think so." The reporter slowly untwisted himself and tried to stand, letting out a long hiss when he tried to put weight on his right foot. "I think I messed up my ankle pretty bad."

"Lemme see," said Schmidt, bending down and gently prodding the injury. "Yeah—it's already starting to swell."

As the pastor helped Frank upright, the reporter's eyes followed the flashlight beam to some kind of metal bar directly at his feet. "Hey," he said, pointing down, "I think we found something."

The tunnel beneath the trapdoor Frank had discovered led due east for about twenty feet, opening up into a much larger space. It was obviously inside the hill they'd spotted. Cold and slightly damp, it smelled strongly of rust and dirt. It was packed with wooden crates on shelves. But not until Bill turned on a light switch did the two men know what they had stumbled upon.

The shelves were laden with hundreds of automatic machine guns: M-249s, M-60s, M-16s—manufactured for the military, strictly illegal for private citizens. On the floor sat hundreds of metal boxes with ammunition. Pushing deeper into the room they found large crates stacked five-high—hand grenades, incendiary devices, concussion bombs, land mines. Against the far wall were rack after rack of shoulder-held launchers, their rockets beside them in bins.

"Let's take pictures and get outta here," Frank whispered, urgency shaking his voice.

Schmidt pulled out his camera and snapped a couple dozen photos. Then he shut off the light, and the two men made their way back along the tunnel.

"Oh, man...I can barely walk on this thing," Frank groaned, his limp worsening with each step.

They emerged from the trapdoor, ready to make their escape. But then they froze. The sound of barking dogs was approaching. And blinking flashlights, held by what they could only assume were skinhead guards, were closing in fast.

55

*Even though I walk through the valley of the shadow
of death, I will fear no evil, for you are with me.*

PSALM 23:4

★★★

"Run!" yelled Bill. Frank labored hard to move fast, but his twisted ankle shot lightning bolts of agony up his leg with every move he made.

"Do you know where you're going?" he managed to gasp as they lurched onward, their pursuers gaining steadily.

"I saw a break in the fence somewhere around here," Schmidt said, wiping beads of perspiration from his eyes. "Maybe we can crawl through it and get back to where we parked."

They looked back to check on the camp guards in pursuit, and missed seeing the lip of an embankment right in front of them. At the bottom of the slope Bill landed about ten feet from Frank, who was now writhing in pain.

"I'm starting to reconsider the wisdom of this plan," the journalist quipped after getting his wind back.

"Oh no," Schmidt groaned.

"What now?" asked Frank, trying to get back to his feet.

"The camera! It fell out of my pocket somewhere. I...I can't see it."

Within seconds, flashlight beams were flickering above the edge that Frank and Bill had fallen over.

"Forget it," the journalist told him. "You need to keep moving. Go!"

"I can't leave you here!"

"You *are* going to leave me. I can't make it any farther. I'll keep the penlight—I'll tell them I was alone. The moon's finally out, so you should be able to see well enough to get to the break in the fence—*Now go.*"

Bill glanced back up. "Alright," he agreed. "I'll come back for you." With a brief squeeze of Frank's shoulder, Schmidt turned and headed off into the night.

Moments later, the guards reached Frank and aimed their rifles at his head. "Happy New Year, gents!" he joked weakly.

"Shut up!" bellowed one of the soldiers.

Frank ignored him. "I know you're probably wondering why I—"

"I said, shut up!"

Another man hollered down from the lip of the embankment. "Who is it?"

One of the men looked up toward his superior. "Don't know, sir! Never seen him before!"

"Anyone with him?"

"No, sir."

"Well, then, bring him on up."

Four of the guards grabbed Frank roughly and hoisted him to his feet. He gasped with the pain. "Easy there, boys. My ankle's screwed up. I can't walk too well, okay? You know, you should really throw up a few lights around here. It isn't safe and—"

Frank's rambling was cut short as the butt of a rifle jabbed his diaphragm. "I told you to shut up!" ordered the biggest guard.

He was yanked and pummeled up the hill. Horrible thoughts about what would happen next filled his mind. There was no chance of escape. All of the guards were exceptionally beefy and menacing—with one exception.

"Wait a minute," the small guard said, "that…that's the guy who was here yesterday."

"Hey, Todd," Frank called out hopefully. "See, you guys? I'm okay. T.R. will vouch for me."

The man in charge walked up and thrust the end of his shotgun under the journalist's chin. "You know this intruder?" he asked T.R.

The young man was shaking but tried to answer clearly. "Yeah…yes, sir…he…he was talking to Pastor Gruber yesterday and I…I took him on a tour of the camp. He's a…a newspaperman. Erich told me to take him around. I ain't lying, Porter. Erich told me to do it."

"That's alright, T.R., that's alright. You didn't do anything wrong. Looks to me like maybe we've caught ourselves one of them Jew spies from the liberal media."

Frank raised his palms into the air and gave a huge shrug. "Truth be told, guys, I…uh, I'm not Jewish. Really. Tell them, Todd."

But by the time Frank had pivoted around, T.R. was already scurrying back toward the main camp.

Poor kid. He's probably just as scared of these guys as I am.

His thoughts were interrupted by the *thunk* of Porter's shotgun striking the back of his neck. He collapsed like a felled tree.

"Stand him up," barked Porter, who went toe-to-toe with Frank, then leaned in close. "Who sent you," he asked softly, "and where's your friend?"

"No one…no one sent me. I'm just a reporter. Pastor Gruber invited me here. I'm alone. I came here by myself."

"You hear that, boys?" Porter said as he turned to his underlings. "He's all by himself." The other guards guffawed as their leader pressed on. "So I guess we were just seeing things, huh?"

Frank gave a halfhearted nod. "I guess so."

The punch landed squarely on Frank's cheek. It would have

sent the reporter to the ground had he not been firmly held in place by two burly guards. He was immediately struck again—this time in the ribs, as Porter swung his gun forward like a baseball bat. Frank actually felt bones crack.

The soldiers dropped him to the grass and, along with the others, started kicking him with their steel-toed jackboots. He tried to cover up as best he could, curling into a tight ball. Then, tasting blood in his mouth, he began to lose consciousness. He could still hear his attackers, however, and knew the men wouldn't stop until he was dead.

This is the end, he realized.

This is the end.

56

All men make mistakes, but only wise men learn from their mistakes.

SIR WINSTON CHURCHILL (1874–1965)

★★★

It took a while, but eventually Frank could tell he was in a small, dimly lit room. He decided, as his eyes shifted back and forth, that everything looked too solid for him to be in heaven—or hell, for that matter. And he could still feel his battered body, which hurt too much for him to be dead.

By the weak light filtering in from behind the curtains, the journalist guessed it was probably late morning or early afternoon. He also observed with interest the IV drip attached to his left arm and the cast on his foot. He slid his head a fraction to the right, setting off a kaleidoscope of swirling dots in front of him, his unsteady focus finally landing on Pastor Bill, whispering quietly, head down, hands folded in front of him.

"I sure hope I'm the one you're praying for," the reporter muttered around what felt like a mouthful of cotton balls.

Startled, Schmidt leapt out of his chair and crossed to Frank's bed. "Welcome back to the land of the living, buddy."

"How long have I been out?"

"About ten hours."

"Since I'm still alive, I assume you made it back with the cavalry."

"Yes, but not until after you'd been left for dead by the side of the road, just outside the entrance of the camp."

"Now *that* must've been a pretty sight."

"I see you haven't lost your sense of humor. That's good."

"I guess I owe you one, Pastor Schmidt."

"Actually, it was your friend T.R. who saved you—along with an undercover agent the feds had inside the camp. From what I hear, T.R. started running around telling everyone that he needed to see Erich Strom pronto because the boys thought they'd caught themselves a spy and were going to beat him to death. Stark says their undercover guy heard about it and got to you as fast as he could. He's the one who stopped that bunch of animals from killing you."

"So tell me the truth: How bad do I look?"

Schmidt rubbed the bridge of his nose. "Bad. You've got a bruised kidney, four broken ribs, a fractured ankle, a dislocated shoulder, multiple cuts and bruises...and a few dog bites."

"Lovely."

"You said you wanted the truth."

Frank worked his jaw slowly from side to side and heard an unsettling snap each time he moved it. "Have you talked to Stark yet?"

"Yes."

"Did you also happen to talk to..."

"Carlyle?"

"Uh-huh."

Schmidt nodded. "They're both waiting outside in the hallway. She's not too happy with you, that's for sure. Not too thrilled with me either. And FYI, that gal's sweet on you, in case you haven't noticed."

Frank tried to smile, but the stitches in his lip made it impossible. "What makes you think that, Pastor Bill?"

Schmidt chuckled. "Well, she wasn't looking at you with the eyes of a Secret Service agent when you were lying on the ground covered in blood…if you know what I mean."

A soft knock at the door echoed through the room. "Come in," called Frank.

Bristling with pent-up energy, Stark and Carlyle entered and took up positions on either side of the bed.

"Good to see you awake, Frank," said Stark. "How do you feel?"

The reporter made a painful attempt to prop himself up. "I've had better days."

Schmidt picked up his Bible from a chair in the corner. "I'm gonna take off now, if that's okay. Luke's sort of mad at me, so I think I'd better try to explain to him what's been going on."

"We'll be in touch," Stark told Schmidt, who nodded and slipped out. The agent then turned his full attention back toward the injured reporter. "You up to answering a few questions?"

"Yeah," added Carlyle. "Like, how stupid *are* you?"

Stark waved his hand. "Take it easy, Chris."

"I'm just asking," she said, crossing her arms in front of her.

Frank began to explain. "As you know, Bill found out about a stash of weapons on Gruber's property. Now, correct me if I'm wrong, but without proof, there would have been no way for you to get a search warrant."

"If you had simply notified us, we could have had our undercover agent get all the proof we needed," Carlyle remarked.

"Did I know you had an agent in the camp? Excuse me for not wanting to see anyone else killed before you could go in there and do something. Bill and I just wanted to speed things up a little. We didn't want to pass up an opportunity to catch Gruber red-handed."

Stark absentmindedly began scratching his neck. "But Schmidt lost his camera somewhere during your little adventure. Which means we've got nothing. And you almost got yourself killed to boot."

Frank took a deep breath. "I…uh, wouldn't say we got nothing."

Starks stopped scratching. "What do you mean?"

"Go get my coat, and reach inside the lining. There's a hidden pocket on the left side."

Carlyle grabbed the jacket, and after a quick search, pulled out Frank's small, silver Samsung. "Your cell phone?"

"That's not just any cell phone," the reporter said. "That happens to be the best videophone on the market today. And on its memory card you'll find at least five minutes of digital footage taken where we found the weapons cache, complete with close-ups."

Carlyle tossed the phone to Stark. Sure enough, the footage showed the weapons, just as Schmidt had described them.

"But we still have a problem," Stark noted grimly as he glanced up.

"What's that?" inquired Frank.

"The nature of this evidence. You two had no business even being on the property. You were trespassing, so this is inadmissible as evidence. It was illegally obtained."

"Well, what if it wasn't illegally obtained?" the journalist responded.

Stark and Carlyle looked at each other. "I don't follow you," replied Stark.

"I was *invited* to the compound, specifically for last night's celebration. I was there as a guest."

Carlyle stepped forward. "Who invited you?"

"Karl Gruber."

The agent arched her eyebrow incredulously. "Do you have any proof of that?"

"On my recorder, the one I used for the interview, you can hear him inviting me to the camp for New Year's Eve."

Stark was excited now. "Okay, Frank. This is very important. Was there any kind of lock on the trapdoor you guys entered? A sign that said 'Restricted,' maybe? *Anything* that would indicate this room was off limits to the public?"

"Nope, nothing," Frank said, shaking his head.

Stark pocketed the phone and turned to his partner. "I'm going to run this over to one of our local contacts. The courthouse is closed today, but I can still obtain an emergency order through Washington. While I'm doing that, I need you to begin coordinating an operational task force. Get hold of McBride and have him bring three strike teams down from L.A.: units four, five, and seven. I want Navarro to draw up detailed blueprints of the camp and the underground room based on Schmidt's info. I'll contact you for an update in…" he checked his watch, "…three hours." Not missing a beat, Stark headed for the door. "I'll bring the car around."

Carlyle started to leave, but paused at the foot of the bed, pinning Frank with a pensive stare. "Why did you lie to me?" she began.

"I wasn't thinking. I wanted to tell you, but I…couldn't. I didn't mean to…" He stopped, knowing there was nothing he could say to make things right.

"Just so you know, I came to your room last night with some champagne. I figured you'd be tired after *working* so many hours, and…" she looped a stray piece of hair behind her ear, "…I thought maybe you wouldn't want to spend New Year's Eve alone."

The journalist was stunned. "Chris, I'm…sorry."

"So am I," she said, and brushed out of the room.

57

★ ★ ★

Duncan Phelps pecked out a final e-mail on his keyboard as he spoke loudly on the phone. "Lance," he declared, "I was completely wrong about the War Room. You were right—it does indeed exist. I wanted you to hear that personally from me before tonight's operation got underway."

"Well, I appreciate that," replied the former director of the Secret Service. "But to be honest, I'm still not convinced that Gruber's underground storage facility *is* the War Room."

The Secretary of Homeland Security clenched his teeth. "Of course it is," he barked. "It's a well-concealed underground enclosure, jam-packed with illegal ordnance, in a white-supremacist enclave. If that's not a war room, what is?"

"True," Vaughn agreed, rolling a golf ball back and forth across his desk, "but still—"

"You worry too much," interjected Phelps, finishing up a memo on his computer. "We're going to get rid of that whole stinking camp once and for all. Then you'll see—everything will be fine. And I want you to know that tomorrow morning at the press conference I'm going to make sure the public is aware of the fact that you were the one who warned us about the War Room in the first place. Give credit where credit is due, I always say."

Vaughn caught the ball before it rolled off the edge of his desk. "I'm not interested in getting any special recognition for merely doing my job, Duncan. I just want us to be right about this."

58

*Those things which are precious are
saved only by sacrifice.*

PFC DAVID KENYON WEBSTER (1922–1961)

★ ★ ★

Strike teams A and B approached Gruber's camp. They hugged the line of trees bordering the open field near the front gate, moving stealthily forward. The darkness helped maximize the effectiveness of their camouflage—completely black, right down to their caps and gloves.

As Agent Stark led Unit A closer to the compound, his mind flashed back to Vietnam. He was once more leading an assault on a small, isolated camp of combatants; perilously close to women and children. His heart and soul burned at the awful memories.

This is it, he promised himself, gesturing for his men to halt until he could survey the property. *After tonight, I'm through.*

Stark looked forty feet behind him at Unit B, then gave the signal for *all clear.* The men moved out from the cover of the woods and approached swiftly, stopping about ten yards from the gate. No guards were posted. And the floodlights that normally illuminated the front of the compound were off.

Stark didn't like it.

Unit C, under Carlyle and McBride, had already worked its way around to the rear of the compound and was entering the break in the fence through which Schmidt had escaped.

According to the map, it would take them only a few minutes to reach their objective. Once they accessed the weapons cache, the plan called for McBride to fire off a flare, indicating that Units A and B could make their presence known and serve the search warrant on Gruber. The logistics team had projected that resistance would be minimal because so many families lived in the camp.

Stark moved his men past Unit B and pushed open the unlocked gate. Both squads entered and formed up inside the fence.

Then, in the midst of the darkness, a sound grabbed the men's attention: *thud...thud.*

The agents saw nothing. But each one registered the dull thumps under their feet, like ripe avocados hitting the ground.

Thud...thud, thud.

It took a few seconds, but Stark finally remembered where he'd heard that noise before—the jungles around Khe Sanh, on patrol. "Grenade! Take cover!" he yelled as loud as he could, just as floodlights lit up the perimeter like it was high noon.

Stark's next command was drowned out by the deafening explosions. Two agents were killed instantly. Shrapnel ripped through the whole squad. Those who could still stand fought to pull the more critically injured men to safety, barely avoiding the automatic gunfire that began hitting them from several points.

By the time chaos broke out near the gate, Unit C had reached the weapons cache. Most of the squad had already taken up positions when they heard the explosions and machine guns. "Oh, man," McBride exclaimed. "I hear at least one 50-caliber. And a lot of AK-47s."

Carlyle faced her team. "Agents one through twelve follow me. The rest of you stay here and keep the location secure. Anyone not with us is to be considered hostile."

The agent's walkie-talkie squawked to life. "This is Stark. Do you copy? Come in, Chris. Come in!"

"Go ahead," Carlyle shouted, as she and the others bolted toward the conflict.

Stark was hunkered down with three others behind the stairs leading up to an office building. "Listen carefully," he yelled, poking his head up to identify enemy positions. "You need to approach from the southwest. Do not, I repeat, *do not* come straight in from your location. That will take you directly into their line of fire. Make a lateral move west when you get a hundred yards from the main complex, keep going until you reach…" he checked his map, "…a cluster of cabins. Head straight through them, then back toward the gunfire. You should come up right behind them."

"Affirmative. On our way."

Stark continued assessing the situation, developing and relaying an attack plan on the fly. "Hostiles are concealed at four points: inside a metal toolshed; behind a gutted van; near an electrical supply shack; and outside the perimeter in the woods facing the camp. Stay low and keep moving. Take up a position, and when I say *now*, open up with everything you've got."

"Roger that," Carlyle said, leading her team forward.

They reached the row of cabins and raced between them. Abruptly, a door swung open and a man appeared with a double-barreled shotgun. Windows in other cabins shattered as rifles were punched through them. The shotgun blast missed everyone. But the automatic gun-fire that followed took out several of Carlyle's men. One of them received a direct shot to his forehead and died instantly.

"Return fire!" shouted Carlyle, who dropped and rolled, squeezing off four rounds. The man with the shotgun fell, then lay still. The other agents opened fire, forcing the shooters inside the cabins to back away from the windows and take cover.

Stark, meanwhile, had located the combatant in the woods by watching for the flash of his gun. He moved to within range, lying on the ground just inside the fence. From there he sent a barrage of rounds into the targeted area. No more flashes came from the woods. From his new vantage point, Stark observed his men returning fire, but their chances of an effective counterattack were slim without help.

Finally, he glimpsed Carlyle approaching from the distance, but with only about half of her team. *It might be enough,* he guessed. He picked up his walkie-talkie. "This is Stark. Come in, Chris."

"Go ahead."

"Are you ready?"

"We're moving into position...Ready," Carlyle replied.

"Hold on." Stark waited for just the right moment—a lull in the enemy's fire, a sure sign they were reloading. At last.

"Now!" he shouted to Carlyle, who gave the order to advance.

The camp guards immediately turned away from Units A and B to deal with the assault coming from behind them, giving Stark and his men the opportunity to make their move. Stark was up first, running forward with a stinger grenade in his hand. He got to the toolshed and tossed it in through an open window. The blast took out the four occupants.

But just as Stark was about to sprint for the gutted van, he saw his partner heading for a large boulder nearby. "No! Stay down!" he shouted. Too late. A bullet caught her in the shoulder. Then, two more rounds found their mark in the center of her chest. "Chris!" he screamed. Without hesitation, Stark scrambled toward Carlyle, hitting the enemy's positions with short bursts from his assault rifle.

He grabbed the back of her collar and dragged her into a ditch near the fence. "Chris—Christine!"

Carlyle's eyes fluttered open, then closed again. "I'm...I'm okay." She grimaced, inhaling with difficulty. "My shoulder's only grazed. And the other two rounds hit my vest."

Stark gasped with relief and put his hand gently on Carlyle's cheek. "You know what, kid? You're the best partner I've ever had."

"Thanks," she mumbled, her eyes wide with surprise. "And,

um…thanks for pulling me out of there." Not until her partner slumped over did she realize her friend and mentor had taken a hit. "Stark!" Carlyle rolled him over and pulled open his vest. There was a gaping wound directly beneath his armpit where the vest had left an opening. "You're gonna be okay, Eddie. Take it easy."

"No. I don't think so, Chris." Stark was already finding it hard to breathe. "Hey, you…you called me by my first name."

Tears welled up in Carlyle's eyes and spilled onto the ground, mixing with her partner's blood. She looked around. The remaining agents had finally taken control of the situation, and the surviving compound guards were in custody.

"Eddie, listen. The gunfire's stopped. We got 'em. You did it."

"Make sure…do a complete sweep," he added weakly.

"I will."

"Don't…don't forget to…"

Special Agent Eddie Stark took a final, shuddering breath, and fixed his eyes for the last time on the only person he truly cared about.

59

*There is no greater grief than to remember
days of joy when misery is at hand.*

DANTE ALIGHIERI (1265-1321)

★★★

Frank was perched uncomfortably on an orange plastic chair in the hallway outside the hospital's small chapel. He probably shouldn't have been out of bed, but as long as the Vicodin was enabling him to endure being upright, he was going to be there.

Some minutes later, Pastor Schmidt emerged, closing the chapel's door behind him.

Frank stood up slowly, using his crutches for balance. "How is she?"

Bill considered the question for a second or two before answering. "A little in shock, as you might imagine. She and Agent Stark were extremely close. It's going to take a while for her to adjust." Schmidt frowned at Frank, who was having difficulty just standing. "You should be resting, you know."

The journalist took a deep breath. "No, I...I need to see her. Do you think that'd be okay?"

"I do. In fact, seeing you might actually make her feel a lot better."

Frank looked down. "Well, the last time I saw her she was, uh...pretty upset with me. Had every right to be, but I—"

The pastor interrupted. "Listen, less than twenty-four hours ago Christine lost someone very dear to her. That's what she's dealing with. And just so you know, we spoke briefly, and she understands why you did what you did." He patted his friend's arm. "You made a mistake. You know it—she knows it. That doesn't matter much to her anymore. Not now."

Frank fidgeted nervously. "But what should I say?"

"You don't have to say anything. Just be there for her."

"Well, if you think that'll help..." he said, grinding the tip of his crutch into the cracked linoleum floor. He hesitated for a long moment, and then spoke, choosing his words carefully. "Is there anything I should know before I go in? About the raid last night, I mean?"

Schmidt exhaled loudly. "It was bad, Frank. Real bad. Four agents killed, including Stark, and a dozen others injured. Obviously, someone tipped them off before the operation."

The reporter cocked his head to the side in disbelief. "How is that possible?"

"I have no idea."

"I heard the camp's been emptied and Gruber's in custody. But what about Strom? Did they get him?"

Bill rubbed his chin. "I don't think so. Now that you mention it, I don't remember hearing his name come up at all. I guess he must've been away at the time of the raid. I don't know."

"I'm sure he'll turn up eventually. Probably not around here, though. Not after last night." Suddenly, Frank remembered someone else. "What about T.R.?"

"No word on him, either. He wasn't even on the list of non-hostile occupants escorted off the property."

"Huh...that's odd. Well, thanks for checking on that for me."

"No problem," Bill said, glancing at his watch. "Listen, I'd like to stay, but I've gotta get going. It's already noon, and I need to start making arrangements for the special prayer service we're having tonight. "

"I understand. Don't worry about me. I'll give you a call to-morrow."

The pastor squeezed Frank's good shoulder and strode down the hallway.

Carlyle was standing with her back to the doorway when Frank hobbled into the chapel. She didn't turn around, but continued staring out the window at the hospital's rose garden. A fountain bubbled gently at the center of it—the soothing music of water running over pebbles. Even more captivating were the countless blooms that graced the courtyard and hung over its weathered wooden benches.

"Chris?"

The grief-stricken agent remained still, her eyes locked on the serene lushness of the garden. "Hi," she said, still looking away, her voice a mere rustle in the room.

Frank took a tentative step forward. "Is there anything I can do?"

Pulling her gaze from the window, she turned. "He liked you a lot."

Frank paused. "Did he?"

"Yes. He thought you were gutsy."

"I...I guess that's better than being thought of as stupid."

Her lips twitched upward slightly at the corners. "Well, he said you were that too."

The journalist chuckled, then winced from the pain in his ribs. It was almost time for another pill.

"You'd better sit down, Frank."

"No, no—I'll be fine," he said. "So, are you heading back to L.A.?"

Christine nodded. "Of course, there are a lot of details that need to be worked out first. Washington will want to investigate the whole operation—try to find out what went wrong, and who's to blame for the ambush. They're fairly certain the weapons cache was the War Room we've all been looking for, though. So the investigation on that front is pretty much officially over."

Frank reached out and leaned against the pew in front of him. "Christine, are you going to be okay?"

Her face grew tight with unshed tears. "Soon, yes. I believe so."

"If there's anything you need...anything at all..."

The tired agent straightened her back imperceptibly and walked back toward the window. She paused for a few seconds, then asked, "Do you think we could just hang out here for a while? Maybe go and sit in that garden out there? It looks so beautiful, doesn't it?"

Not for the first time, Frank noticed the auburn gleam of her hair and the deep green of her wide-set eyes. "Yes," he answered. "Very beautiful."

60

A hidden connection is stronger than an obvious one.

HERACLITUS (540-480 B.C.)

★★★

Frank's article, "Homegrown Terror: The Truth Behind the December Attacks," went to print in mid-April, coinciding with the major news of the verdict that had just been handed down in *United States of America v. Karl Gruber.*

Gruber, like The Dirty Dozen before him, was found guilty. Although he still couldn't be directly tied to the Nordic Brotherhood or the December terrorist attacks, the testimony given by three disaffected members of Yahweh's Holy Temple was conclusive. Gruber was given a sentence of fifty years to life in a federal penitentiary for possession and distribution of illegal guns, possession of military-grade explosives, possession of stolen goods, aiding and abetting terrorists, obstruction of justice, obstruction of a federal investigation, and concealing evidence relating to terrorist acts.

The presiding judge further declared, "Karl Gruber initiated a synergistic wave of racial animosity that encouraged his followers to imperil innocent lives. Although the pastor's rhetoric is indeed protected by the First Amendment, his propensity and ability to incite disenchanted youths to acts of violence makes him a danger to society."

Frank Delafield was the only reporter with cutting-edge, up-to-date information on Gruber, which made every other journalist green with envy, especially when they saw his exclusive interview: "Karl Gruber: Man of God, Man of Hate." Once the media at large started referencing the story and interview, sales of *BTI* magazine took off like a rocket.

Angus Reid was giddy with success. "I knew I'd pegged a winner when I found you, Delafield," he babbled over the phone. "You're a purebred bloodhound with a nose for news. I told that to Roy Ashton at the *L.A. Times* just this morning. 'Yes, sir,' I said, 'that guy's got a *gift.*'"

The journalist cracked a lopsided grin as he sat in the visitors' room of the Southern Sector Detention Facility in Florida.

"Thank you, Angus. Happy to be of service."

"Now don't you get me wrong, Frank. Just 'cause you got lucky this time doesn't mean I think you should pull any more 007 stunts. You hear me?"

"Sure, sure. I hear you." He pulled out his digital recorder and placed it on the metal table in front of him. "Listen, Angus, I'm afraid I gotta go. But I promise I'll buzz you when I get back in town. Okay? You take care of yourself." He flipped his cell phone closed just as the guard brought in a prisoner and seated him in the chair opposite Frank.

Dressed in a wrinkled jumpsuit, the guy looked like he hadn't slept or eaten in weeks.

The muscular guard at the young man's shoulder briefly addressed the reporter. "Let me know if he gives you any trouble. I'm right outside the door."

Frank couldn't even begin to imagine how this skinny punk in handcuffs and shackles would be able to give *anyone* trouble.

"Hi, Sammy," he said. "Thanks for agreeing to talk with me."

SamHack slowly raised his bloodshot eyes to meet those of his interviewer. "I...I just want people to know I didn't do anything wrong. I had nothing to do with those terrorist attacks. I…I'm not guilty."

"That's not how the jury saw it."

Sammy jerked suddenly. His shackles clattered against the chair. "That stupid jury didn't understand half of what was said! They weren't even paying attention most of the time! Buncha idiots, all looking at me like I was some kind of monster. They'd already made up their minds I was guilty." He stopped for a moment, and swallowed several times. "Now look at me. I'm gonna be in here for the rest of my life."

Frank spent the next few hours recording Sam's tale of woe, hearing about how he'd been scapegoated by his militia, then railroaded by the feds. The prisoner started detailing lots of information that seemed to support his contention that he knew nothing whatsoever about the December attacks.

The journalist hadn't originally intended the interview to be about whether or not Sammy was guilty, but that's what the topic quickly became as he started seeing that many of the facts presented in the government's case against SamHack were not really "facts" at all.

It soon became clear to Frank that the guy had been set up to take a long, hard fall. SamHack theorized it was probably because he hadn't paid income taxes on the hundreds of thousands of dollars he'd made from selling video-game characters and assets online. But prosecuting him for tax evasion would have cost the government far more than a quickie terrorism trial, where a guilty verdict was almost assured.

Finally, the conversation came to a close, and Frank began packing up his things. "Did you read the article I sent you about the December attacks?" he asked. "I was wondering what you thought of it, particularly the part where I explained how the terrorists probably used Internet chat rooms or e-mail to schedule meetings in the War Room."

"I read it."

"And?"

SamHack massaged his right wrist where the handcuffs had left a thin welt. "You want the truth?"

"Of course."

"You got it all wrong, man."

"Did I?"

"And I'll tell you something else." His leg started bouncing like a jackhammer under the table. "The feds...they didn't find the War Room."

Frank froze. "What do you mean?"

"You remember all those names you listed—the names of the terrorists found on those papers from the house—you know, Thor, IronCross..."

"Yeah...VampireKiller, ReichMan, PsychoSS, WhiteFury... what about 'em?"

"Those *aren't* screen names for chat rooms or abbreviated e-mail addresses." SamHack leaned forward. "Those are the names of characters in a video game—a really violent MMORPG."

"'MMORPG'? I don't follow you."

"Massively Multiplayer Online Role-Playing Game. It's an online game that's loaded up on a single computer or bank of computers—dedicated *servers*. Players from just about anywhere in the world can log on if they have the password, then jump on a program called Teamspeak to talk to other players in real time."

"Okay."

"Well, last year I was searching online for a different MMO to play and I hacked into this game. I know the server was probably near L.A. because I traced the connection route from my computer."

"Alright. Go on."

"So, like I said, I hacked into this server. And once I was in the game, I was surrounded by all these video characters dressed as Nazis. They were sort of like the toons you can create in Return to Castle Wolfenstein. Some looked like Hitler's SS, others resembled Nazi infantrymen, or Gestapo officers. Get the picture?"

"I think so. Toons are animated characters, right?"

"Yeah. But listen to this—I checked out their player names and they were super-racist. Some of them were totally sick, like Jew-Basher, SonOfAdolf, CoonHunter…you know, like that. And all of them were stalking computer-generated toons that resembled Jewish rabbis or some other minority. The Nazis were shooting them down with machine guns or blowing them up. It was really graphic."

"That's all very interesting, Sammy, but what does this have to do with the War Room?"

"I'm getting to that. When I hacked into the server and started looking around this game, I overheard some other players on Teamspeak talking about a War Room where they were gonna meet, so I went, uh, exploring, you know, through the game's environment. I finally ran across this huge statue of Adolf Hitler in the middle of a forest, and right next to it was a stone doorway with a sign on it saying ENTER THE WAR ROOM. So I went inside and it was enormous, like the Cave of Skull Rock in World of Warcraft, only it's decorated with German stuff from World War II—a picture of Hitler, a Nazi flag, swastikas, and eagles. The place kinda freaked me out. I'd never seen anything like it."

Sammy continued. "Then this other character walked in on me—someone called the Reichsmarschall. He asked me to identify myself and demanded the security password. Of course I didn't have the password, so I turned toward the nearest exit and hit COMMAND-RUN. That's when my computer lost its connection and I dropped out of the game. Whoever was controlling the server probably figured out I wasn't supposed to be there and that I'd hacked my way in. Anyway, I'd forgotten all about the War Room until I read your article."

The reporter chewed the inside of his lip intently. "Could that server have been located anywhere near Rosamond in the Antelope Valley?"

"Around Bakersfield?"

Frank nodded. "Just south of there."

"I suppose. Sure...easily."

The journalist suddenly remembered the video game he'd found in the California City house. "Sam, did you happen to find out the name of that game you hacked into?"

"Sure. It was called Rise of the Fourth Reich."

Even before SamHack had finished saying the title, Frank was headed for the door. "I'll be in touch," he said over his shoulder as he sprinted down the hall, popped his cell phone open, and began calling Agent Carlyle.

61

If you want to know the end,
look at the beginning.

AFRICAN PROVERB

★ ★ ★

Delafield raced back to Orlando International Airport, ignoring every speed limit sign he passed. Even so, the trip took him two hours. He was able to catch an early flight out, but because of weather delays and a long layover in Chicago, he didn't land at LAX until after 10:00 p.m.

When he came out of the terminal, Carlyle greeted him from behind the wheel of her black sedan, ready to go at the curb of the pickup lane. "Well, it's about time," she remarked as he opened the passenger-side door.

Frank slid in beside her, his clothes wrinkled and exhaustion pinching his features. "You're telling me." He chucked his suitcase into the backseat and slammed the door. "Where's the new partner I've been hearing so much about?"

"He'll meet us there."

They took off immediately for Rosamond. Frank had told Schmidt the same information he'd already given to Christine—that the War Room might not have been located yet, and that a very grave threat remained. "I'd like to come by and go over some new material," he'd explained. "If the server is indeed located in Rosamond, which SammyHack thinks is a definite possibility, then we need to find out who's running it. Once we know that, we'll be able to identify the person behind the December attacks."

Bill had responded doubtfully. "I'd like to help...but I don't know anything about video games."

"Actually, I just want to go over SamHack's description of the War Room with you, point by point. Maybe it'll remind you of something you've seen before. Also, you said Luke plays video games and knows a lot about the Internet, so I was hoping he might be able to help us figure out what's going on."

"Oh...I see," Schmidt replied. "Well, that sounds fine, then. Luke isn't home yet, but by the time you get here, he should be back."

Carlyle had been the one to suggest they talk to Bill's grandson. She thought Luke probably had more knowledge about video games than any of the agents she could have contacted on such short notice. Furthermore, Washington higher-ups were extremely reluctant to act on the new theory, especially Duncan Phelps, who scoffed at the notion of a video game being used as a tool for terrorists. He was riding high on his recent successes and didn't want anyone raining on his parade.

As they sped north on I-5, the journalist recounted the SamHack interview to Carlyle. Because the War Room existed in the virtual world, that would explain not only why no one had yet found it, but also why the feds could not apprehend the Reichsmarschall and Der Neue Führer. They were simply characters in an online game—characters who could meet safely *inside* the game, not only with each other, but also with their followers. It was a brilliant way to conceal both their activities and identities. The Reichsmarschall and Der Neue Führer could be anybody... sitting at any computer in the country.

"If you're right about this, Frank..." Carlyle tapped her thumbs on the steering wheel, "...they could be planning another attack right now."

Frank closed his aching eyes and rubbed them, letting the agent's words soak in. "Christine, this is one time I seriously hope you're wrong."

62

★ ★ ★

They pulled up to Pastor Schmidt's house close to midnight. Despite their crushing fatigue, they had to talk to the pastor and his grandson. By morning, with any luck, Carlyle would have something to offer Washington politicians to justify a new investigation based on SamHack's assertions.

Bill answered the door quickly. "What took you so long? I thought your plane landed three hours ago."

"My connection was delayed," replied Frank sourly.

"Well, at least you finally made it." He extended his hand toward Agent Carlyle. "Good to see you again, Christine."

"Thanks for agreeing to meet with us. I know it's a crazy hour."

"No problem...no problem at all. I just hope I can be of some assistance."

Frank glanced around the living room. "Is Luke home yet?"

The pastor gestured impatiently. "No. And I have no idea where he is."

"Exactly how many places could he be at this time of night?" asked Frank.

Schmidt thought for a moment. "Wait a minute—maybe he came home and went straight to his studio."

"Studio?" asked Carlyle.

"Yeah, it's out back. I had it built for him when he was a teen-ager so he could have a place to himself whenever he wanted to write or record music. Nothing fancy—it's more like a big shed with rooms. That must be where he is. Just last week he was holed up there all night, working on some project he wanted to finish."

"Can we go and see if he's there now?"

"Sure, just let me grab my coat." Schmidt went to the closet. "The place is usually locked up tight, but the other day I saw where he keeps his spare key."

"You don't think he'll mind if we just barge in?" Carlyle asked.

Bill shrugged. "Even if he's there, I usually have to pound on the door for ten minutes. Besides, I'd kinda like to see what he's done with the place. I don't think I've been in there for years."

When the pastor opened the studio door, the first thing he noticed was the music. Frank and Christine heard it too, but none of them recognized it. It sounded like some kind of men's chorus.

"Luke?" Bill shouted into the dimly lit studio.

No answer.

Christine stepped in, followed by Frank, who stopped near the sound-control board in the first room. He looked around. There was a storage alcove to the left, but otherwise he saw nothing. "Hmm...now what?"

Schmidt scratched his head. "I'm not sure. I'm really surprised he's not here."

"Gentlemen!" Carlyle yelled from inside the next room. "You might want to take a look at this."

63

★★★

Frank and Bill joined Christine in the adjoining room. What they saw made them stop short. Along the far wall stood a long table with planting trays filled with soil. Against the adjacent wall was a large desk with an elaborate computer setup, including a huge monitor.

The music they'd heard upon entering the studio was drifting out of the system's speakers. Schmidt finally recognized it and went pale as he stood there listening to *Das Lied der Deutschen*, "The Song of the Germans":

Deutschland, Deutschland, über alles, über alles in der Welt!
Wenn es stets zu Schutz und Trutze
Brüderlich zusammenhält!
Von der Maas bis an die Memel,
Von der Etsch bis an den Belt:
Deutschland, Deutschland über alles,
Über alles in der Welt!

On the opposite wall was a Nazi flag surrounded by black-and-white photos dating from the time of Hitler's rule: a parade of troops and artillery, a group of Brownshirts marching, Wehr-macht soldiers, Waffen-SS officers, and the like. Enshrined at the center of the flag was a portrait of Hitler in a beige uniform, complete with black tie and swastika armband. Beneath the picture in a glass box was a large reproduction of the German Iron Cross, First Class—the decoration earned by Der Führer in World War I.

Frank's attention was eventually drawn to a calendar lying open on the desk. He flipped through several of its pages. They were mostly covered with indecipherable symbols, but he was able to make out three dates circled in red: December 8, December 26, April 20. He then spied on a nearby shelf several books with titles such as *The Mushroom Cultivator, Mushrooms Demystified,* and *Nature's Toxic Wonders.*

No one spoke for what seemed like a very long time. Finally, Carlyle broke the silence.

"Bill, we need to find out where Luke is—and fast. Now, think—where could he be?"

The pastor stood unmoving, his eyes fixed on the flag and the portrait of Adolf Hitler.

"Bill!" Christine yelled loudly.

He jerked and blinked rapidly. "I…I don't understand. How could he…it can't be," he stammered, his voice thin.

"Christine?" Frank interrupted, holding out the calendar.

She stepped over. "What is it?"

He pointed to the month of December. "See these circled dates?"

Carlyle's breath caught in her throat. "The terrorist attacks."

Frank flipped forward to April, putting his finger on another day circled in red. "And the twentieth. Chris, that's tomorrow."

Schmidt turned slowly toward his two companions. "What is this?" he muttered, as if searching for an explanation other than the one already forming in his mind. But before they could say anything, an answer came out of the shadows of the first room.

"*What is this?*'" the Reichsmarschall said, his words leaden with disdain. "This, old man, is the future." Luke stepped into the doorway, coolly leveling at them the rifle that had killed Mindy Laughlin. "The future of the Aryan race. The future of America. The future of the world."

Bill began to tremble, not only with grief, but also with rage. "Luke," he commanded, "put that gun down."

"Shut up!" screamed his grandson, his face contorted. "I've listened to you long enough. You betrayed your people. You betrayed my father. Lied about him and…about everything he believed!"

The pastor shook his head fiercely. "I told you the truth."

"*No.* My father—*he* spoke the truth! He stood for honor, for God, for this country—and for the white race. I remember seeing you destroy the pamphlets he wrote when I was little. But today his words are on Web sites all over the world—and I've read every one of them!"

A tear spilled down the pastor's weathered cheek. "Luke… please. I…I loved your father. He was my son! But he was wrong and misguided. I was wrong and misguided. Please, whatever you've done…whatever you're thinking of doing, it's not too late. Put the gun down."

While Bill spoke to his grandson, Carlyle inched her hand toward the holster at the small of her back.

Luke spotted the movement and swung his rifle around. "I wouldn't do that if I were you! Take that gun out nice and slow, and drop it on the floor!"

The agent met his gaze. "You know I can't do that."

"Alright, then—you'll be the first to die." He pointed his weapon at her head.

"You won't get away with this," Frank said forcefully, attempting to pull Luke's focus away from Christine.

Luke laughed in disbelief. "Oh, really? Is that what you think— Mr. Delafield? Mr. Journalist? Mr. Investigative Reporter?" He dropped the rifle to his waist. "Well, here's a scoop for you! I've *already* gotten away with it. By this time tomorrow, our country will have a new president—*Der Neue Führer*. He will bring about the glorious empire so many of us have longed to see, the empire that is our destiny—the Fourth Reich."

At that moment, a voice boomed out from behind Luke. *"Freeze. Don't move.* Drop the weapon. Do it now! Then put your hands up and turn around."

Luke pivoted, and his face took on an expression of shock and confusion.

"No, no…it's okay," he insisted. "I'm on your side. You're Erich Strom, right? From Gruber's camp?"

Erich kept his pistol aimed at the young man, and took a step forward. "I said, *drop your weapon.*"

Luke glared at Strom, trying to decide what to do. In that moment, Bill lunged clumsily for the rifle. His grandson had just enough time to turn and fire. The shot hit Schmidt in the stomach, knocking him to the floor. Strom immediately squeezed off three rounds, striking Luke in the neck, side, and shoulder.

Silence.

"You okay, Coletti?" Carlyle asked after a moment. Her unholstered gun locked on Luke, who lay motionless in front of her.

"Yeah, I'm okay," Mike replied from the doorway. He moved in closer and kicked the young man's weapon into the corner, then knelt down and checked his pulse. "But I'm not sure about this one."

"Mike Coletti?" gasped Frank.

Carlyle nodded. "My new partner."

"Also known as Erich Strom," the reporter added.

An ambulance arrived fifteen minutes later and rushed Bill and Luke away. Frank wanted to accompany the injured pastor, but he felt he had to stay with Coletti and Carlyle and help them figure out what to do next.

Christine paced the interior of the studio, and gestured toward her partner. "How much do you know about computers?"

"Why?"

She hastily explained that they now believed Luke might be the organizer of the December attacks. The computer in front of them was likely the server he had been using to communicate with other white supremacists across the country. "That's not all," she continued. "According to the calendar we found on the desk, it looks like another attack is scheduled for tomorrow."

"Happy Birthday, Adolf," Frank muttered as he poked through the trays of dirt on the table.

"Happy what?" Coletti asked, leafing through one of the books on mushrooms.

"Tomorrow is Hitler's birthday," he repeated. "White supremacists are big on dates, numbers, memorials. So whatever's planned for tomorrow will be a sort of tribute to Hitler—a birthday present. Which means its going to be a *major* deal. Luke said that by this time tomorrow, our country would have a new president."

Carlyle yanked out her cell phone. "Okay, we're going to have to put extra men on Beckett. Let him know what's going on—"

"Hold it, hold it," interjected Coletti. "Remember, the previous attacks were extremely unconventional. For all we know, one of the president's own bodyguards might be the assassin. Or maybe they've planted a bomb under his car, or even in the White House. Let's take a second here and think it through."

Carlyle tapped her phone against her chin as she thought. "April 20…I know something special is going on, but I can't remember—"

"Do you know what the president has scheduled?" Frank asked Coletti.

"Nothing big," he answered. "Just his quarterly prayer breakfast. He'll be there…maybe a few senators…probably most of the Cabinet."

"A bomb?" Carlyle suggested.

"I...don't think so," Frank offered slowly. "Christine, look at those books on the shelf. They're all about growing mushrooms. And these trays..."

"Are you saying what I think you're saying?" she asked.

Coletti stiffened with alarm. "I think he's right. Toxic mushrooms. I bet they're going to try to poison the president."

Carlyle flipped open her cell phone and started punching the keypad. "These breakfasts usually start at 8:00 a.m. Right now, it's going on five o'clock in Washington, which means the cooks are already starting on the food. Let's find out what's on the menu."

Mike sat down at Luke's server and pulled out his PDA. "There's this guy I know over at the Bureau. A real techno-geek—knows everything about computers. With his help I should be able to tap into the system logs. Once I do that, it'll only take a few hours to trace the IP addresses of the computers that have been logging into this server. By early morning, I'm guessing we'll finally know who Der Neue Führer is."

64

★★★

ONE WEEK LATER:

Frank waited patiently for his order to be filled. Despite the racket of the coffee grinders and espresso machines, he could still hear the other customers at his favorite L.A. coffee stop chatting noisily about the unexpected arrest in connection to the December terrorist attacks. Recent events had been so sensational that even total strangers struck up conversations about the latest special updates and network exclusives that were continuing to interrupt scheduled TV programming. The mysterious figure known as Der Neue Führer—the evil mastermind behind the attacks that had crippled America nearly five months earlier—had been taken into custody the morning after a shooting in Rosamond, California, involving two Secret Service agents, a tabloid journalist, a pastor, and the pastor's grandson, who had apparently been living a double life for many years.

Newspapers and magazines were continuing to release a steady stream of articles about the complex saga: profiles of key players; an interview with SamHack of the Dirty Dozen; stories on the history of Nazism in the U.S.; and assorted pieces on video games, the

Internet, homeland security, and so on. The majority of the reports, however, concentrated on the architect of the terrorist acts—who, if his plot had succeeded, would have been the nation's next president.

"One double espresso! One mocha cappuccino!" shouted the barista.

Frank picked up the order and maneuvered his way across the crowded café to a table in a corner next to the window. "Here you go," he said, carefully placing the foamy cappuccino in front of Christine. He set down his own coffee and took a seat. "So how are things in Washington?"

"Well, the whole administration is still reeling. All the usual damage control that kicks in after a scandal of this magnitude."

"I'm not sure there's ever been a scandal of *this* magnitude."

"Yeah, you're probably right about that."

"So what happens now?"

"After Beckett nominates a new vice president, the Justice Department will have to figure out how in the world they're going to put our former one on trial for treason, murder, sedition, terrorism, and a handful of other felonies."

Frank leaned back. "I still can't believe it."

"You're not the only one."

"I mean, Vice President Mayhew would have poisoned not only the president, but at least half the Cabinet."

Carlyle raised her eyebrows, still a bit shaken by how close the U.S. had come to being taken over at the highest government levels. "Ladies and gentlemen, I give you the President of the United States, Martin Mayhew...closet Nazi."

Frank took a sip of his espresso. "That about says it all."

"And Mayhew would have picked a new Secretary of Defense, Secretary of State, Attorney General, and Secretary of Homeland Security—all of them undoubtedly from his radical Aryan movement. And whichever people he was going to choose are still in Washington somewhere. No doubt about that. Maybe in Congress, maybe somewhere else. We're just going to have to ferret them out."

"Whew! Forget about background checks on baggage handlers in the airports. Let's pay attention to whether or not our elected officials are goose-stepping maniacs."

Carlyle rolled her eyes. "You do have a way with words, Delafield."

Frank smiled. "It comes with the job. Speaking of which, is there anything else going on that, uh…I should know about?"

Carlyle mopped up a damp ring from under her cup. "Once a reporter, always a reporter."

He made a hurt face.

"Oh, relax. I'm just yanking your chain. Let's see…Duncan Phelps hasn't come out of this looking very good. After all, he was the one who kept insisting there was no War Room. Beckett's already asked for his resignation, but that won't be made public until next week, so keep it under your hat."

"Who's gonna replace him?"

"Probably Lance Vaughn, the former director of the Secret Service."

"Is he a good man?"

"I think so."

Frank nodded, and took another slow gulp of coffee. "By the way," he added, "thanks for getting SamHack released."

"My pleasure. Without him, we'd all be in big trouble now." She scooted her chair forward and rested her elbows on the table. "Listen, I've been meaning to ask you, have you spoken to Bill lately?"

The journalist looked out the window at the bright, morning sky. "He's not doing so well, Chris. Luke's death hit him hard."

"I can imagine. I hope he's going to be okay." She paused, regarding Frank. "What about you?" she asked. "How are *you* doing?"

Frank studied Christine for a moment. He knew he wasn't the

same man he'd been when they'd first met. Not because of the story he'd gotten, or the dangers he'd faced, or the injuries he'd endured. *She* had started to change him.

"I think…" he began, "if everything goes well, I'm actually going to be able to take something very, very good away from this whole experience."

65

*When we lose one blessing, another is often most
unexpectedly given in its place.*

C.S. LEWIS (1898–1963)

★★★

TWO MONTHS LATER:

Bill Schmidt sat alone in his den, paging through a collection of old photo albums and dog-eared scrapbooks. He gazed for hour after hour at pictures of his long-dead son, David. There was one of him as a baby crawling on the grass, another of him riding his first bicycle—and Bill's most treasured picture, the two of them together on a hunting trip when David was thirteen. The pastor eventually moved on to snapshots of Luke opening Christmas presents as a toddler…sitting at his first computer when he was twelve…and finally, leading worship services at church.

"I loved them so much, God," he whispered softly. "I don't understand."

As he continued praying, a broken soul pleading for comfort as well as answers, a timid knock on the front door broke into his lonely meditations. He wasn't expecting anyone, and it was getting late. Perhaps it was another member of the congregation dropping by to offer some support. The pastor sighed, then grimaced at the sudden stab of pain from his still-healing gunshot wound.

Even though he really didn't want to see anyone, he dutifully got up and answered the door.

It was a stranger. A young man Bill had never seen before. "Can I help you, son?"

The skinny youth shuffled his feet back and forth, shifting his focus repeatedly from the pastor to the ground. For a moment it looked as if he was going to turn and leave. But then he seemed to gather his resolve, and spoke. "I, uh...I..."

Bill inched forward. "It's alright, son. You don't have to be scared. Do you need something?"

"Uh, yeah. I need a...place to stay." He handed Bill a smudged business card with tattered edges. "I...this is from someone at your church. I met him in town. He said to come here. I ain't got no money, but I can work if you need anything done around here."

The young man looked as if he hadn't bathed in weeks. His clothes were torn in places, and his hair was matted.

"Are you in some kind of trouble?" the pastor asked in a kind tone.

"No, nuh-uh. I just got nowhere to go."

"Any family?"

No answer.

Bill noticed the scuffed guitar case strapped to the boy's back. "Do you play?" he asked, nodding toward it.

The youth reached up and lightly fingered the strap. "Yes," he replied, a glimmer flashing briefly in his dull eyes.

"Are you good?"

He shrugged. "I don't know. I guess."

Bill pondered the choice before him—turn the kid away, or invite him to stay. It was an easy decision to make.

"What's your name?"

"Todd. Todd Ryan," the boy answered. "My friends call me T.R."

Schmidt straightened up and angled his head to the left. "T.R.? Weren't you the guy who..." Bill stopped.

Todd swallowed anxiously. "Who what?"

"Uh...nothing, don't worry about it. Never mind." The pastor swung open the door and stepped aside. "Well, T.R., why don't you come on in? It's almost time for supper."

> *All things work together for good to*
> *those who love the Lord, to those who*
> *are called according to his purpose.*
>
> **ROMANS 8:28**

A nationally recognized authority on popular culture and religion, **Richard Abanes** has spent nearly 15 years in the field as an author and journalist. In 1997 he received not only The Myers Center Award for the Study of Human Rights in North America for his "outstanding work on intolerance in North America," but also the Evangelical Press Association's "Higher Goals in Christian Journalism Award." Among his nearly two dozen books are *What Every Parent Needs to Know About Video Games* and the bestselling *The Truth Behind the Da Vinci Code*.

A published poet and accomplished vocalist, **Evangeline Abanes** has participated in television and film projects and worked in church-support roles such as youth counselor and worship leader. *Homeland Insecurity*, coauthored with her husband, Richard, is her first novel.

HARVEST HOUSE
PUBLISHERS

WHAT EVERY PARENT NEEDS TO KNOW ABOUT VIDEO GAMES
Richard Abanes

Do you know enough to make good choices for your kids?

Packed with the latest information on the pros and cons of video and computer gaming, this concise, easy-to-follow guide helps you understand a form of entertainment that's become a part of the daily lives of millions of children and young adults. Bestselling author Richard Abanes—an experienced video-gamer himself—offers balanced discussions of

- positives and negatives of game-playing and game content
- the rating system—where it's helpful, where it's not
- family-friendly selections…and those that aren't
- terminology and genres, such as *sports, role-playing, shooter*
- ways to go beyond just what is shown in a game and evaluate its overall message

You'll come away with a better picture of what is appropriate for you and your family—so you can enjoy the good, use caution with the bad, and steer clear of the ugly.

To read a sample chapter, go to
www.harvesthousepublishers.com

What Is Fact? What Is Fiction?
**THE TRUTH BEHIND
THE DA VINCI CODE**
Richard Abanes

"All descriptions of artwork, architecture, documents, and secret rituals in this novel are accurate."

With those startling words, *The Da Vinci Code*—author Dan Brown's megaselling thriller—kicks you into high gear. After 454 nonstop pages, you've discovered a lot of shocking facts about history and Christianity…or have you?

Award-winning investigative journalist Richard Abanes takes you down to the murky underpinnings of this blockbuster novel and movie that has confused so many people. What do you really learn when the *Code's* assumptions are unearthed and scrutinized?

- **The Code:** Jesus was married to Mary Magdalene, whom he named leader of the church before his death.

- **The Truth:** This fantasy has no support even from the "Gnostic gospels" mentioned in the *Code,* let alone from the historical data.

- **The Code:** Since the year 1099, a supersecret society called "The Priory of Sion" has preserved knowledge of Jesus and Mary's descendants.

- **The Truth:** Today's "Priory of Sion" was founded in the early 1960s by a French con man who falsified documents to support the story of Jesus' "bloodline."

- **The Code:** As a "Priory" leader and pagan goddess-worshipper, Leonardo da Vinci coded secret knowledge about Jesus and Mary into his paintings.

- **The Truth:** Da Vinci had no known ties to any secret societies. Any obscure images in his paintings likely reflect his personal creativity.

Probing, factual, and revealing, *The Truth Behind the Da Vinci Code* gives you the straightforward information you need to separate the facts from the fiction.

To read a sample chapter, go to
www.harvesthousepublishers.com

THE CHAMBERS OF JUSTICE SERIES
Craig Parshall

The Resurrection File

When Reverend Angus MacCameron asks attorney Will Chambers to defend him against accusations that could discredit the Gospels, Will's unbelieving heart says "run." But conspiracy and intrigue—and the presence of Mac-Cameron's lovely and successful daughter, Fiona—draw him deep into the case...toward a destination he could never have imagined.

Custody of the State

Attorney Will Chambers reluctantly agrees to defend a young mother from Georgia and her farmer husband, suspected of committing the unthinkable against their own child. Encountering small-town secrets, big-time corruption, and a government system that's destroying the little family, Chambers himself is thrown into the custody of the state.

The Accused

Enjoying a Cancún honeymoon with his wife, Fiona, attorney Will Chambers is ambushed by two unexpected events: a terrorist kidnapping of a U.S. official...and the news that a link has been found to the previously unidentified murderer of Will's first wife. The kidnapping pulls him into the case of Marine colonel Caleb Marlowe. When treachery drags both Will and his client toward vengeance, they must ask—*Is forgiveness real?*

Missing Witness

A relaxing North Carolina vacation for attorney Will Chambers? Not likely. When Will investigates a local inheritance case, the long arm of the law reaches out of the distant past to cast a shadow over his client's life...and the life of his own family. As the attorney's legal battle uncovers corruption, piracy, the deadly grip of greed, and the haunting sins of a man's past, the true question must be faced—*Can a person ever really run away from God?*

The Last Judgment

A mysterious religious cult plans to spark an "Armageddon" in the Middle East. Suddenly, a huge explosion blasts the top of the Jerusalem Temple Mount into rubble, with hundreds of Muslim casualties. And attorney Will Chambers' client, Gilead Amahn, a convert to Christianity from Islam, becomes the prime suspect. In his harrowing pursuit of the truth, Will must face the greatest threat yet to his marriage, his family, and his faith, while cataclysmic events plunge the world closer to the Last Judgment.

*To read sample chapters of Craig Parshall's books,
go to www.harvesthousepublishers.com*

Deliver Us from Evelyn
Chris Well

Kansas City, the heart of America—where the heartless Evelyn Blake lords it over the Blake Media empire. The inconvenience she suffers when her billionaire husband, Warren, mysteriously disappears is multiplied when nearly everybody starts asking, "Where is Blake?"

Rev. Damascus Rhodes (his current alias) figures a man of the cloth can properly console the grieving Mrs. Blake.

Detectives Tom Griggs and Charlie Pasch are feeling the heat from on high to get this thing solved.

An unidentified blogger is writing on the Web, spilling Blake Media corporate secrets and hinting at a long-hidden relationship with the company's missing owner.

By the end of this twist-and-turn thriller, some characters find unexpected redemption...and more than a few are begging, *Deliver us from Evelyn...*

"Clever, snappy, and streetwise!"

—**Creston Mapes,** author of *Dark Star* and *Full Tilt*

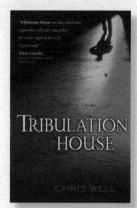

Tribulation House
Chris Well

It's not the end of the world—which could be a problem...

Mark Hogan has it all. The job. The family. A position on the board at church. All he's missing is a boat. Not just any boat—a 2008 Bayliner 192.

When Reverend Daniel Glory announces that the Rapture is taking place on October 17 at 5:51 AM, Hogan realizes his boat-buying days are numbered. So he does what any man in his situation would do—he borrows a load of money from the mob.

Not that there's any risk involved: After all, when the Rapture comes, Hogan will be long gone. The mob will never find him.

But when Jesus fails to come back on schedule, Mark Hogan finds that the mob is in no mood to discuss the finer points of end-times theology...

"Chris Well's hilarious new mystery is not to be missed. Even though it's an amusing romp, it's not light on spiritual truths. I highly recommend it!"

—**Colleen Coble,** author of *Fire Dancer* and *Midnight Sea*

To read sample chapters of Chris Well's books, go to www.harvesthousepublishers.com